會展
實用英語

（讀寫篇）

Practical
Event
English

會展實用英語編委會 編

崧燁文化

目錄

前言

Chapter 1 The MICE Industry and the World Expo 會展業和世博會

Chapter 2 MICE Planning 會展策劃

Chapter 3 Event Sponsorship 會展融資

Chapter 4 Event Marketing 會展營銷

Chapter 15 Event Evaluation 會展評估

Chapter 16 Handling Problems and Complaints 會展問題與投訴處理

前言

　　《會展實用英語》分為讀寫篇和聽說篇。本套教材的編寫宗旨如下：透過介紹歐美會展業的先進理念和實踐經驗，結合會展業的各個部門和整個工作流程，深化聽、說、讀、寫、譯等英語語言技巧訓練，幫助會展從業人員熟悉英語國家綜合文化知識和國際會展業的背景知識，提高會展從業人員用英語進行會展管理與服務的交際能力。針對實際工作需求，按照國際會展流程，透過大量練習，幫助上崗人員和會展從業人員進一步擴大詞彙量，掌握綜合運用語言的能力，更好地開展國際會展業務。

　　《會展實用英語》（讀寫篇和聽說篇）教材內容涉及會展業和世博會概況、會展策劃、會展融資、會展營銷、談判、物流、展臺搭建、會展訊息管理、會展餐飲服務、會展財務、出展管理、展覽現場管理、安保與風險管理、會前會後旅遊、會展評估、會展問題與投訴處理等領域。

　　《會展實用英語》（讀寫篇）的每章包括三個部分：第一部分是閱讀訓練，第二部分是案例分析，第三部分是公文寫作。閱讀訓練部分圍繞一篇介紹理念和業務的課文，設置了熱身練習、課前提問、核心語言點講解、小組討論、寫作練習、翻譯等小區塊。案例分析部分以一篇與課文相關的案例為引子，向學生提出實際工作中會出現的問題，引導學生思考並找出解決辦法。公文寫作部分所選的公文類型都是與會展工作密切相關的。除了對範例進行註解，列出該類型公文的寫作要點外，還設計了「自己動手做」的區塊供讀者練習掌握。本書既可作為會展、旅遊等行業從業人員的職業培訓教材，也可作為會展、旅遊等專業院校和培訓機構的參考用書。

　　本書在原內部使用教材《會展英語》的基礎上，彙集了所有參編人員的集體智慧。參加本書編寫的人員有：吳雲（第1、2、6、11章），邢怡（第8、13、14、15章），吳楊（第3、4、10章），朱艷華（第9、16章），歐陽黎靜（第5章），莊婷（第12章），徐藤崗（第7章）。傅國林老師也為本書做了許多工作，在此表示衷心感謝。

　　由於編者水平有限，若有疏漏之處，懇請批評指正。

編者

Chapter 1 The MICE Industry and the World Expo 會展業和世博會

▌Section A Reading Assignment

Warming-up Activity

Go over the following terms with your teacher.

MICE 會展	incentive travel 獎勵旅遊	convention 大會	seminar 討論會
manufacturer 廠商	supplier 供應商	venue 會展場地	exhibitor 參展商
contractor 承包商	OHP（overhead projector） 高射投影儀	AV（audio-visual） 聲像	shell scheme 含基本隔間裝潢的攤位
logistics 物流/後勤	incentive travel package 獎勵旅遊包價套餐	literature 宣傳材料	exhibition manual 會展指南
DMC（Destination Management Companies）目的地管理公司			

Pre-reading Questions

Answer the following questions without referring to the text.

1.What is the role of MICE industry in the country's economy?

2.Why do we need meetings?

3.How do you define "incentive travels"?

4.Is it that when people speak of modern exhibitions they mean only the venue owners?

5.What is a meeting broker?

6.What kinds of MICE organizers are there in your place?

7.What is the role of those intermediaries in MICE process?

Text

What Is MICE?

The term MICE, coined from meetings, incentive travels, conventions and exhibitions, has gained its popularity in China since the mid 1980's. The phenomenal growth in the number and diversity of MICE has given rise to new business opportunities and tourism implications. MICE management has become recognized as a separate field of study in a growing number of educational institutions.

A "meeting" can be defined as an event at which people gather from afar, exchange messages, and make decisions. However, it is too generic a term to be inclusive. This is partly because there are diverse meeting needs, ranging from international conferences to corporate training sessions, and partly because the emerging technologies make it possible for people to see each other without meeting face-to-face.

Anyway, be it a convention or seminar, the importance of such an event lies not only in what is said from the platform but also in the total atmosphere of the event.Furthermore, feeling elated at the end of a meeting does not make credit to the increased number and diversity of meetings alone. Meetings, especially at the international level, are inherently information-oriented and problem solving. Experience needs to be shared, as does the knowledge about the world and human being themselves. Everything can be the topic of a meeting.

Another lucrative aspect is incentive travel. Incentive travel aims to entertain, reward, and motivate those who work directly or indirectly with the organization for their increased levels of performance. For management, incentive travel provides an opportunity to share experiences and ideas and build up loyalty to the company.

Incentive travel deals more with hospitality than convening. It includes receptions, dinners or banquets, and hours to interesting destinations.

Last, exhibitions are a fast-growing segment of today's MICE industry. The country's booming economy increases the need for trade and commerce. Manufacturers or suppliers seek opportunities to display their products in public, as do buyers to secure desirable products. Exhibitions provide such opportunities. There the sellers explain or sometimes demonstrate the value, beauty, and particular interest of their products or services.

Besides, exhibitions serve as a cost-effective way of launching new products, securing new markets, strengthening existing customer interest, and thus improving upon market share. The modern exhibition is clearly structured, taking in venue owners, exhibition organizers, and contractors from the supply side, and exhibitors and visitors from the demand side.

Then who are the professional MICE players?

1) Independent Meeting Planners. They are flexible, negotiable, and well experienced experts assisting directly with a client's

planning. The planners provide consultants who become part of the meeting organizing committee. They function as intermediaries and manage all details on behalf of the group. Some planners are even technically competent to provide a range of technical support, including OHP, AV equipment, and computer technology. They are private companies, able to access any suppliers to meet the client's requirements.

2) Destination Management Companies (DMC). A DMC is a company that specializes in the organization and logistics of meetings and events. No matter what the event or the occasion, destination management companies will always find a surprising and tailor-made solution.

In addition to transportation and theme events, a full service DMC can provide audiovisual support, temporary help, entertainment, interpreters and other services. They may act on behalf of the organizer to negotiate hotels and meeting facilities, as a travel agency, as an agent subcontracting for any services the event requires or function in a variety of support roles. The influence of a local DMC can result in agreements that could not be easily accomplished by an outsider. They are often familiar with the reactions of many other groups as to what they are and have been doing, so they know what does and what doesn't work. Destination management companies remain behind the scenes while ensuring that everything runs according to the plan.

3) Incentive Travel Companies. These companies deal directly with arranging incentive travel packages for corporations wishing to reward or motivate their staffs or their customers. These packages are usually "first class", often involving an exotic or popular resort

location. These companies see to all the details of the incentive program. They negotiate with airlines and hotels and then package the transportation, lodging, and meeting accommodations, meals, tours and entertainment. They often prepare the promotional literature and may even get involved in setting the goals of the program.

4) Full Services Contractors. They offer a comprehensive range of the services and products that are essential for the creation of successful congresses, corporate meetings, exhibitions, and special events of any size. The services offered include concept and design, project management, production, graphics and decoration, installation and dismantling, destination management, transport and warehousing. They can also provide anything from electrical services, furniture and shell schemes to online exhibitor manuals.

Check-in

Do you have any questions about the text? If any, ask your teacher.

More Terms

accommodation 下榻	package tour /travel 包價旅遊	booth decoration 展台裝修	corporate meeting 公司會議
meeting facility 會議設施	literature 宣傳資料	A/V equipment 視聽設備	event contractor 會展服務承辦商
dismantle/move out 撤展	plan 策劃	intermediary 中介公司	conference planning company 會議策劃公司
consultation 商談	installation 安裝	planner 主辦方	shell booth 框架式展台

Important Vocabulary

coin	[kɔɪn]	v.	創造
phenomenal	[fɪˈnɔmɪnl]	a.	顯著的
diversity	[daɪˈvɜːsətɪ]	n.	多樣性
implication	[ɪmplɪˈkeɪʃən]	n.	含義
generic	[dʒɪˈnerɪk]	a.	一般的
diverse	[daɪˈvɜːs]	a.	不同的
corporate	[ˈkɔːpərət]	a.	公司的
rendezvous	[ˈrɒndɪvuː]	n.	會面
vis-à-vis	[ˌviːzɑːˈviː]	adv.	面對面地
stimulation	[ˌstɪmjuˈleɪʃən]	n.	激勵
elate	[ɪˈleɪt]	v.	使興高采烈
inherently	[ɪnˈhɪərəntlɪ]	adv.	固有地
lucrative	[ˈluːkrətɪv]	a.	獲利的
motivate	[ˈməutɪveɪt]	v.	給予動機

hospitality	[ˌhɒspɪˈtælətɪ]	n.	殷勤款待
convene	[kənˈviːn]	v.	召集會議
secure	[sɪˈkjuə(r)]	v.	獲得
subcontract	[sʌbkənˈtrækt]	v.	分包・轉包
exotic	[ɪɡˈzɒtɪk]	a.	異國的
resort	[rɪˈzɔːt]	n.	渡假勝地

Useful Expressions

to gain popularity	頗受歡迎
to give rise to	引起，使發生
to become recognized as	被公認為
to serve as	用做
to share experience and idea	分享經驗和思想
to build up loyalty	提高忠誠度
to launch new products	發佈新產品
to improve upon	提高，改善
to function as	用做
on behalf of	代表
a tailor-made solution	考慮周到的解決方案

Language Focus

1.The phenomenal growth in the number and diversity of MICE has given rise to new business opportunities and tourism implications.

會展業在數量和種類方面驚人的發展帶來了新的商機和旅遊熱潮。

Implication 有多個抽象意義，在此句中根據上下文翻譯其具體含義「熱潮」。

implication：n. 牽連，涉及，密切關係，捲入

例：This issue has grave implications for unemployment.

這是一個嚴重關係到失業的問題。

2....and partly because the emerging technologies make it possible for people to see each other without meeting face-to-face.

……另一個原因是層出不窮的技術使得人們有可能不用面對面就能看到對方。

3.Meetings, especially at the international level, are inherently information-oriented and problem solving.

會議，尤其是國際會議，其本質是發布訊息和解決問題。

Information-oriented 和 problem solving

皆為形容詞短語，分別翻譯為動詞短語「發布訊息」和「解決問題」。

4.Incentive travel deals more with hospitality than convening.

與其說獎勵旅遊是聚會還不如說它是友好款待。

More of 的意思是「更大程度上的」。

例：He is more of a musician than a poet.

與其說他是詩人還不如說他是音樂家。

5.The modern exhibition is clearly structured, taking in venue owners, exhibition organizers, and contractors from the supply side, and exhibitors and visitors from the demand side.

現代展覽業結構劃分明晰，包括（展覽）場館地主、展覽承辦和承包方（供應方）、參展商和觀眾（需求方）。

Group Discussion

Discuss the following topic in group. Select one on the team to make a presentation before the class.

Define the terms by giving examples.

▬ MICE

▬ Independent Meeting Planners

▬ Destination Management Companies

▬ Incentive Travel Companies

▬ Full Services Contractors

Writing Activity

Summarize the text （Paras 1-7） by outlining major points. Write a few lines about the MICE industry.

Translating Activity

Complete the following by translating the Chinese given in the brackets.

1.Exhibits, （舉行時無任何議程） _____, are called trade fairs.

2.When （大型展覽對公眾開放時） _____, they are referred to as consumer shows, such as home shows, flower and garden shows, auto shows and boat shows, （在這些展覽上通常適當收取入場費） _____.

3. （儘管運輸和招待服務費用上升） _____, there has been an increasing need to hold a variety of meetings for a number of purposes：（為了跟上日益變化的技術步伐） _____, to keep sales goals on track, （為了激勵和獎勵團隊） _____； and many more.

4.Another organization relating to world expositions is the IAEM. （根據國際博覽會管理協會的規定，當「博覽會」一詞用於商業展覽時，它大概可分為兩類：專業展覽和公眾展覽。） _____.

5.It sets policies for bidding on and holding world expositions. （透過競標，世界博覽局將世博會舉辦權授予申辦國。） _____.

6.The world exposition is an international event of showing industrial goods. （世博會是由總部在巴黎的世界博覽局管理的。） _____.

Section B Case Study

Read the following passage before solving the problems that ensue.

Types of Meetings

Hello, everybody. Today we will talk about meetings. Do you know what a meeting is and how many types of meetings there are?

There is more than one word for meeting, but they differ from each other in practical use.

The most commonly used word is convention. The dictionary tells us that a convention is a meeting of people for particular matters. Today's convention usually includes a general session and smaller meetings. Most conventions are held once a year.

A conference is similar to a convention. Everyone at the conference takes part in the discussion. The word conference is often used in the scientific area. It may or may not be a smaller meeting.

If large groups come together at a regular period of time, they take part in a congress. A congress may be held for several days. It is commonly used in Europe and in international meetings.

Small groups often hold seminars. Members can speak and get to know each other's experience and knowledge. When many people go to a seminar, it becomes a forum.

At a forum, there are speakers of different sides. They talk to the audience at the forum. The audience is usually allowed to ask questions, so there should be many microphones at the forum.

When none of the above terms applies to the gathering, it can be called a meeting. This is especially true when all members come from the same company to discuss matters, such as stockholder meetings, boarding directors meetings, etc.

I now hope you are able to better understand those different words for "meeting" and use them in a proper way.

Problem Solving

How do you solve the following problems? Outline your assertion.

1.Why is it important to know the exact meaning of each meeting term?

2.Give as many meeting terms as your memory can serve.

Section C Format Writing

Acquaint yourself with the following. Finish the exercises that ensue.

Exhibition Manuals 會展指南

Sample

The 11th ADIPEC

ADIPEC in brief

Started in 1984, ADIPEC—the Abu Dhabi International Petroleum Exhibition and Conference—has been a platform for the oil and gas industry to examine and evaluate the latest products, services, and technology the world has to offer. A steady growth over the years has helped ADIPEC become the largest and most informative Oil and Gas Exhibition and Conference in the Middle East.

ADIPEC is supported by Abu Dhabi National Oil Company and its Group of Companies, as well as the society of Petroleum Engineers.

Why Abu Dhabi plays host to ADIPEC

Abu Dhabi—the capital city of United Arab Emirates—accounts for more than 50% of the country's reserves and 85% of the country's actual output. With the third largest proven oil resources in the world, UAE currently has an estimated output of 2.5 million bpd, which is projected to increase to 4 million bpd in the coming years.

This by itself offers tremendous growth and expansion potential for the oil and gas industry—with the result that almost all major companies already present in the city. Further, Abu Dhabi is just a 2-hour flight away from other Arab countries—making it easily accessible and extremely convenient for travel.

Why ADIPEC 2004 is crucial for your company

ADIPEC is a forum that goes beyond the traditional buyer-seller meet. It is, in fact, a platform that enables local and international suppliers to make a detailed presentation of the latest products, services, and technology, to a specialized audience who is drawn entirely from the region's oil and gas industry. Further, this audience will be participating in the event with specific project needs—be it assessment of their procurement or contract needs.

ADIPEC facts

ADIPEC 2002—the 10th in the series—witnessed the participation of 935 exhibitors, representing both local and international oil and gas related companies, from 48 countries. Nearly 20, 535 visitors—most of them decision makers and high-ranking officials from around the world—attended the event. Their presence helped in making a final decision in either specifying or recommending the purchase of one or more of the products exhibited.

The ADIPEC conference

Running simultaneously with the Exhibition, the International Petroleum&Gas Conference will witness the presentation of Technical Papers authored by well-known engineers and scientists from the oil and gas industry.

In 2004, the theme for the Technical Papers will be：

"Managing resources and opportunities for the maturing global Oil & Gas industry."

The Papers presented at the 11th ADIPEC will be selected from abstracts submitted to the Technical Committee. Deadline for submission of abstracts is 1st November, 2003. For more details, visit the Conference page of the ADIPEC WEBSITE：www.adipec.com or e-mail us at adpec @ ec.ae.

The venue

The purpose-built, state-of-art Abu Dhabi International Exhibition Center-considered one of the most advanced Exhibition Centers in the Middle East—will form the venue of ADIPEC 2004. It offers a hassle-free ambience coupled with all the facilities of an international venue.

The organizer

General Exhibitions Corporation (GEC) acts as a supervisory body for all exhibitions and conferences held in the capital city. With vast experience as an event organizer, GEC has helped put up highly successful events at local, regional and international levels. To ensure the success of ADIPEC 2004, a core team of specialists are at hand to coordinate and supervise the event.

Questions about the Samples

Supply answers to the following questions based on your understanding of the format writing.

1.What is the mission of ADIPEC?

2.Why was Abu Dhabi selected to be the host city of the event?

3.What does "bpd" stand for?

4.What is the exhibitor benefit of the event?

5.What parallel activity will be held during the event?

Notes of Format

Always bear in mind the following.

「會展指南」是一個會議或展覽的說明書，其目的是向潛在讀者簡要介紹該會議或展覽的宗旨、類型、史料、特點、舉辦地、承辦方和主辦方、舉辦設施或場館等情況。「會展指南」一般包括以下內容：

1.Brief introduction of the event 會展的簡要介紹

2.Mission of the event 會展的宗旨

3.Why_____ (name of the venue city) plays host to_____ (name of the event) 為什麼由 _____ （城市名）來舉辦這個會展

4.Format （open to the public or to the trade or professionals）類型

5.Facts 史料

6.Agenda 日程安排

7.Venue and organizer 場館和主辦方

Do It Yourself

Work out a company profile with the Chinese prompts.

上海環球展覽公司成立於 1980 年，是一家以承辦中國國內和海外科技產品展覽為主的股份制機構。公司以促進上海科技產品進步，經濟與社會發展和各國、各地區人民之間的友好合作及貿易往來為宗旨，自成立至今，已和 60 多個國家和地區開展了富有成效的展覽合作。公司占地 25, 000 平方公尺，分為 1 號館和 2 號館，展區面積共有 16, 000 平方公尺，適合舉辦各種商業性或藝術性展覽會、研討會、時裝表演等活動。

Reference Answers

Reference Answers to Translating Activity

1.held without any type of program

2.large scale exhibitions are open to the public where a modest admission fee is typically charged

3.Despite rising costs for transportation and hospitality service to keep abreast of today's ever-changing technology to meet for group motivation and rewards

4.According to the IAEM, when the term "exposition" is applied to commercial shows, expositions generally fall into two types：trade shows and customer shows

5.And on basis of the competitive bids, it makes the award of a world exposition

6.It is regulated by the BIE in Paris

Answers to Questions about the Samples

1.The mission of ADIPEC is to provide a platform for the oil and gas industry to familiarize and evaluate the latest products, services and technology the world has to offer.

2.Because of its important position in the country's oil reserve and output.

3."Bpd" stands for "barrel per day".

4.It enables local and international suppliers to make a detailed presentation of the latest products, services and technology.

5.Some well-known oil and gas engineers and scientists will present Technical Papers at the International Petroleum & Gas Conference.

Reference Answer to Do It Yourself

Shanghai Global Exhibition Company (SGEC), founded in 1980, is a holding company mainly involved in organizing international or regional scientific and technical exhibitions. The mission of the company is to speed up scientific and technological progress, economic and social development of Shanghai as well as enhancing friendly cooperation between the Chinese people and the peoples of other countries and regions worldwide. Since its foundation, SGEC, has conducted fruitful and successful exhibition cooperation with more than 60 countries and regions. The company's building area covers a land of 25, 000 square meters, comprising two exhibition halls with an exhibition area of 16, 000 square meters for commercial or artistic shows, seminars, fashion shows, etc.

Chapter 2 MICE Planning 會展策劃

▍Section A Reading Assignment

Warming-up Activity

Go over the following terms with your teacher.

convention center 會議中心	action plan 行動計劃	corporate sales 公司銷售	training session 培訓會議
attendance 參加會議/展覽的人數	function 聚會	post meeting tour 會後旅遊	spouse program 攜帶配偶計劃
lead-time 從籌畫到會議/展覽實際舉行時的時間段	leisure amenity 休閒設施	interpersonal communication 人際溝通	customer need 客戶需求
to close a sale 達成銷售協議/做成一筆生意	to salvage a cancellation 挽救一個解約	to screen prospects 篩選潛在客戶	sales effort 銷售力度

Pre-reading Questions

Answer the following questions without referring to the text.

1.What is the director of the meeting sales department supposed to do?

2.Why do we need the meeting market?

3.How do you define "lead-time"?

4.Can you describe the differences between the corporate sales and the association sales as regards to their individual characteristics?

Text

Who Plans and Holds Meetings?

The marketing department is the first contact that the meeting group has with the convention center. The director of marketing initiates the sales effort by setting objectives and monitoring the action plans. It is also his or her job to administer, coordinate and supervise the activities of the sales department executives, who, in turn, are responsible for coordinating and directing the efforts of the sales staff. Due to the existence of various segments of meeting industry, the sales department may have different divisions that focus on corresponding markets. To sell a meeting, the sales department must know the meeting market inside out.

Today's meeting market falls into four major categories according to profitability : corporate sales, association sales, incentive meetings, and non-profit organizations.

The corporate meeting market includes company management meetings, planning, recruitment and sales meetings, and training sessions in off-company locations. Attendance of such meetings varies in size and is obligatory. The company organizing the meeting pays for all fees incurred and wants it to succeed achieving its organizational goal. Organizers and delegates are highly demanding for service standards. Prior to the meeting, the meeting venue works with the meeting organizer to plan the event and ensure that all the details are carefully agreed upon. Nowadays, the guaranteed meeting packages are the common practice to satisfy the wants of meeting groups.

Another lucrative market is the large number of professional and trade organizations that hold conventions on a regular basis. These meetings are voluntary and therefore have a variable attendance. Although most associations do not generate large revenue in the area of accommodation, food and beverage, they often hold functions such as annual dinners, post meeting tours, and spouse programs. This market is a major source of revenue for convention centers. Then what do association delegates look for? They want adequate meeting space, enough guest rooms, an attractive location, adequate exhibit space, and good service.

With respect to major national and international conventions involving hundreds or thousands of delegates, the lead-time may range from one year to ten years or more. The larger the convention, the greater the lead-time. Cities like Beijing, Shanghai and Hong Kong have provided dedicated facilities that attract major national and international conventions.

For such large conventions, climate factors, modern convention facilities, and leisure amenities are additional influences in deciding which venue to book. The role of the convention and visitors bureau is to promote the area and act as an information provider.

Sales tools are another aspect the sales department should not ignore due to their inherent nature. Sales tools for soliciting and following up convention business range from interpersonal communication media, such as personal calls and telephone calls, to mass media, such as direct mail and radio television advertising.

For most convention companies, personal calls receive top billing, primarily because large amounts of volume business can be generated through direct face-to-face dialogue with customers. It is rare for a customer to make a meeting commitment merely on the basis of looking at an ad, a brochure, or a form letter. The buyer and seller must personally get together.

The major constituents of personal sales calls are the environment where the meeting occurs, objectives that should be met during the visit, the presentation itself and the following up. Often you make appointments to meet with potential customers. You can also create visibility and make contacts by either visiting or actually participating in customer conventions and trade shows. There are times when the customer initiates the contact. Whatever the case, the sales executive must be astute enough to recognize the possibility of identifying potential customers. Objectives can include : to establish positive image or ameliorate a negative one, to discover customer needs, to obtain an advance commitment, to close a sale and get a definite booking, or to salvage a cancellation. The basic working technique in most sales presentations is to simply let the customer or potential buyer talk, which may involve responses to a series of probing questions or statements. The presentation allows for the immediate countering of objections and affords direct negotiating opportunities. An important step in following up a sales call is to send the prospect additional information, brochures, or other literature. It can also involve scheduling another sales call to make a presentation before a large site selection committee. Or, it may consist of scheduling a customer or committee visit to the convention venue.

Telephone calls are cost-effective, especially for screening prospects and for follow-ups. Next to personal visits, the phone affords the best means for communication between buyer and seller, and offers the opportunities for two-way, give-and-take communication, focusing precisely on items of interest to the specific buyer. Due to technological advances, the feasibility of using the telephone as a primary selling tool has been greatly enhanced. Nowadays we can use conference calls, linked facsimile transmission techniques, computer links, and closed-circuit TV hookups.

The actual use of sales tools often follows a specific sequence. Rarely is one particular tool used alone. And the tools should facilitate developing business from each targeted market segment.

Check-in

Do you have any questions about the text? If any, ask your teacher.

More Terms

venue 會議地點	form letter 格式信函	personal call 登門銷售	telephone call 電話銷售	direct mail 直接郵寄廣告

give-and-take 互讓	site selection committee 選址委員會	meeting commitment 會議委託	advance commitment 預約委託	closed-circuit TV hookup 閉路電視連接
presentation 介紹	literature （廣告用的）宣傳印刷品	prospect 有前途的候選人	brochure 小冊子	to follow up 後續回訪
objection 異議	cancellation 取消（預訂）	potential customer 潛在顧客	definite booking 正式預訂	targeted market segment 細分目標市場
facsimile transmission 傳真傳送	two-way communication 雙向溝通	to solicit and follow up convention business 招攬會議業務及後續回訪		

Important Vocabulary

initiate	[ɪˈnɪʃɪeɪt]	v.	開始
administer	[ədˈmɪnɪstə]	v.	管理
segment	[ˈsegmənt]	n.	部分
recruitment	[rɪˈkruːmənt]	n.	招聘
obligatory	[əˈblɪgətrɪ]	a.	必須的
incur	[ɪnˈkəː]	v.	蒙受
voluntary	[ˈvɔlʌntrɪ]	a.	自願的
solicit	[səˈlɪsɪt]	v.	徵求；懇求
primarily	[praɪmərɪlɪ]	adv.	主要地
constituent	[kənˈstɪtjuənt]	n.	構成物
visibility	[vɪzəbɪlətɪ]	n.	可見性
astute	[əˈstjuːt]	a.	敏銳的
ameliorate	[əˈmiːlɪəreit]	v.	改善
salvage	[ˈsælvɪdʒ]	v.	搶救
probe	[prəub]	v.	探索
counter	[ˈkauntə]	v.	抵消，反抗
feat	[fiːt]	n.	功績
feasibility	[ˌfiːzəˈbɪlətɪ]	n.	可行性
facilitate	[fəˈsɪlɪteɪt]	v.	促進

Useful Expressions

to set objectives	確立目標	to focus on	集中
to fall into	分為	to be demanding for	對……要求苛刻
prior to	在……之前	on a regular basis	定期
in respect of	在……方面	to establish positive image	樹立良好形象
by grace of	承蒙		

Language Focus

1.It is also his or her job to administer, coordinate and supervise the activities of the sales department executives, who, in turn, are responsible for coordinating and directing the efforts of the sales staff.

他或她的工作是管理、協調和監管銷售主管人員的活動，而銷售主管人員則負責協調和指導銷售人員的銷售工作。

2.Rarely is one particular tool used alone.

一種工具通常與其他工具一起使用。該句運用「反說正譯」法，將「不單獨使用」翻譯成「與其他工具一起使用」。

Group Discussion

Discuss the following topic in group. Select one on the team to make a presentation before the class.

▬ personal sales calls

▬ telephone sales calls

▬ the key items associated with personal sales calls

▬ the part the telephone plays in convention and group sales

Writing Activity

Summarize the text by outlining major points. Write a few lines about the MICE market and sales tools.

Translating Activity

Complete the following by translating the Chinese given in the brackets.

1. （如果細分目標市場是公司培訓會議）_____, the objective might be to acquaint the market with a new training facility you have under construction.

2. （登門銷售的優點之一就是）_____that it is a personalized two-way communication.

3.The particular type of sales call used_____ （通常涉及要實現什麼樣的重點目標）.

4.（儘管各種銷售手段都能用於招攬會議業務及後續回訪）_____, there is a general ranking of their potential effectiveness.

5.（接下來要做的就是發直接郵寄廣告、獲取最新有希望的候選會議客戶名單、寄送最新會議小冊子）_____and finally a concentrated program of sales calls.

6.（選擇適當的銷售手段將促進溝通渠道的暢通，如果成功的話，就可以促成）_____ the sale of meeting facilities that will benefit both buyer and seller.

Section B Case Study

Read the following passage before solving the problems that ensue.

The Convention Marketing Mix

There are at least six elements in the convention marketing mix, each beginning with the letter P. Selling a meeting begins with the product orientation. Many meeting organizers try to sell their meetings with little or no regard for what potential customers need, want and will pay. They fail to consider other elements of their marketing mix as they sell with a single product concept.

"Place" refers to the location and setting of the meeting. It can be a particular building, space, set of venues, or the atmosphere and the design created. Meeting products are distributed and sold to the clients in a convenient place. If done properly, the place can enhance the client's enjoyment. To make the place come alive, the programming element should never be neglected.

The meeting industry is a people industry. The staff are one essential ingredient in making the meeting success. It is necessary to develop a team spirit and customer orientation among staff. The interaction between customers, the setting and the staff constitute a large part of the convention service activities. Promotion refers to the communications tools, including advertising, public relations, and sales promotions. However, promotion requires ongoing rapport and image building.

The meeting product must be priced right and a package is often used to combine elements offered for sale at a single price. When selling packages, the distribution network becomes important. Intermediaries of various types will be required, such as travel agents, tour companies, computerized ticketing agents, and others.

Problem Solving

How do you solve the following problems? Outline your assertion.

1.What is the difference between marketing and sales?

2.Compare two local convention hotels in terms of : physical features, personnel, service, location and image.

Section C Format Writing

Acquaint yourself with the following. Finish the exercises that ensue.

Business Letters 商業信函

Sample 1

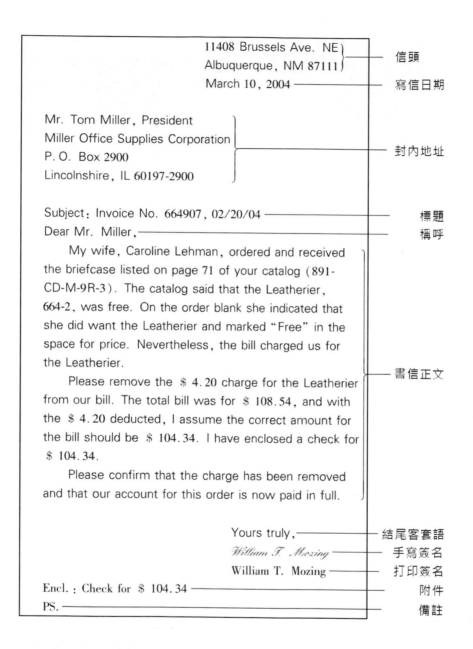

11408 Brussels Ave. NE — 信頭
Albuquerque, NM 87111
March 10, 2004 — 寫信日期

Mr. Tom Miller, President
Miller Office Supplies Corporation — 封內地址
P. O. Box 2900
Lincolnshire, IL 60197-2900

Subject：Invoice No. 664907, 02/20/04 — 標題
Dear Mr. Miller, — 稱呼

My wife, Caroline Lehman, ordered and received the briefcase listed on page 71 of your catalog (891-CD-M-9R-3). The catalog said that the Leatherier, 664-2, was free. On the order blank she indicated that she did want the Leatherier and marked "Free" in the space for price. Nevertheless, the bill charged us for the Leatherier.

Please remove the $ 4.20 charge for the Leatherier from our bill. The total bill was for $ 108.54, and with the $ 4.20 deducted, I assume the correct amount for the bill should be $ 104.34. I have enclosed a check for $ 104.34. — 書信正文

Please confirm that the charge has been removed and that our account for this order is now paid in full.

Yours truly, — 結尾客套語
William T. Mozing — 手寫簽名
William T. Mozing — 打印簽名

Encl. : Check for $ 104.34 — 附件
PS. — 備註

Sample 2

THE BRITISH MACHINERY COMPANY

Bingley Road, Birmingham

ENGLAND（信頭）

24 November, 2003（日期）

Messrs. Tada & Co.,

Marunouchi, Tokyo

Japan（收信人）

Attention of J. R. Smith （請……注意）

Gentlemen, （稱呼）

Re：British Machinery （標題）

（正文）

Our market survey informs us that you are interested in the import of machinery. We shall be pleased to receive your enquiries for machinery made in Britain. Our Machinery Division mainly acts as an export agent on a commission basis.

In order to prepare quotations, however, we would need some additional information with respect to the questions which are on the attached sheet and more particularly the checked ones.

Looking forward to receiving your early reply, and assuring you that your requirements will have our very best and prompt attention. Yours sincerely, （結尾客套語）

THE BRITISH MACHINERY COMPANY（公司名稱）

E. f. Bigelow（手寫簽名）

E. F. Bigelow, Manager （影印簽名）

Encl.：Copies of catalogues of our products.（附件）

PS.（附筆）

Sample 3

National Restaurant Association （NRA）

One IBM Plaza, SUITE 2600, Chicago, Illinois 60611

312/787-2525

January 17, 2004

Dear Exhibitor：

A new year means new budgets and higher sales projections for your company. The NRA restaurant, Hotel-Motel show will be five of the most important sales days of the year to attain these goals.

May 17-18-19-20-21, are the dates for the Annual NRA Show, to be held in Chicago at McCormick Place. Industry attendees at this show have averaged over 85,000 for the past three years, making this the largest, most important yearly event in the food service and lodging field.

To help join the growing list of 648 exhibitors who already contracted for the exhibit space, we have enclosed for your review a space sales brochure, which includes floor plan and cost information relative to your company exhibiting.

Call us collect so that we may discuss exhibit locations that are still available—don't delay, do it TODAY.

Sincerely yours,

GJR

Convention Director

GJR：JT

Encl.

Questions about the Samples

Answer the following questions based on your understanding of Sample 3.

1.Whom is this letter intended for?

2.What event will the reader of this letter be likely to attend?

3.How many contracts has the event organizer secured?

4.Who dictated this letter? And who typed this letter?

5.What items are enclosed in this letter?

Notes of Format

Always bear in mind the following.

英文商業信函主要組成部分

1. 信頭（Heading）

信頭的主要內容是發信人的公司名稱、地址、聯繫號碼、發信日期，有時還有發文編號等。商務信函中信頭一般都是印就的，只需填寫發文編號和日期即可。日期的寫法注意以下幾點：

寫日期時，月份名稱可以寫全稱或用縮寫字。但是 May，June，July 不縮寫；九月（September）是前四個字母的縮寫（Sept.），其餘月份為三個字母的縮寫。如：Jan.（January），Feb.（February），Mar.（March），Apr.（April），May，June，July，Aug.（August），Sept.（September），Oct.（October），Nov.（November），Dec.（December）。

日期的順序常有兩種：英國式和美國式。在英國式的寫法中，以日為先，月份為後；美國式則與之相反。

2. 封內地址（Inside Address）

　　封內地址應為收信人的公司名稱和地址。通常有下列幾個部分：公司名稱、門牌號碼和街名、城市或鎮名、州縣名和其郵政編碼、國名。

　　英文地址的寫法與漢語相反，即按從小到大的地址單位書寫。如中國上海市光明路 123 號，郵政編碼：200103。其英語地址為：123, Guangming Road, Shanghai 200103, P.R.China。郵政編碼或區號應跟在直轄市、省或州名的後面，國家名的前面。

　　又如：

Director of Exhibition Development Dept.

California Exhibition Center

18 Songbird Road

Oakland

CA 94611

U.S.A.

3. 稱呼（Salutation）

　　一般用 Dear Sirs,（英國式）或 Gentlemen：（美國式）。注意，不能單用 Sirs，而且 Gentlemen 不能用單數。

4. 書信正文（Body of the Letter）

　　信的正文是信函的主體，是最重要的部分。通常可分為三部分：引言、目的和結束語。正文部分中引言的功能是用來提及寫信的相關訊息。如「I was very happy to have received your letter dated March 12」， 或「Please forgive me for not writing to you for such a long time」。陳述寫信的目的時，要開門見山，簡單明瞭，言簡意賅。結束語一般是用來表達希望、願望和要求的。如「I look forward to your early reply」。

信函的主要目的是傳遞訊息，因此撰寫信函時要注意做到簡要（conciseness）、清楚（clearness）、有禮貌（courtesy），符合語法規則，並有針對性。分段要正確，每段限於一個主題。

5. 結尾客套語（Complimentary Close）

商務信函中最常用的稱呼及相稱的結尾客套語如下：

客氣稱呼	結尾	解釋
Dear Sir(s),	Yours faithfully,	英國式的正規用法
Gentlemen:	Yours sincerely, Yours truly,	美國式用法，比較隨意

結尾客套語的第一個詞的頭一個字母要大寫，標點用逗號。

6. 簽名（Signature）

第一行用作機構的名稱，全部用大寫字母；第二行用於簽名，多用鋼筆手寫體；第三行用於寫簽名人的頭銜（如 President，Director，Manager 等）或所屬部門。其他組成部分：

a）請某人注意（Attention of）

用於寫信人在發信給一個單位時希望把信遞交給某個具體成員。

b）標題（Subject）

信函中加上標題，便於讓對方一看就知道信的內容。標題的第一個詞或主要詞的第一個字母要大寫。在標題前可用 Re：或 Subject：，意為「事由」。Re 是拉丁文，不是 regarding 的縮寫。

c）附件（Enclosure）

如信中有附件，則應在左下角註明 Encl. 或 Enc.，之後要標明物件品名和數量。

d）附筆（Postscript）

在正文後頭，如需補充事項，可以附言。在商務信函中是計劃欠周的標誌，但特殊情況下可以造成正面作用，如有些經理在打好了的信函上偶爾附筆以示隨意親切。「P.S.See you at the Interexpo China next month.」又或營銷推廣人員為了加深印象常常把最有說服力的論點歸納在附筆中。「P.S.I learn the forum is great.」

信函常用句型

1. 私人書信常用開頭語

（1）I'm very happy to receive your letter of 16th April.

我收到了你 4 月 16 日的來信，十分高興。

（2）Thank you for your letter of 16th April written from Shanghai.

謝謝你 4 月 16 日從上海寫來的信。

（3）I had been looking forward to hearing from you and you can imagine my pleasure when I got your letter.

我一直盼望你的來信。你能想到我收到你的信時心裡有多高興。

（4）I hope you can forgive me for putting off writing you for so many days.

耽擱了這麼多天才回你的信，希望得到你的諒解。

（5）I was so glad to get your letter of 16th April and to learn that all's good with you.

我收到了你 4 月 16 日的來信，並得知你一切都好，十分高興。

（6）It was a great pleasure to get your letter telling me about your recent trip.

你來信跟我說了你前不久的旅行，我看了很高興。

（7）I'm sorry that I didn't write you as soon as I got your letter, but I've been very busy.

沒有及時回覆你的來信，我很抱歉。不過我前一陣確實很忙。

（8）Please forgive me for having delayed my answer to your letter.

請諒解我這麼遲才給你回信。

2. 私人書信常用結束語

（1）I hope this will not greatly inconvenience you.

但願那件事情不會給你添麻煩。

（2）I look forward to seeing you soon.

期待早日與你見面。

（3）I wish you every success.

祝你成功。

（4）I hope you'll get well soon.

希望你早日康復。

（5）I wish you every happiness on the coming trip.

祝你旅行愉快。

（6）Please remember me to your mother.

請代我向你母親問好。

（7）I hope you won't mind my not going.

我無法前往，請多包涵。

3. 商業書信常用開頭語

（1）This letter is to inform you that we have lately obtained a patent for an improved method of aluminum soldering.

我們改進的鋁銲接法最近獲得專利權，特此函告。

（2）In response to your letter of the 16th respecting the account, I will send you a check shortly.

16 日貴函關於結帳一事，謹此告知，我們將很快寄去支票。

（3）We received your letter dated 6th February.

您 2 月 6 日的來信收悉，多謝。

（4）We confirm our call of last week respecting our offers to you.

關於上週本公司透過電話給您的報價，我們特此予以確認。

（5）We have received your letter of 16th May, and confirm our today's telegram as per the copy enclosed.

我們收到您 5 月 16 日的信，我們已於今日發電報確認，請參閱所附該電抄件。

4. 商業書信常用結束語

（1）We thank you for your inquiry.

謝謝您的詢價。

（2）We thank you for your past favor, and I trust that you will continue the same in future.

感謝您往日的盛情，我相信您今後會一如既往。

（3）Please accept our apologies for the inconvenience this matter has given you.

對此事給您帶來的不便，請接受我們的歉意。

(4) We trust that this business may prove to our mutual advantage.

我們相信這一交易對雙方都有利。

(5) We hope to have your further orders for serges at an early date.

我們希望早日收到您的嗶嘰訂單。

(6) Enclosed please find the invoice of 80 bales of wool bought by your order.

依照您的訂單隨函附上 80 包羊毛的發票，請查收。

(7) We enclose for realization drafts as per the list at foot.

按照本函下列清單，附上應兌現的匯票。

Do It Yourself

Work out a company profile with the Chinese prompts.

下面是一封書信的部分訊息。將下列所給訊息按照其在書信的適當位置重新排列。

a. 標題：Re：Request for a Synopsis

b. 收信人：Dr. Maclean

c. 收信人地址：21, Pheasant Road, Newington, CT06111, U.S.A.

d. 寫信人：Osamu Nakamura, Program Coordinator

e. 寫信人地址：9-6-35 Rokuban-cho, Chiyoda-ku, Tokyo 102-8353, Japan

f. 發信日期：March 10, 2004

g. 結尾客套語：Yours sincerely,

h. 附件：Encl.：Journal of the Symposium

Reference Answers

Reference Answers to Translating Activity

1.If the target segment is corporate training meetings

2.One of the advantages of personal calls is

3.is usually related to achieving a key objective

4.Although all forms of sales tools can be used in convention business solicitation and follow-up

5.It could be followed by a direct mail campaign to obtain an up-to-date prospect list, a mailing of the new convention brochure

6.The selection of the proper sales tool will enhance a communication process that, if successful, will result in

Answers to Questions about the Samples

1.Food service and lodging exhibitors.

2.The NRA restaurant, Hotel-Motel Show.

3.648.

4.The Convention director with initials G.J.R.dictated the letter, while the secretary with initials JT typed this letter.

5.A space sales brochure

Chapter 3 Event Sponsorship 會展融資

▌Section A Reading Assignment

Warming-up Activity

Go over the following terms with your teacher.

property 酒店（旅遊會展接待服務場所）	demographics 人口統計學	revenue 收入	upscale 高端的
manufacturer 生產者，廠商	motive 動機	print media 出版媒體	brochure 小冊子
retailer 零售商	distributor 分銷商	merchandise 商品	brain storm 腦力激盪法

Pre-reading Questions

Answer the following questions without referring to the text.

1. How do you find potential sponsors for an event?

2. What would you do to design an attractive sponsorship package?

3. What is your definition of sponsorship?

Text

Identifying Potential Sponsors

Over the past decades there have been varied definitions of sponsorship. According to the International Event Group, or IEG, Inc. of Chicago, Illinois, sponsorship is "cash and/or an in-kind fee paid to a property（typically in sports, arts, entertainment or causes）in return for access to the exploitable commercial potential associated with that property." The Exordium Group, an industry strategy company headquartered in Cupertino, California, describes it as "a mutually beneficial relationship most often between a corporation and event or rights holder, for the purpose of enhancing a product or corporate brand." Sponsorship is fast becoming the fourth arm of marketing, in addition to advertising, promotions, and public relations.

Sponsorship becomes more valuable if the event organization is able to offer precise targeting that matches the marketing objectives of the prospective sponsor. The growth in sponsorship is due primarily to the need by advertisers to find alternative marketing channels to inform, persuade, promote, and sell their products and services. However, the number of events that require sponsorship has also grown in recent years.

Without sponsorship, many events would not be financially feasible. Other events would not be able to achieve their specified goals and objectives. Suffice it to say that more often than not, sponsorship provides the grease that allows the event wheel to function smoothly.

Historically, sponsorship has its earliest modern origin in professional sporting events. These events have always appealed to the widest demographics and were therefore the perfect event product for sponsorship. Sponsorship is a uniquely American invention brought forth from the need of advertisers to reach certain markets and the need of event organizers to identify additional funding to offset costs not covered by normal revenue streams, such as ticket sales.

In recent times there has been a noticeable shift in sponsor dollars away from sporting events and toward arts events. The reason for this shift is that sponsors are seeking more highly targeted upscale demographics, and the arts audience delivers that market segment. Therefore, those events that deliver the higher-income demographics are predicted to benefit most from sponsorship dollars in the future.

Perhaps the best example of sport sponsorship is the 1984 Summer Olympics Games in Los Angeles, California. For the first time in the history of the modern Olympic Games movement, sponsors were aggressively solicited as marketing partners for this unprecedented event. Offers were made, deals were cut, and the Los Angles Olympic Organizing Committee received a net earnings of over $200 million.

From fairs to festivals to hallmark events such as a world's fair, the role of the sponsor has earned a permanent place in the marketing lexicon of events. Following are typical types of sponsors for a variety of events.

Fair : bottler, grocer, automotive, and bank.

Festival : department store and record store.

Sport : athletic wear manufacturer, bottler, brewery, and hospital or health care facility.

School program : children's toy stores, children's clothing stores, and amusement park.

Meeting/conference : printer, bank, insurance, broker, and associate member firms.

There are many reasons for companies to sponsor events. You must first understand these reasons before developing a marketing plan : event managers must look at sponsorship through the eyes of the sponsor. According to the International Events Group of Chicago, there are ten reasons that companies sponsor events :

(1) Heighten visibility :

Visibility is often the first reason that companies sponsor events. Larger events enjoy wide exposure, particularly on television, and also in the print media, and provide traditional sponsor benefits of signage, brochures and so forth.

(2) Shape consumer attitudes :

It is in shaping consumer attitudes that sponsorship can create or change a brand image. Sponsors such as Coca-Cola and Pepsi do not need any more visibility, but they do like to tie in with particular lifestyles.

(3) Narrowcasting :

Sponsorship gives companies an opportunity to reach a niche market.

(4) Provide incentives for retailers and distributors :

Within the walls of retail stores, products are constantly fighting for shelf space. Some companies use sponsorship to ensure good shelf presence, which guarantees the ever-so-important eye contact with their products as customers wheel their carts down the aisles of stories.

(5) Entertain clients :

The opportunity to host clients at an event, especially for those clients who can not get tickets, sometimes pays for the entire sponsorship.

(6) Recruit/retain employees：

During times of low unemployment, companies are required to go to greater lengths to recruit and keep employees, so they often use the sponsorship arena to help attract and retain staff.

(7) Create merchandising opportunities：

Sponsors can use events as merchandising opportunities.

(8) Showcase product attributes：

One of the truly tremendous things about sponsorship is that companies can actually see their products in action at a festival or event, which they cannot do with other forms of media. Event managers who showcase product attributes are providing a great service for sponsors, as they actually show their products to potential customers during an event. Wireless cell phone companies benefit from being in-kind sponsors by donating telephones to event producers, which are then seen in action by attendees.

(9) Differentiate their product from competitors：

Differentiating products from those of competitors is another area in which sponsorship scores high, in as much as an event usually ensures category exclusive, which enables financial institutions and other service industries to stand out from their competitors.

(10) Drive sales：

An increasing number of companies are using sponsorship to drive sales. With the understanding of these reasons, before beginning to identify potential sponsors that fit your event, it is important to remember that sponsorship is neither benevolence nor philanthropy. While you can have both sponsorship and philanthropy (donors) to support the revenue side of your budget, each is a very distinct entity. While philanthropic gifts are given out of a sense of altruism, sponsors are looking for a return on their investment (ROI). It is important to distinguish this type of revenue, as it will help in identifying potential sponsors. Another distinction that needs to be made in identifying potential sponsors is the type of event. This is particularly important when you begin to eliminate potential sponsors from your list based on their corporate policies with respect to the types of events they do and do not sponsor. You then can begin to identify the types of sponsors you are seeking :

1.Title/Presenting Sponsor : Underwrites a majority of the event.

2.Host/Supporting Sponsor : Underwrites specific areas of an event such as bars or food and beverage.

3.Tiered Sponsor : Monetary level determines the amount of exposure for sponsors' products, services, and individual leaders. Media sponsors (print, radio, television, Web site sponsors, etc.) and co-sponsors are typical examples of this kind of sponsors.

4.In-kind Sponsor : Often overlooked, in-kind sponsors provide their goods or services at no cost to the event for a sponsorship level that is related to the retail cost of the goods or services provided.

Once you have decided on the type of sponsor—or, more likely, the combination of sponsors—you can begin your research into entities that are interested in sponsorships and are a match with the audience and type of event you are producing. When you begin to brainstorm for potential sponsors, you must be aware that sponsors are everywhere ; they are not located just among the large multinational corporations, but also can be found at the corner store. Do not eliminate sponsors from your list because you think they are too small. You must remember that when you are looking for sponsorship, one of the first rules of thumb in budgeting is that everything has a price. This includes sponsorships. Again, the sponsorship is not a donation. It is a business deal where you are agreeing to promote in the sponsors'goods and/or services in return for the value of your event to them. Not only does the servicing of this agreement have a price tag that impacts the expense side of your budget, it also has costs associated with it. Budgetary issues then become one of the first items to review when looking at potential sponsors. Is the ratio of expense to revenue to service in the agreement worth the effort to secure the sponsorship?

Check-in

Do you have any questions about the text? If any, ask your teacher.

More Terms

sponsorship 贊助	in-kind 實物，非現金所得的貨物、商品或服務，而不是現錢	cause 理想；目標，事業	hallmark event 特點活動
amusement park 遊樂園，樂園	heightening visibility 提高曝光率，提高知名度	narrowcasting 窄帶廣播	title sponsorship 冠名贊助

Important Vocabulary

headquarter	[ˌhedˈkwɔːlə]	v.	以……做總部，設總公司於……
prospective	[prəˈspektɪv]	a.	預期的
alternative	[ɔːlˈtəːnətɪv]	a.	選擇性的，二擇一的
feasible	[ˈfiːzəbl]	a.	可行的，切實可行的
grease	[griːs]	n.	潤滑脂
demography	[dɪˈmɒɡrəfɪ]	n.	人口統計學
unprecedented	[ʌnˈpresɪdentɪd]	a	空前的
permanent	[ˈpəːmənənt]	a.	永久的，持久的
lexicon	[ˈleksikən]	n.	詞典
bottler	[ˈbɒtlə]	n.	從事裝瓶飲料的企業
grocer	[ˈgrəusə]	n.	食品商，雜貨店
brewery	[ˈbruːərɪ]	n.	釀酒廠
recruit	[rɪˈkruːt]	v.	補充，徵募
retain	[rɪˈteɪn]	v.	保持，保留
arena	[əˈriːnə]	n.	競技場，舞台
benevolence	[bɪˈnevələns]	n.	仁愛心，善行

philanthropy	[fɪˈlænθrəpɪ]	n.	慈善事業
entity	[ˈentətɪ]	n.	實體
altruism	[ˈæltruːɪzəm]	n.	利他主義，利他
eliminate	[ɪˈlɪmɪneɪt]	v.	排除，消除

Useful Expressions

in return for	作為……的報答
suffice it to say that. . .	說……就足夠了
to go to great lengths/ go (to) all [any] lengths	竭盡全力；走極端；什麼都做得出

Language Focus

1.Suffice it to say that more often than not, sponsorship provides the grease that allows the event wheel to function smoothly.

只要說贊助通常是活動順利進行的潤滑劑，就足以說明這個問題。

2.Sponsorship is a uniquely American invention brought forth from the need of advertisers to reach certain markets and the need of event organizers to identify additional funding to offset costs not covered by normal revenue streams, such as ticket sales.

贊助是典型的美國式創造，它因以下兩種需求而產生：廣告客戶需要影響特定市場；活動組織者需要獲得額外的資金，來抵消正規收入來源——如門票銷售——所不能沖抵的成本。

Group Discussion

Discuss the following topic in group. Select one on the team to make a presentation before the class.

Why do a lot of companies sponsor events?

Guidelines for Discussion

— heighten visibility

— shape consumer attitude

■ narrow casting

■ provide incentives for retailers

■ entertain clients

■ showcase product attributes

Writing Activity

Summarize the text by outlining major points. Write a few lines about online marketing tools.

Section B Case Study

Read the following passage before solving the problems that ensue.

Sponsorship of ICT 2002

Capture immediate market exposure, global market recognition for your organization, and support the goals of the International conference on Telecommunications （ICT） conference by becoming an ICT 2002 sponsor. Besides exposure advantages, sponsors will meet personally with world-class influential decision-makers and support the development of the telecommunications technologies. Sponsors may demonstrate their products or services to buyers and decision-makers as exhibitors of the ICT 2002 Conference.

To become a sponsor of ICT 2002, contact the ICT 2002 "Sponsorship contact person." All sponsorship events are sold on a first-come, first-served basis. All exhibition booth assignments are made on a first-paid, first-assigned basis.

Sponsor Levels and Benefits

Several levels of sponsorship are available to ICT 2002 sponsors. Benefits are commensurate with level of sponsorship, which is determined by the total cash contributions.

Add to your organization visibility and prestige in the global telecomm-unications business and among its leaders by becoming an ICT 2002 sponsor!

ICT 2002 sponsors are acknowledged in all publications printed after a commitment to sponsor is made. If you don't see an opportunity below that interests you, contact the ICT 2002

Conference Secretariat. We will customize an appropriate sponsorship opportunity for your organization. Here is our contact number or visit our website :

Mr. FANG Dongbo

Tel : 0086 10 62282808/62281774 Fax : 0086 10 62281774

Http : //www.bupt.edu.cn/ict2002

The sponsors will be favored for specific technical presentations during the normal program, by request only. The topics and the forms of contributions—slides only, or text and slides—will be discussed with the organizers during the signature of the sponsorship contract.

Main Platinum Sponsor （minimum US $50,000)

Benefits :

Exhibition space : equivalent of ten （10) modules of 9 sq. m. each （90 sq. m.）, which include basic furniture, carpeting, lighting, AC supply.

Ten （10) full ICT 2002 conference registrations.

Organization name and logo printed in the ICT 2002 Program Guide on a dedicated page with special mention as Main Sponsor.

Organization name and URL placed on the ICT 2002 Website on dedicated page.

Complimentary listing in the On-Site Sponsor Directory, which includes a description of sponsor's organization profile.

Custom signage at entrance to Exhibition Hall.

Invited talk in Business Session.

Gold Sponsor （US $25,000 to US $49,999)

Benefits：

Exhibition space：equivalent of five（5）modules of 9 sq. m. each（45 sq. m.），which includes basic furniture, lighting, AC supply.

Six（6）full ICT 2002 conference registrations（Free）

Organization name and logo printed in the ICT 2002 Program Guide on a

dedicated page.

Organization name and URL placed on the ICT 2002 Website（two Gold Sponsors on a page.

Complimentary listing in the On-Site Sponsor Directory, which includes a description of sponsor organization profile.

Custom signage at entrance to Exhibition Hall.

Invited talk in Business Session.

Silver Sponsor （US $15,000 to US $24,999)

Benefits：

Exhibition space：equivalent of three （3）modules of 9 sq. m. each （27 sq. m.），which includes basic furniture, carpeting, lighting, AC supply

Four （4）full ICT 2002 conference registrations

Organization name and logo printed in the ICT 2002 Program Guide on a dedicated page

Organization name and URL placed on the ICT 2002 Website （three Silver Sponsors on a page)

Complimentary listing in the On-Site Sponsor Directory, which includes a description of sponsor's organization profile.

Custom signage at entrance to Exhibition Hall.

Invited talk in Business Session.

Bronze Sponsor (US $10,000 US to $14,999)

Benefits :

Exhibition space : equivalent of two (2) modules of 9 sq. m. each (18 sq. m.) , which includes basic furniture, carpeting, lighting, and AC supply. Two (2) full ICT 2002 conference registrations.

Organization name and logo printed in the ICT 2002 Program Guide (two Bronze Sponsors on a dedicated page) .

Organization name and URL placed on the ICT 2002 Website (four Bronze Sponsors on a page) .

Complimentary listing in the On-Site Sponsor Directory, which includes a description of sponsor's organization profile.

Custom signage at entrance to Exhibition Hall.

Invited talk in Business Session.

Sustaining Sponsors I (US $5,000 to US $9,999)

Benefits

Five (5) full ICT 2002 conference registrations.

Organization name and logo printed in the ICT 2002 Program Guide.

Organization name and URL placed on the ICT 2002 Website.

Complimentary listing in the On-Site Sponsor Directory, which includes a description of sponsor's organization profile.

Sustaining Sponsors II （US $2,500 to US $4,999）

Benefits：

Three （3） full ICT 2002 conference registrations.

Organization name printed in the ICT 2002 Program Guide.

Organization name and URL placed on the ICT 2002 Website.

Complimentary listing in the On-Site Sponsor Directory, which includes a description of sponsor's organization profile.

Sustaining Sponsors III （US $1,000 to US $2,499）

Benefits：

One （1） full ICT 2002 conference registrations.

Organization name printed in the ICT 2002 Program Guide.

Organization name and URL placed on the ICT 2002 Website.

EVENT SPONSORS：

Individual sponsors and "consortia" of sponsors are expected to cover the costs of the events associated to the ICT 2002 listed below. The sponsors may express their own interest for sponsoring one or more events of the ICT 2002 within the sponsorship amount contracted.

GALA EVENING SPONSORS （4×US $2,500）

Total sponsorship required—US $10,000

Date—June 25th, 2002

This unique and festive evening is the social highlight of ICT 2002. A tempting array of hors oeuvres and refreshments and selected Romanian wines are to be served. Your organization may distribute their own logo'd items, such as napkins or cups. A custom banner, provided by the ICT 2002 Conference, will also be displayed during the Gala.

OPENING RECEPTION AND COCKTAIL SPONSORS (4×US $2,500)

Total sponsorship required—US $10,000

Date—June 24th 2002

Establish your organization's presence at the ICT 2002 kick-off event—the attendee's first impression of the conference. Assorted hors oeuvres and refreshments are served. Custom signage is provided. During the reception, the sponsor may distribute their own logo'd items, such as napkins or cups. CONFERENCE LUNCH SPONSORS (4×US $5,000)

Total sponsorship required—US $20,000

Date—June 23-26, 2002

Increase your organization's recognition with a strong presence at an ICT 2002 plated luncheon. As sponsor, your organization receives custom signage at the lunch entrance and during the lunch, your organization may distribute their own logo'd items, such as napkins or cups.

TOTE BAGS SPONSORS (4×US $3,000)

Total sponsorship required—US $12,000

As a sponsor of the tote bags, your organization will work with the ICT 2002 Conference Secretariat to design a custom ICT 2002 tote bag. Every conference attendee receives the tote bag, complete with your organization's name and logo, and filled with all conference-related materials.

CUSTOM T-SHIRT SPONSOR （4×US $3,000)

Total sponsorship required—US $12,000

In sponsoring the conference T-shirt, your organization will work with the ICT 2002 Conference Secretariat to design a custom ICT 2002 T-shirt. Every conference attendee will receive the T-shirt, complete with your organization's name and logo.

SOCIAL EVENT SPONSORS （4×US $3,000)

Total sponsorship required—US $12,000

Date—June 22-27, 2002

Social events （e.g. opera, theatre, tours, etc.) will be determined and timely announced by the organizing committee （please contact：ICT2002 @ bupt.edu.cn for special events).

INTERNET ACCESS ROOM—EXHIBITION HALL （5×US $2,000)

Total sponsorship required—US 10,000

One of the most popular rooms during ICT 2002 conferences, the Internet Access Room is open 14 hours each day, during all four days, to conference and exhibition attendees. The Exhibition Hall Internet Access Room has direct, high-bandwidth connections through the Internet, with over 30 computers and docking stations. The Conference Center Room has 5 computers and also hubs for attendees' laptop computers. As sponsor, your organization receives custom signage in the Access Room.

REFRESHMENT/COFFEE BREAKS （4×US $1,250）

Total sponsorship required—US $5,000

Date—June 23-26, 2002

Take advantage of the time after the morning Plenary Session and during the afternoon session break to promote your organization. As sponsor, you receive custom signage and may distribute your own logo'd items, such as napkins or cups. Covers two refreshment breaks daily.

AWARDS SPONSORSHIP （10×US $1,000）

Total sponsorship required—US $10,000

Date—June 26th, 2002

We expect more than 10 such awards to be given. Commonly, these awards are internationally published via our Organization Committee and may be granted for innovative proposed publications, outstanding presentations, encouraging young authors, or awarding special demos.

Notes：

AC supply：變頻電源

URL：Uniform Resource Locator 統一資源定位系統

Problem Solving

How do you solve the following problems? Outline your assertion.

Problems

1.How many levels of sponsorship are available to ICT 2002 sponsors?

2.What could we do to offer benefits to the sponsors?

My Solutions

Solution to Problem 1 : _____

Solution to Problem 2 : _____

Section C Format Writing

Acquaint yourself with the following. Finish the exercises that ensue.

Part 1 Visiting Card 名片

上海世博會事務協調局

張　　三

項目經理

地址：上海延安中路１０００號　　電話：86-21-×××××××

郵遞區號：200040　　傳真：86-21-×××××××

Bureau of Shanghai World Expo Coordination

Tom　　Zhang

Program Manager

Add：No. 1000，Yan'an Road（M）　　Tel：86-21-×××××××

Shanghai 200040，P. R. China　　Fax：86-21-×××××××

```
┌─────────────────────────────────────┐
│                                      │
│              張　三                  │
│           訪問教授                    │
│                                      │
│               SACE-SIFT 中美研究所    │
│                 世界與社會研究         │
│                    臺奇學院           │
│            特洛伊市，紐約州 XXXXX - XXXX │
│        電話：XXX - XXXX 傳真：XXX - XXX - XXXX │
│               電子郵箱：zhs@sage.edu  │
│                                      │
└─────────────────────────────────────┘
```

```
┌─────────────────────────────────────┐
│                                      │
│              ZHANG SAN               │
│            Visiting Professor        │
│  SAGE-SIFT Institute of Sino-American Studies │
│   Department of Global & Community studies    │
│            The Sage Colleges         │
│ Troy，New York ×××××-××××Tel；×××-××××Fax；×××-×××-×××× │
│            E-mail；zhs@ sage. edu    │
│                                      │
└─────────────────────────────────────┘
```

Notes of Format

Always bear in mind the following.

名片的使用，是為了便於社交和處理公務。其寫法是將本人的名字寫在名片中間或略高於中間的地方。名字用全稱，前面可加上學銜、職位等稱呼，但頭銜的字體應小於名字的字體。上方應寫上工作單位。下方應寫地址、電話和傳真號碼以及電子郵件地址，也可加上手機號碼以便聯繫。其字體一般與頭銜字體一致，小於名字的字體。

Do It Yourself

Suppose you are newly recruited to work as the deputy director of Customer Service Department of Shanghai New International Expo Center.Design a visiting card for yourself with the following information.

上海新國際博覽中心 客戶服務部

地址：中國上海浦東新區龍陽路 2345 號

電話：86-21-××××××××

傳真：86-21-×××××××

郵編：201204

Part 2 Memo 內部通知

Sample 1

MEMO

TO： All Staff

FROM：Joy Lin

DATE：March 10, 2004

SUBJECT：VISIT OF AMERICAN DELEGATION

Staff are informed that this visit will occur on Monday March 15, 2004.

The next morning there will be a presentation to the group by senior staff and an opportunity for discussion between delegates and among ourselves.

All staff are welcomed and please inform me of your arrival before March 13.

Sample 2

To：Mr.M.Qin

From：Sally

Date：29 February, 2004

Sub：Booking Done

A single room with bath and shower has been reserved for Mr.Yocio Yamakuchi at the Garden Hotel from 3 March to 6 March as you have instructed.

Sample 3

FAX MEMORANDUM

TO :   David Blenchevinz

DMB Speaker's Bureau

FROM : Harry Freedman

ABC Woman's Corps

DATE : May 30, 2005

Re :   SALLY JESSY RAPHAEL'S CONTRACT

Enclosed is a faxed copy of the contract and check for Sally Jessy Raphael's speaking engagement for our "Women Who Lead" awards luncheon on Thursday, July 8, 2005.

I also have enclosed copies of correspondence for this event and draft samples of our "SAVE THE DATE" card.

As we discussed, I need photos of Sally Jessy Raphael in order to complete our "SAVE THE DATE" cards and to go with our press releases.As you know, the "season" gets jam packed in Palm Beach so the earlier we get information out to committee and press, the better the response.

Thanks!

Questions about the Samples

Choose the best answers to the following questions based on your understanding of the format writing.

1.Who wrote this memo?

A.Harry Freedman.

B.David Blenchevinz.

C.Sally Jessy Raphael.

D.NOT MENTIONED.

2.For whom is this memo intended?

A.Harry Freedman.

B.David Blenchevinz.

C.Sally Jessy Raphael.

D.NOT MENTIONED.

3.The memo is about_____.

A.the photos of Sally Jessy Raphael

B.the contract with a speaker

C.the press releases

D.the awards luncheon

4.A copy of contract has been （is） _____.

A.sent together with the memo

B.faxed to David earlier

C.sent to David before the "SAVE THE DATE" card

D.sent to the press

5.Items sent together with this memo also include _____.

A.photos of Sally Jessy Raphael

B.copies of communication letters for this event

C.draft samples of our "SAVE THE DATE" card

D.all of the above

Notes of Format

Always bear in mind the following.

備忘錄屬於簡易公文，主要用來提醒督促對方，或補充正式文件的不足，是各部門書面聯繫的一種手段。

撰寫備忘錄時應遵循 POSE 原則，即：

· Positive

使用正面語氣，如使用「Please do be on time」，而不是「Don't be late for the meeting」。

· Only

一文一事，如有多項事務通報，最好分開撰寫。

· Short

句子段落寧短勿長，備忘錄屬非正式公文，應儘量做到清晰簡潔。

· Easy

通俗易懂，不要讓收到備忘錄的人還要花時間去查閱生詞。

Do It Yourself

Suppose you are to send a memo for the HR director to all staff on the May Day holiday, which starts at 4：00 p.m.on April 30 and ends at 9：00 a.m.on May 8.Complete the Memo.

```
┌──────────────────────────────────────────────┐
│ FAX MEMORANDUM                                 │
│ TO：                                           │
│ FROM：                                         │
│ DATE：                                         │
│                                                │
│ Re：                                           │
└──────────────────────────────────────────────┘
```

　　五一放假時間自 4 月 30 日下午 4 點起至 5 月 8 日上午 9 點止。希望各位放假前能完成自己計劃中的工作。祝各位假期愉快。

Reference Answers

Answers to Do it Yourself of Part 1

```
┌──────────────────────────────────────────────────────┐
│      Shanghai New International Exposition Center      │
│                  Cindy   Wang                          │
│            Customer Service Department                 │
│                                                        │
│  Add：No. 2345，Long Yang Road，Pudong   Tel：86-21- ××××××××  │
│       Shanghai 201204，P. R. China       Fax：86-21- ×××××××× │
└──────────────────────────────────────────────────────┘
```

Answers to Questions about the Samples of Part 2

1.A2.B3.B4.A5.C

Reference Answer to Do It Yourself of Patr 2

```
┌──────────────────────────────────────────────────────────┐
│ MEMO                                                       │
│ TO：         All Staff                                     │
│ FROM：       Cindy Wang                                    │
│ DATE：       April 25，2006                                │
│ SUBJECT：    LABOR DAY HOLIDAY                             │
│ The Labor Day Holiday will start on 4 p. m. April 30，and end on 9 a. m. May 8. │
│ All staff is expected to finish the work planned.          │
│ Have a good time！                                         │
└──────────────────────────────────────────────────────────┘
```

Chapter 4 Event Marketing 會展營銷

Section A Reading Assignment

Warming-up Activity

Go over the following terms with your teacher.

cross promotion 交叉宣傳 利用某媒體來宣傳另一媒體。例如，一個電視網可在其各個頻道上交叉宣傳各姐妹頻道的節目。	niche market 縫隙市場，也稱利基市場，是指在市場中通常北大企業所忽略的某些細分市場	direct marketing 直效行銷，指任何與消費者或商務客戶直接溝通，以獲取回應的方式。所得回應包括發出訂單（直接訂購/Direct Order），諮詢更多資料（衍生導引性銷售/Lead Generation），及／或光臨店鋪或其他商務地點購買指定產品或服務（衍生人流）等。	electric commerce（e-commerce）電子商務
web site 網頁	statistics 統計，統計數字	stunt 特技表演，絕技	startup 啟動

media coverage 媒體報道	product launch 產品發佈	focus group 焦點團體訪談	questionnaire 調查表，問卷
cost/ benefit ratio 成本效益比率；性價比	publicity 宣傳；推廣；廣告	profile 資質；簡介；個性及生平的簡要描述	virtual conference 虛擬會議

Pre-reading Questions

Answer the following questions without referring to the text.

1.How do you promote an event to a target market?

2.What role does the Internet play in the event marketing?

3.What is the difference between advertising and public relation?

Text

Online Event Marketing

The Internet can be a highly efficient tool in the overall marketing programs of event management organization.At the same time, it can be a major financial burden if an event management organization does not formulate specific goals for its Internet marketing policy. The objectives for each event management organization may vary, depending on company size, dynamics of operations, financial and staff resources, location, overall development strategy, and client base. The web site for a small event management startup will differ from that of a large multinational event management conglomerate.Major marketing concepts enhanced by online tools include brand building, direct marketing, online sales and online commerce, customer support, market research, and product or service development and testing.

Brand Building.Online marketing, combined with television, media, and print is a major brand-building tool.The biggest advantage the Internet has over television and old-fashioned media is the favorable cost/benefit ratio.Event management organizations can achieve a much higher return on their marketing investments in Internet promotions than in a traditional campaign.It is very important to submit your company's profile to all of the major search engines.Submitting your company's profile to most search engines is free, so there is no reason not to do it.

Direct Marketing.According to Bruce Rvan, vice-president and general manager of Media Metrix, a research firm that studies Web users' characteristics and profiles, more than 80 percent of personal computer (PC) owners have at least one college degree.Their average household income is about $ 50,000 per year, well above the $35,000 U.S. household average.These consumers could be a prime market niche for event management organizations.Customers with household income of less than $40,000 per year often cannot afford to contract a professional event manager.By placing well-designed information and ads about your event management services on the Internet, you gain immediate direct contact with your target market group.In addition, larger competitors have no significant advantage over smaller organizations on the Internet.

Online Sales.An online sales concept is more applicable to companies that sell consumers goods, not services.However, event management organizations can still benefit greatly from Internet electronic commerce features.Event management organizations conduct registration, ticket sales, and distribution of materials over the Internet.All of these are segments of event sales.By putting them online, event management companies achieve financial savings and preserve resources that can now be reallocated.

Among the most important problems of online commerce is the problem of security.If an event management organization conducts financial transactions over the Internet, the security of clients' personal financial information is a top priority.Data that contain information, such as credit card and social security numbers, are very sensitive.It is important to ensure that these data are protected.Since this is a critical point, it is highly recommended that you involve security professionals in this aspect of your web site development.

Customer Support.Event customer support is one of the areas where the Internet can be truly indispensable.Industry analysts predict that in coming years, many event management companies will shift their telephone customer support services to the Web. This does not mean that telephone-based services will disappear ; however, they will become a secondary source that customers will use if they need to get a more detailed response or resolve a problem.The primary source for customer support will be the Internet.

The first step in shifting at least part of their customer support services online is to start a "Frequently Asked Questions" (FAQ) Web section.Simply by adding this section to an event management organization web site an organization can achieve better customer service and improve efficiency.The next step after posting an FAQ page is to personalize online customer service.This can be accomplished by adding the following interactive feature to a customer support site. A customer is asked to type his or her question and submit an e-mail address.Then the customer receives an answer within a certain time frame via either e-mail or telephone.By adding this feature an event organization can achieve much more personalized customer service and can also collect very valuable data about its clients.

Market Research.Increasingly, event management organizations are recognizing the Internet potential for market research.Burke Inc., a leading international market research firm with a history of over 65 years, conducts online focus group meetings for its client in addition to face-to-face interviews and telephone surveys.Using Internet technology, the company is able to bring together participants from different parts of the world for small, real-time chat sessions.Clients can observe these chat sessions from anywhere in the world.

Web sites can be used to conduct market research by surveying visitors.This information can be effective if the process is well planned.Unfortunately, many Web sites require users to complete online registration forms without providing incentives.As a result, users often submit incorrect information or simply ignore the forms. This behavior can be explained by the desire of users to guard their privacy online and fear that their e-mail addresses will be sold to third parties.The best way to overcome this constraint is to build a sense of trust between event organization and clients or to compensate users for submitting their data.

Product or Service Development and Testing.The Internet is an ideal place for event companies to test new products/services before they are launched.An event organization can post information about a conference that it is planning to organize online and monitor the interest that users express toward the conference.By doing this, the organization can see a market's reaction to the conference before they invest large amounts in actual planning.This refers to the first stage of successful event management event research.One of the biggest advantages of the Internet over other marketing tools is real-time contact.Marketing professionals con use a number of special technical features to leverage this point.Chat rooms, live broadcasting, and time-sensitive promotions are only a small part.The Internet allows marketing professionals to change and update content in almost no time and hence ensure that customers have the most recent information.

Check-in

Do you have any questions about your reading assignment? If any, ask your teacher.

Important Vocabulary

formulate	[fɔːmjuːleɪt]	v.	闡明
conglomerate	[kənˈglɒmərət]	v.	聚集
niche	[nɪtʃ]	a.	瞄準機會的
applicable	[ˈæplɪkəbl]	a.	可適用的，可應用的
registration	[ˌredʒɪˈstreɪʃən]	n.	註冊，報到，登記
distribution	[ˌdɪstrɪˈbjuːʃən]	n.	分配，分發，配給物
reallocate	[rɪˈæləkeɪt]	v.	再分配，再指派
transaction	[trænˈzækʃən]	n.	辦理，處理，交易
indispensable	[ˌɪndɪˈspensəbl]	a.	不可缺少的，絕對必要的

personalize	[ˈpɜːsənəlaɪz]	v.	使人格化；賦予個性
constraint	[kənˈstreɪnt]	n.	約束，強制，局促
compensate	[ˈkɒmpenseɪt]	v.	償還，補償，付報酬
leverage	[ˈliːvərɪdʒ]	v.	通過槓桿作用進行影響

Useful Expressions

Frequently Asked Questions(FAQ)	常見疑問
focus group meeting	焦點小組會談
time-sensitive promotions	限時促銷

Language Focus

1.The biggest advantage the Internet has over television and old-fashioned media is the favorable cost/benefit ratio.

互聯網與電視及其他傳統媒介相比，最大的優勢在於令人滿意的成本收益率。

2.Since this is a critical point, it is highly recommended that you involve security professionals in this aspect of your Web site development.

既然這一點十分關鍵，你最好在進行網頁開發時借助一些專業安全控制人員的力量。

3.The Internet allows marketing professionals to change and update content in almost no time and hence ensure that customers have the most recent information.

互聯網營銷人員可以即時更改和更新內容，因而確保顧客獲得最新訊息。

Group Discussion

Discuss the following topic in group.Select one on the team to make a presentation before the class.

What market concepts can be enhanced by online tools?

Guidelines for Discussion

— brand building

— direct marketing

— online commerce

— customer supporting

— market research

— product/service development and testing

Writing Activity

Summarize the text by outlining major points.Write a few lines about online marketing tools.

Section B Case Study

Read the following passage before solving the problems that ensue.

Clever E-mail

Not since the invention of the printing press has advertising been changed as dramatically as with the introduction of the Internet.For example, the number of Internet users in the event industry grew from 50 percent to over 80 percent between 1096 and 1098.Event marketing has now fully embraced the electronic marketplace.Reggie Aggarwal, CEO of Cvent.com, a leading Internet event marketing firm, told the Convention Industry Council Forum attendees that "the fastest, most precise, easiest, and most cost affordable way to reach prospective event attendees is through e-mail." According to Aggarwal, the penetration of the Internet will be 100 percent and will be equal to or even replace traditional television and radio in some segments as an electronic source for daily information and communications.

Cvent.com is one example of how the technological revolution is driving the event management industry.Aggarwal started the firm after he used e-mail invitations and reminders to promote registration for a local association that he directed.He soon discovered that he could increase the response rate significantly and better target his prospects using e-mail communications.For example, Cvent.com technology enables meeting planners and event managers not only to send e-mail messages, but also to note whether or not they have been read.Direct-mail marketers cannot monitor whether or not their communications are read, as they can only note when a purchase or inquiry has been received.This innovation gives Cvent.a competitive edge in event market because they can determine quickly whether or not the e-mail event invitation has been opened and read.If it has been opened, the event marketer can assume that there is interest and build upon that interest with follow-up communications.This customized marketing approach is one of the many benefits of the new technologies that are being developed to assist event marketers.

When developing event marketing, Internet marketing must be considered a central part of any strategy.For example, regardless of size, all events should have a Web presence through either a dedicated Web home page, banner on an existing Web home page, or link to a separate page.

Problem Solving

How do you solve the following problems? Outline your assertion.

1.How do you make use of the Internet to do the market survey?

2.What could we do to ensure the security of electronic commerce?

Section C Format Writing

Acquaint yourself with the following.Finish the exercises that ensue.

Part 1 Invitation Letter 邀請信

Invitation Letter （1）

English Department

Pujiang University of Foreign Languages

Shanghai, 200001

P.R.China

Feburary 29, 2004

Professor Kevin Coster

English Department

Pitsburgh State University

Pitsburgh, KS 72344

USA

Dear Professor Coster,

All of our English teachers who attended your lecture on British Drama over in the States were deeply impressed by your thorough knowledge and profound understanding of the subject.We would like to know if you could come, as our guest of honor, to the National Seminar on Shakespeare, which is to be held on our campus between October 11 and 17, and deliver a speech on whatever subject that interests you.

You would, of course, receive our standard honorarium to cover traveling and other expenses.

Please let us know as soon as possible if you can come and tell us when you can make the trip.

Sincerely yours,

　(signature)

WU Zheren

Chairman

English Department

Invitation Letter （2）

Dear Sir or Madam,

[organization] would like to have someone from your company speak at our conference on ［topic］.

As you may be aware, the mission of our association is to promote ［target］.Many of our members are interested in the achievements your company has made in ［field］.Enclosed is our preliminary schedule for the conference which will be reviewed in weeks.I'll call you ［date］ to see who from your company would be willing to speak to us.I can assure you that we'll make everything convenient to the speaker.

Yours faithfully,

［name］

［title］

Notes of Format

Always bear in mind the following.

Most of the business letters are typed.It has been customary to set it out in the semi-indented style （半縮進式或混合式）（Invitation Letter 1）.Many readers like this style because the blocked （頂格式的） inside name and address is compact and tidy.The indented paragraphing is easy for reading.Others dislike the indentations because they waste the typist's time.Therefore the blocked style （頂格式或平頭式）（Invitation Letter 2） has now come to be much more widely used than before.

常用句型：

1.We are deeply impressed by your thorough knowledge and profound understanding.

我們對您淵博的知識和深刻的見解記憶猶新。

2.We would like to know if you could...

不知您能否前來……

其他類似表達法有：

I would like to invite you to...

我請您……

Is there any chance of your coming...

您是否能前來……

We would be very happy if you could come...

如蒙光臨，不勝榮幸。

I should be cheerful if you could come to...

您如果能來……就太叫人高興了。

I cordially invite you to join us.

我真心地邀請您來參加我們的活動。

I would like to take this opportunity to invite you to...

藉此機會，我想邀請您……

3.You would receive our standard honorarium to cover traveling and other expenses.

我們將按照常規給您報銷差旅及其他費用。

4.Please let us know as soon as possible if you can come and tell us when you can make the trip.

請您盡早與我們聯繫，並告知能否成行及具體時間。

5.Please accept our warm welcome and sincere invitation.

請接受我們熱情的歡迎和誠摯的邀請。

6.I can assure you that we'll make everything convenient to the speaker.

可以向您保證的是，我們將為發言人提供一切便利條件。

Do It Yourself

Write an invitation letter according to the given information.

The G.Manager assistant of DDCC, Teresa Wang, is inviting the acting president David Chapman of Marshal International Chemicals Corp.located on 987 Lincoln Street, Los Angeles （CA95345） to visit her corporation to celebrate its tenth anniversary from August 1 to 3.She also arranges for Mr.Chapman to meet Mr.Liu, the general manager of DDCC for a talk.They will talk about their future cooperation.

Part 2 Invitation Card 邀請卡

INVITATION

On the occasion of the thirty-eighth

anniversary of the founding

of Pujiang University

the office of the president of Pujiang University

requests of the honor of your presence

at a reception to be held

in the Guest House of the University

On Sunday, 24th December, 2001

from 7:00 p. m. to 9:00 p. m.

Reserve

INVITATION

Mr. Robert Shenstone

Director of Jinjiang Hotel

presents his compliments to

Mr. and Mrs. Dickenson

and requests the pleasure of their company

at a dinner party

in honour of Mr. Xie Jin

Chief Executive of Simons

on Saturday, December 28, 2001

at seven o'clock p. m.

at restaurant in Jinjiang Hotel

Reply if declining Tel: 66666666 Dress: Informal

```
┌─────────────────────────────────────────┐
│              INVITATION                   │
│      The Organizing Committee of          │
│      the Guangzhou Spring Trade '01       │
│        requests the pleasure of           │
│       Mr and Mrs. Heny Verner's           │
│      presence at the Opening Ceremony     │
└─────────────────────────────────────────┘
```

Notes of Format

Always bear in mind the following.

　將大寫的「請柬」寫在頂端中央。正式的請柬中，行文用第三人稱。請柬內容應包含：時間、地點、被邀者和邀請者。其形式較為固定。如果要求給予答覆，在請柬左下角註明。服裝若要有要求，寫明 Dress （Formal/ Informal），即「著裝（正式／非正式）」。

常用短語：

1.on the occasion of 值此……之際

2.presence at 出席

3.company of 陪伴

4.in honor of 以……的名義

常見句型：

1.On the occasion of the thirty-eighth anniversary of the founding of Pujiang University...

值此浦江大學成立三十八週年之際……

2....request the honor of your presence at a reception to be held...

恭請您大駕光臨於……舉行的招待會。

類似的表達法有：...requests the pleasure of their company at a dinner party...

3.Reply if declining. 如不能出席，敬請回覆。

4.R.S.V.P.：repondez s'il vous plait （＝ please reply）.

請賜覆。（正式請柬用語）

Do It Yourself

為慶祝開開集團成立八週年，請以開開集團董事會的名義向客戶發出舉行招待會的請柬，招待會的時間和地點由你定。

Part 3 Acceptance and Regret 回帖與辭謝

```
                        REGRETS
              Mr. and Mrs. Henry Verner
              regret that a previous engagement
              prevents their acceptance of
         the kind invitation of the Organizing Committee
              of the Guangzhou Spring Fair '01
                to the Opening Ceremony
              On Sunday, April the fifteenth
                 at nine o'clock a. m.
                at the White Swan Hotel
```

```
┌─────────────────────────────────────────────────┐
│                   ACCEPTANCE                      │
│            Mr. and Mrs. Henry Verner              │
│               accept with pleasure                │
│   the kind invitation of the Organizing Committee │
│        of the Guangzhou Spring Fair '01           │
│             to the Opening Ceremony               │
│          On Sunday, April the fifteenth           │
│               at nine o'clock a. m.               │
│             at the White Swan Hotel               │
└─────────────────────────────────────────────────┘
```

Notes of Format

Always bear in mind the following.

頂端中央寫明「回帖」或是「辭謝」。行文使用第三人稱。如不能接受邀請，最好能說明原因。不論是否接受邀請，都應在回覆中將時間、地點、邀請人、被邀請人複述一遍。

Do It Yourself

根據邀請函練習中的請柬各寫一封接受回帖和辭謝回覆。

Reference Answers

Reference Answer to Do It Yourself of Part 3

REGRETS

Mr. White

regrets that a previous engagement

prevents his acceptance of

the kind invitation of KaiKai Group

to the reception for the eighth anniversary

of the founding of KaiKai Group

at Jadeite Ballroom in Hilton Hotel

on Satuday, 18th november, 2006

from 7:00p. m. to 9:00p. m.

ACCEPTANCE

Mr. White

accepts with pleasure

the kind invitation of KaiKai Group

to the reception for the eighth anniversary

of the founding of KaiKai Group

at Jadeite Ballroom in Hilton Hotel

on Satuday, 18th november, 2006

from 7:00p. m. to 9:00p. m.

Chapter 5 Negotiations 談判

Section A Reading Assignment

Warming-up Activity

Go over the following terms with your teacher.

deal-breaker 交易破壞者	trade journal 行業雜誌	bottom-line 首要的，關鍵的	tactics 戰術，策略	stalemate 僵持，對峙
upfront 開誠布公的	intermediary 中間人，調解人	counterbalance 抗衡，抵消	prioritize 把事情的優先順序排好	

Pre-reading Questions

Answer the following questions without referring to the text.

1.Why is it important to set your main objective before negotiation?

2.How can you get information about the party you are going to negotiate with?

3.What will you do if there is deadlock in negotiation?

Text

Negotiating Tactics

Employing the right negotiating tactics is more important than ever in today's volatile business environment.Following are the eight fundamental steps to winning at the negotiating game, collected from the business people and experts in the field：

1.Take Stock of Your Weaknesses

Not everyone is born a great negotiator.In fact, most people don't have a clue about how to get what they want—other than to make demands and dig in their heels.

People let negotiations get away from them because they haven't figured out how to handle problems.They resort to using emotions instead.

Before you are faced with a negotiation, take time to learn the basics.One way to do that is to sign up for a reputable training session. Many trade and business organizations, colleges and universities, and private consulting firms run seminars on negotiating.

In addition, there are dozens of books on the market covering this topic.

2.Determine Your Bottom-line Goal

It's a lot easier to deal with a jerk who knows what they want than with a nice person who doesn't.

Many people get confused over the number of issues introduced in a negotiation and lose sight of their bottom line.

Before you can negotiate effectively, you have to identify the one thing you must come away with.Not five or ten things.It's got to be one tangible, concrete objective.If you can't tell whether or not your goal has been achieved, then it's not solid enough.

Paul Geffner, co-founder and former owner of Captain Video, a California videostore chain, and founder and owner of Escape from New York Pizza, a restaurant chain based in San Francisco says, "I always prioritize in a negotiation, so I know what the one or two deal-breakers are."

Before he starts negotiating with suppliers, banks and others, Geffner determines which issues he would back down on to achieve his main objective.

For instance, he says, "I'll never sign a lease where the landlord gets a percentage of the gross.If I'm working hard, why should they get a portion of my success? But I'll compromise on a rent increase based on the Consumer Price Index."

3.Learn as Much as Possible about the Other Party

The more you know about the person with whom you're negotiating, the better-off you'll be."Do your homework," suggests Neil Lerner, director of the Small Business Development Center at the University of Wisconsin School of Business in Madison.

Lerner suggests that if you're negotiating with a business, collect company brochures, annual reports, trade journals, and newspapers that cover local business news.Lerner also suggests searching the Internet and commercial databases for information on who else might be negotiating for the same thing you're after.

Don't be shy about asking around."Talk to other companies you know that have dealt with the person with whom you're negotiating," says political scientist and mediation specialist Linda Stamato.Get a feel for their reputation.Stamato is a mediator at Rutger's Center for Negotiation and Conflict Resolution and a professor at the Bloustein School.

4.Establish a Relationship before the Negotiation Begins

The worst place for the first meeting with the individuals with whom you're negotiating is the negotiation table."Try to get to know them on a personal level," says Lerner.

Paul Fox, president of Fox Performance Training, a firm in Ellington, Conn.that specializes in negotiation training for managers, suggests being upfront about negotiation issues.

"Tell the other party you'd like to have a pre-meeting so you can get acquainted," Fox says. "Let them know you realize this is an important negotiation for both of you and you believe both can benefit by getting a sense of how each other operates.Explain that you want to help them achieve their goal as much as you want to achieve your own."

Arrange a casual lunch or dinner, pick the other party up at the airport, or just chat over the phone.

It also can be helpful if, as Rain Forest Café's Schussler advises, you can get to know the people who are nearest the other party. "Most people skip this step, but this minor investment of time can really pay off," Fox says.

5.Create and Stick to an Agenda

Negotiations often assume a life of their own, veering off into areas not related to the core objectives of both parties.Formulating a blueprint helps keep the discussion on track and reduces the chances of extraneous issues working their way in.For the blueprint to be acceptable, however, both parties must have input.

"Ahead of time, lay out what you'd like to see happen," says Stamato. "Jointly develop a flexible, reasonable plan outlining what you want to talk about and how to go about making that happen."

Make a copy of your consensus and distribute it to the members of both negotiating teams.That way, if the subject jumps the tracks, you can call attention back to the plan.

However, it may not be a good idea to make your itinerary too rigid, warns Stamato.Don't do anything that forces the other party into a corner and makes the other person feel threatened.

6.Don't Let the Talks Get Personal

Emotions can run high when there's a lot at stake, and it's easy to vent frustration by lashing out at the other party.If the other party starts down this path, the best approach is to sit back and listen, says Lerner."Just don't get into it," he says.Don't cave in to the other person. Refuse to fight on their level.

Jot down what the other party is saying.That will often reveal clues about what's really bothering the other party besides the issues on the table. "A good tactic is to increase the number of variables over which you're negotiating," Lerner adds.For example, if both parties are hot under the collar over price, try focusing on the services that accompany that price.

"Maybe you can stage deliveries over time rather than insisting that the other party take all the product at one time," says Lerner."Or perhaps you can provide extra training—not just about your product but about the industry itself.These things have a value attached to them.Spread out your range of negotiable items."

7.If There is Stalemate, Find the Underlying Cause

"Stalemate usually develops over small things, not the large matters," says Michael Hoesly, founder and principal of Hoesly and Co.in Madison, an intermediary and adviser to companies seeking strategic partnerships or seeking to buy or sell firms. "Fear and uncertainty are often what kills the deal," he says.

Hoesly cites a case in which an acquisition was about to be clinched.At the last minute, the potential buyer refused to extend medical coverage to the owner's wife, who had a history of cancer.The deal began to unravel.

Hoesly says, "The complete stalemate wasn't really about the insurance issue.The owner thought the buyer was being cheap toward his sick wife.He was really afraid his wife's cancer would return.The buyer thought the seller was being unreasonable asking for unlimited benefits.But his real fear was that the magnitude of the claim would bankrupt him."

After talking through their anxieties the two parties reached settlement placing a ceiling on the dollar amount of medical claims reimbursed.

8.When a Deadlock Looks Hopeless, Buy Time

If there's deadlock, experts suggest, take a time out to think about what's been said.Break for coffee or say that you must go back to your office to confer with others.Take the time to review what you've been arguing about and try to approach another way.

When all else fails, you can bring in an impartial third party to act as a counterbalance. "It helps to have someone present who's not impassioned about the issue," notes Hoesly.A professional mediator agreed upon by both parties can often break a deadlock and get negotiations back on track.

As the experiences and suggestions business people as well as specialists in the field indicate, negotiators are made, not born.With careful forethought and perhaps measure of training, just about anyone can develop the ability to win the best deal possible.

Check-in

Do you have any questions about your reading assignment? If any, ask your teacher.

Important Vocabulary

tactics	[ˈtæktɪks]	n.	戰術，策略
volatile	[ˈvɒlətaɪl]	a.	反覆無常的，短暫的
jerk	[dʒɜːk]	n.	蠢人，無賴
tangible	[ˈtændʒəbl]	a.	有形的，確切的
prioritize	[praiˈɒrətaɪz]	v.	把事情的優先順序排好
upfront	[ʌpˈfrʌnt]	a.	開誠布公的
extraneous	[eksˈtreɪnɪəs]	a.	與正題無關的，外來的
intermediary	[ɪntəˈmidiərɪ]	n.	中間人，調解人
cite	[saɪt]	v.	引述
stalemate	[ˈsteɪlˌmeɪt]	n.	僵持，對峙
clinch	[klintʃ]	v.	最終解決
forethought	[ˈfɔːθɔːt]	n.	事先籌劃，預謀
counterbalance	[ˈkauntəbæləns]	n.	抗衡，抵消

Useful Expressions

dig in their heels	固執己見
resort to	採取（手段），訴諸……
bottom line	基本論點，決定性因素
back down	放棄，屈服
mediation specialist	調解專家
get a feel for	開始熟悉
pay off	行得通
jot down	（簡要地）記下
hot under the collar	憤怒的

Language Focus

1.If the subject jumps the tracks, you can call attention back to the plan.

如果談判偏離主題，你可以將談判重點拉回到計劃之中．

2.Emotions can run high when there's a lot at stake, and it's easy to vent frustration by lashing out at the other party.

當談判到了勝敗關頭，雙方有時無法控制情緒，很容易就會互相攻擊來發洩沮喪情緒．

3.When a deadlock looks hopeless, buy time.

當出現看似無可救藥的僵局時，給自己多爭取點時間．

4.Ten Rules for Negotiating：

· Find out how many points are to be negotiated.

· Start from an extreme position.

· Assume the other person owes you a concession.

· Don't concede without exchange.

· Don't give what you can sell.

· Exaggerate the value of your concessions, minimize the value of the other person's.

· If they insist on "principle", expect a concession in return.

· Only threaten what you are prepared to carry out.

· Don't show disrespect to the other person.

· If you're happy with the result, don't shout "I've won!"

Group Discussion

Discuss the following topic in group.Select one on the team to make a presentation before the class.

What are the appropriate strategies in negotiation?

Guidelines for Discussion

— your weakness

— your bottom-line goal

■ the other party

■ agenda

■ emotions

■ stalemate or deadlock

Writing Activity

Summarize the text by outlining major points.Write a few lines about negotiating tactics.

Section B Case Study

Read the following passage before solving the problems that ensue.

To Be a Skilled Negotiator

The common theme running through all of the definitions of negotiating is that two or more parties, who have both common and conflicting interest, interact with one another for the purpose of reaching a mutually beneficial agreement.Effective negotiation does not involve bludgeoning the other side into submission.Rather, it involves the more subtle art of persuasion, whereby all parties feel as though they have benefited.There is no simple formula for success.Each situation must be assessed within its own unique set of circumstances.The successful negotiator must choose the appropriate strategy, project the correct personal and organizational images, do the right type of homework, ask the most relevant questions, and offer and request the appropriate types of concession at the right time.Negotiating within one's own culture is sufficiently difficult, but the pitfalls increase geometrically when one enters the intercultural arena.

Being a skilled negotiator in any context entails being a intelligent, well-prepared, creative, flexible, and patient problem solver.International negotiators, however, face an additional set of obstacles not ordinarily encountered by domestic negotiators. As we have explained, one very important obstacle to international negotiations is culture.Because culture involves everything that a people have, think and do, it goes without saying that it will influence or colour the negotiation process.The very fact that one party in a negotiation will usually travel to the country of the other party establishes a foreign negotiating setting for at least one party, and this strangeness can be a formidable barrier to communication, understanding, and agreement.

There are other barriers as well.For example, international negotiation entails working within the confines of two different, and sometimes conflicting legal structures.Unless the negotiating parties are able to both understand and cope with the differing legal requirements, a joint international contract may be governed by two or more legal systems.Another barrier may be the extent to which government bureaucracies in other countries exert their influence on the negotiation process, a problem not always understood by Westerners whose governments are relatively unobtrusive in business negotiations.

And finally, an additional obstacle that goes beyond cultural differences is the unpredictable geopolitical realities of the two countries of the negotiating parties.Sudden changes in governments, the enactment of new legislation, or even natural disasters can disrupt international business negotiations either temporarily or permanently.

Now that we see the importance to international negotiations of these non-cultural obstacles, it should be apparent by now that success in negotiating international business contracts requires a deep understanding of the culture of those on the other side of the table.The reason for this cultural awareness, however, is not for the purpose of bringing the other side to its knees—to make them do what we want them to do.Nor is it to accommodate them by giving up some of our own strongly adhered-to principles.Rather, an appreciation of the important cultural elements of the other side is essential if one is to get on with the business at hand so that all parties concerned can feel as though they are better off after the negotiations than before.Moreover, it is equally the responsibility of both sides in the negotiating process to understand the cultural realities of their negotiation partners.Inter-cultural communication, in other word, is a two-way street, with both sides sharing the burden and responsibility of cultural awareness.

Problem Solving

How do you solve the following problems? Outline your assertion.

1.There are barriers in cross-cultural negotiation.

2.Government bureaucracies exert their influence on the negotiation process.

▌Section C Format Writing

Acquaint yourself with the following.Finish the exercises that ensue.

Contract 合約

Sample 1

Sales Contract

Contract No.

Date：

The Sellers undertake to sell and the Buyers undertake to buy the under-mentioned commodity on the terms and conditions stipulated in the text below and the appendix attached：

1.COMMODITY：

Quantity, Unit Price and Shipment are stipulated in the appendix.

2.SPECIFICATIONS：

3.PACKING：

Packed in new polypropylene woven bags, each containing approx.50 kilos, gross for net.The bags should be sound and suitable for ocean transportation.The bags shall be properly marked with the name of commodity, weight, country of origin and date of packing in English.

4.TERMS OF SHIPMENT：

a) The Sellers shall advise the Buyers by fax within 5 working days after the completion of loading, the name of the carrying vessel, the date of departure, the name of commodity, the invoice value and the quantity actually shipped.

b) The Sellers shall give the Buyers, by fax, 15 days prior to the Vessel's ETA （estimated time of arrival） at the port of discharging, advising the vessel's latest ETA at the discharging port.If there is any change in Vessel's ETA, a notice shall be given to the Buyers or their Agent in time by ship Owners or their Agent at the port of discharging.

c) The Buyers undertake to accept the Captain's Notice of Readiness （NOR） given by the Captain in time.Laytime for discharging shall commence at 14 hrs if NOR is given at or before noon and at 08：00 hrs the next working day if such NOR is given in the afternoon.Time lost in waiting for berth and shifting shall be counted as discharging time.

d) Discharging the cargo at the rate of 250 metric tons per hatch per weather working day of 24 consecutive hours, Sunday and Holiday excluded unless used.Rate of demurrage as per Charter Party/subject to a maximum of USD 6, 000 per day or pro rata for any part of a day. Half demurrage for dispatch.

e) Discharging cost including night shift surcharges, tally charges, sorting charges etc.are for buyers' account.

f) The Sellers should inform the Buyers the carrying vessel's principal particulars before shipment.

g) If the age of the carrying vessel is over 20 years, the overage insurance premium is to be for Sellers' account.The overage insurance premium payable as per PICC's schedule. (Claim for overage premium to be supported by official invoice of the insurance company.)

5.INSURANCE：

All Risks and War Risk including risks of heating, sweating, caking, molding, spontaneous combustion howsoever and whatsoever caused, risks of shortweight, quality inconformities with the loading description at the destination shall be covered by the Buyers from warehouse to warehouse.

6.TERMS OF PAYMENT：

On or before _____ the Buyers must open an irrevocable letter of credit for 100%of the contract value in favor of _____ Trading Limited payable at sight through

Bank of China, China or any Prime Bank in China which is acceptable by the Sellers.The irrevocable letter of credit shall be unrestricted for negotiation at any bank in Hong Kong.The payment of the L/C is to be effected by T/T.

The Letter of Credit shall be valid in Hong Kong until the 30th day after the date of shipment.

If the fully operational Letter of Credit has not been advised to the Sellers on or before _____, the Sellers have the choice either to extend the shipment month or declare the Buyers default as per GAFTA No.10 Clause 24.

Documents Required：

a) Commercial Invoice in triplicate.

b) Full set of Clean On Board Shipping Bills of Lading, each consisting of three original and three non-negotiable copies, made out to order and blank endorsed, marked "Freight Prepaid," indicating 1% empty bags shipped along with cargoes free of charge.

c) Original Certificate in quadruplicate （one original and three copies） indicating the country of origin producing the said commodity.

d) Technical Inspection of the Process and Bacteriological Examination of the product in quadruplicate （one original and three copies）, indicating XXX.

e) Certificate of Sampling/Analysis in quadruplicate （one original and three copies）, indicating XXX.

f) Sanitary Certificate of the said commodity in quadruplicate （one original and three copies）.

g) Certificate of Weight in quadruplicate （one original and three copies）, indicating the number of bags and the actual weight loaded.

h) Certificate of Packing in quadruplicate （one original and three copies）.

i) Pre-shipment Survey Report in quadruplicate （one original and three copies） indicating that the cargo shipped on board of the carrying vessel has been treated with antioxidant, bagged and stored in well ventilated place.

7.REMARKS：

a) All certificates issued by SGS.All shipping documents shall be written in English or Spanish together with English translation attached.

b) All documents presented later than 21 days after the date of shipment but within 30 days after the date of shipment are acceptable.

c) The issuance date of all certificates later than Bill of Lading date are acceptable, but the inspection date/sampling date must not be later than Bill of Lading date.

d) Charter Party Bills of Lading and Third Party Documents are acceptable at presentation.

e) All banking charges including commission in lieu imposed by Buyers'Bank are for Buyers' account and all banking charges including commission in lieu imposed by Sellers' Bank are for Sellers' account. Acceptance Commission, if any, is for Buyers' account.

f) All import duties, taxes and dues present or future is to be for Buyers' account.

8.INSPECTION：

Quality and quantity of the commodity stating in the documents required in the Clause 7 inspected by the independent surveyors at the port of loading shall be final.

9.FORCE MAJEURE：

The fulfillment of this Contract is subject to the usual force majeure practice and GAFTA contract No.10, clause 22.

10.ARBITRATION：

Should any dispute arise between the contracting parties, it shall be settled through friendly negotiations.But if no agreement can be reached, the disputes arising out of the execution or performance of this contract shall be submitted by the parties for arbitration. Arbitration shall be conducted by China International Economic and Trade Arbitration Commission in Beijing in accordance with its procedure rule.The award given by the Arbitration Commission shall be final and binding upon both parties.The fees for arbitration shall be borne by the losing party.

11.The Buyers to return one copy of this Contract duly signed in confirmation, however, failure of the Buyers to return same duly signed documents will not in any way affect or alter the validity of this Contract.

12.All other terms not in conflict with the above-mentioned shall be as per GAFTA Contract No.10.

This Contract is made in two originals in English, both are equally valid.

ACCEPTED BY THE BUYERS： ACCEPTED BY THE SELLERS：

Buyers' Name   Sellers' Name

Buyers' Address：   Sellers' Address：

Sample 2

Contract made and entered into this ［date］, by and between ［name of Seller］, of ［address］ ［city］, ［state］, herein referred to as "Seller," and ［name of Buyer］, of ［address］ ［city］, ［state］, herein referred to as "Buyer."

Seller hereby agrees to transfer and deliver to Buyer, on or before ［date］, the following goods：

Buyer agrees to accept the goods and pay for them in accordance with the terms of the Contract.

Buyer and Seller agree that identification shall not be deemed to have been made until both parties have agreed that the goods in question are appropriated and the requirements of performance of said contract with the Buyer are fulfilled.

Buyer agrees to pay for the goods at the time they are delivered and at the place where he receives said goods.

Goods shall be deemed received by Buyer when delivered to address of Buyer as herein described.

Until such time as said goods have been received by Buyer, all risk of loss from any casualty to said goods shall be on Seller.

Seller warrants that the goods are now free from any security interest or other lien or encumbrance, that they shall be free from same at the time of delivery, and that he neither knows nor has reason to know of any outstanding title, or claim of title, hostile to his rights in the goods.

Buyer has the right to examine the goods on arrival and has ［number］ of days to notify Seller of any claim for damages on account of the condition, grade or quality of the goods.That said notice must specifically set forth the basis of his claim, and that his failure to either notice Seller within the stipulated period of time or to specifically set forth the basis of his claim will constitute irrevocable acceptance of the goods.

This agreement has been executed in duplicate, whereby both Buyer and Seller have retained one copy each, on ［date］.

_____ ［signature］

Notes of Format

Always bear in mind the following.

1. 英文合約由當事人（parties），敘述（recital），正文（habendum），附錄（schedule），證明（attestation）五大部分構成。其中敘述部分由 WHEREAS 加雙方願望等訂立合約的基礎構成，附錄常用動詞短語替代句子，但不是每個合約都有。

2. 英文合約中充滿 notwithstanding，without prejudice to，subject to，where as，here of，here to，here in 等用詞和「This contract is made and entered into by Party A and Party B, whereas」和「If and whenever」等用句。瞭解其具體含義和用法可以更準確掌握合約條款的含義。

3. 正式用語：

因為 by virtue of ／在 …… 之前 prior to ／關於 as regards ／ concerning ／事實上 in effect ／開始 commencement ／停止做 cease to do ／其他事項 miscellaneous ／理解合約 comprehend a contract ／認為 deem ／願意做 intend to do

4. 合約的訂立，變更，終止的英語表達：

合約的訂立 make，enter into，form，conclude，execute

合約的變更 alter，change，modify

合約的終止 terminate

英語文件中常與合約搭配的動詞還有 cancel，discharge，rescind 和 revoke.

5. 爭議的解決：

關於英文合約中爭議的解決，一般先約定友好協商解決，協商未果，則在協定的仲裁機構用約定的規則和語言進行仲裁，很少選擇訴訟解決。

All disputes arising in connection with this contract or in the execution thereof should be settled amicably through negotiations. In case no settlement can be reached, the case in dispute shall then be submitted for arbitration in _____.The arbitration award shall be accepted as final and binding upon both parties.

有關或執行本合約的一切爭議應該友好協商解決。若達不成協議，有關爭議則提交 _____ 仲裁。仲裁裁決為終局的，並對雙方均具有約束力。

6.L/C：Letter of Credit 信用證

7.T/T：Telegraphic Transfer 電匯

8.SGS：瑞士通用公證行，世界上最大的認證機構之一。

9.Clean On Board Shipping Bills of Lading 清潔已裝船提單

Do It Yourself

The words below are often used in contracts.Use some of them to complete the following sentences.You may need to put certain words in the plural.Use a dictionary if necessary.

terminate	clause	ection agreement
condition	binding	compromise party
provide for	arbitration	breach comply with
litigation	out of court	term abide by

1) A contract is an _____ drawn up between two _____.It is divided into _____, , and _____.

2) The contract _____ _____any problems between the two parties.The conditions of the contract are _____ on both parties.If one party does not _____ _____the clauses, this is called a _____ of contract.

3) In the case of a dispute, many contracts provide for _____, but in some cases the dispute results in _____.Most parties reach a _____ without going to court, and the dispute is settled _____ _____ _____.

4) Some contracts are for a fixed period, or _____ ; also, there are ways in which the parties can end, or _____, the contract.

Reference Answers

Reference Answers to Do It Yourself

1) agreement, parties, sections, clauses, conditions

2) provides for, binding, abide by/comply with, breach

3) arbitration, litigation, compromise, out of court

4) term, terminate

Chapter 6 Logistics 物流

▌Section A Reading Assignment

Warming-up Activity

Go over the following terms with your teacher.

inventory 存貨	value-added 增值的	competency 能力	initiate 開始	ultimately 最終地	interrelated 有相互關係的
in isolation 單獨地	prerequisite 先決條件	incorporate 合併‧混合	supply chain 供應鏈	procurement 採購	finished product 成品

Pre-reading Questions

Answer the following questions without referring to the text.

1.What is logistics?

2.Why is logistics important in exhibition industry?

3.What are the differences between the three areas of logistical operation, e.g.physical distribution, manufacturing support and procurement?

Text

The Logistics Value-Added Process

Logistics is viewed as the activity that links an enterprise with its customers and suppliers.Information from and about customers flows through the enterprise in the form of sales activity, forecasts, and orders.The information is refined into specific manufacturing and purchasing plans.As products and materials are produced, a value-added inventory flow is initiated that ultimately results in ownership transfer of finished products to customers.Thus, the process is viewed in terms of two interrelated efforts, inventory flow and information flow.

First, viewing internal operations in isolation is useful to elaborate the fundamental importance of integrating all functions and work involved in logistics.While such integration is prerequisite to success, it is not sufficient to guarantee that a firm will achieve its performance goals.To be fully effective in today's competitive environment, firms must expand their integrated behavior to incorporate customers and suppliers.This extension, through external integration, is referred to as supply chain management.

Second, the basic process is not restricted to for-profit business, nor is it unique to manufacturing firms.The need to integrate requirements and operations occurs in all businesses as well as within public sector organizations.For example, retailing or wholesaling firms typically link physical distribution and purchasing, since traditional manufacturing is not required in them.Nevertheless, retailers and wholesalers must complete the logistics value-added process.The same is true of all public sector organizations that manufacture products or provide other services.

Inventory Flow

The operational management of logistics is concerned with movement and storage of materials and finished products.Logistical operations start with the initial shipment of a material or component part from a supplier and are finalized when a manufactured or processed product is delivered to a customer.

From the initial purchase of a material or component, the logistical process adds value by moving inventory when and where needed.Providing all goes well, a material gains value at each step of its transformation into finished inventory.In other words, an individual part has greater value after it is incorporated into a machine.Likewise, the machine has greater value once it is delivered to a buyer.

Regardless of the size and type of enterprise, logistics is essential and requires continuous management attention.For better understanding it is useful to divide logistical operation into three areas : physical distribution, manufacturing support, and procurement.

Physical Distribution

The area of physical distribution concerns movement of a finished product to customers.In physical distribution, the customer is the final destination of a marketing channel.The availability of the product is a vital part of each channel participant's marketing effort. Even a manufacturer's agent, which typically does not own inventory, must depend on inventory availability to perform expected marketing responsibilities.Unless a proper assortment of products is efficiently delivered, when and where they are needed, a great deal of the overall marketing effort can be jeopardized.It is through the physical distribution process that the time and space of customer service become an integral part of marketing.Thus physical distribution links a marketing channel with its customers.To support the wide variety of marketing systems that exist in a highly commercialized nation, many different physical distribution systems are utilized.All physical distribution systems have one common feature : they link manufacturers, wholesalers, and retailers into marketing channels that provide product availability as an integral aspect of the overall marketing process.

Manufacturing Support

The area of manufacturing support concentrates on managing work-in-process inventory as it flows between stages of manufacturing.The primary logistical responsibility in manufacturing is to participate in formulating a master production schedule and to arrange for timely availability of materials, component parts, and work-in-process inventory.Thus, the overall concern of manufacturing support is not how production occurs, but rather what, when, and where products will be manufactured.Manufacturing support has one significant difference when compared with physical distribution. Physical distribution attempts to service the desires of customers and must therefore accommodate the uncertainty of consumer and industrial demand.Manufacturing support involves movement requirements that are under the control of the manufacturing enterprise.The uncertainties introduced by random customer ordering and erratic demand are not present in most manufacturing operations.From the viewpoint of overall planning, the separation of manufacturing support from outbound （physical distribution） and inbound （procurement） activities provides opportunities for specialization and improved efficiency.

Procurement

Procurement is concerned with purchasing and arranging the inbound movement of materials, parts and finished inventory from suppliers to manufacturing and assembly plants, warehouses, or retail stores.Whereas physical distribution is related to outbound product shipments, purchasing is about inbound materials sorting and assembly.Under most marketing situations involving consumer products, such as a grocery manufacturer that ships to a retail food chain, the manufacturer's physical distribution is the same process as a retailer's procurement operations.Although similar or even identical transportation requirements may be involved, the degree of managerial control and risk related to performance failure varies substantially between physical distribution and procurement.

Within a typical enterprise, the three areas of logistics overlap. Viewing each as an integral part of the overall value-added process creates an opportunity to capitalize on the unique attributes of each while facilitating the overall process.The prime concern of an integrated logistical process is to coordinate overall value added inventory movement.The three areas combine to provide integrated management of materials, semi-finished components, and products moving between locations, supply sources, and customers of the enterprise.In this sense, logistics is concerned with strategic management of total movement and storage.Information Flow

Information flow identifies specific locations within a logistical system that have requirements.Information also integrates the three operating areas.The primary objective of developing and specifying requirements is to plan and execute integrated logistical operations. Within individual logistics areas, different movement requirements exist with respect to size of order, availability of inventory, and urgency of movement.The primary objective of information sharing is to reconcile these differentials.It is important to stress that information requirements should parallel the actual work performed in physical distribution, manufacturing support, and procurement. Whereas these areas contain the actual logistics work, information facilitates coordination of planning and control of day-to-day operations.Without accurate information the effort involved in the logistical system can be wasted.

Check-in

Do you have any questions about the text? If any, ask your teacher.

Important Vocabulary

competency	[ˈkɒmpɪtəns]	n.	能力，權限
procure	[prəˈkjuə]	v.	採購，獲得
initiate	[ɪˈnɪʃɪeɪt]	v.	開始，發起
ultimately	[ˈʌltɪmətlɪ]	adv.	最後地，根本地
interrelated	[ˌɪntərɪˈleɪtɪd]	a.	相互關聯的
elaborate	[ɪˈlæbəreɪt]	v.	闡述，詳盡解釋
prerequisite	[ˌpriːˈrekwɪzɪt]	n.	前提，必備條件
incorporate	[ɪnˈkɔːpəreɪt]	v.	包含，合併
finalize	[ˈfaɪnəlaɪz]	v.	使完成
jeopardize	[ˈdʒepədaɪz]	v.	使受到傷害，損失或破壞
erratic	[ɪˈrætɪk]	a.	不規則的，無常的
overlap	[ˌəuvəˈlæp]	v.	重疊，部分巧合
attribute	[ˈætrɪbjuːt]	n.	歸因，性質
reconcile	[ˈrekənsaɪl]	v.	使......一致，化解
parallel	[ˈpærəlel]	v.	與......相當，相匹敵

Useful Expressions

value added	增值
inventory flow	庫存流動
in isolation	單獨地，個別地
supply chain management	供應鏈管理
operational management	營運管理
to be concerned with	與……相關，涉及
finished product	成品
physical distribution	實物配送

Language Focus

1.While such integration is prerequisite to success, it is not sufficient to guarantee that a firm will achieve its performance goals.

雖然這樣整合是取得成功的先決條件，但這還不足以保證一個公司就能實現其工作目標。

2.Providing all goes well, a material gains value at each step of its transformation into finished inventory.

如果一切順利，材料在製成成品的每個步驟中增加了價值。

3.The uncertainties introduced by random customer ordering and erratic demand accommodated by physical distribution are not present in most manufacturing operations.

實物配送中，客戶隨意訂購和需求反覆無常所帶來的不確定性，在大多數的生產運營中不會出現。

Group Discussion

Discuss the following topic in group.Select one on the team to make a presentation before the class.

What is the concept of integrated logistics?

Guidelines for Discussion

▬ inventory flow

▬ physical distribution

▬ manufacturing support

▬ procurement

▬ information flow

Writing Activity

Summarize the text by outlining major points.Write a few lines about integrated logistics using the following expressions.

logistics 物流。物品從供應地向接受地的實體流動過程。根據實際需要，將運輸、儲存、裝卸、搬運、包裝、流通加工、配送、資訊處理等基本功能實施有機結合。

logistics management 物流管理。為了以最低的物流成本達到用戶所滿意的服務水平，對物流活動進行的計劃、組織、協調和控制。

combined transport 聯合運輸。一次委託，由兩家以上運輸企業或用兩種以上運輸方式共同將某一批物品運送到目的地的運輸方式。

distribution 配送。在經濟合理的區域範圍內，根據用戶要求，對物品進行揀選、加工、包裝、分割、組配等作業，並按時送達指定地點的物流活動。

customs declaration 報關。由進出口貨物的收發貨人或其代理人向海關辦理進出境手續的全過程。

▌Section B Case Study

Read the following passage before solving the problems that ensue.

Event Shipping Services

Exhibitors can avoid high shipping and drayage costs with assistance from operations managers.Encourage exhibitors to ship to the general contractor's warehouse in advance—especially if their targeted move-in date is on a weekend, which can involve overtime drayage rates.Advance shipping enables exhibitors to confirm the arrival of their freight at the show.Additionally, freight arriving at the warehouse in a timely manner will usually be delivered to the booth during the contractor's move-in period at straight-time drayage rates.

Some general contractors also offer shipping services.By appointing them as the preferred or official carrier for the show, the overall pricing for show management on other services, such as furniture rental or carpeting, can often be reduced.

Encourage exhibitors to ask for quotations for international shipping and customs services in advance.The quotations should include both inbound and outbound transportation costs, duties and taxes.

Problem Solving

How do you solve the following problems? Outline your assertion.

1.How can exhibitors avoid high shipping costs?

2.Why is it advisable to appoint the general contractors as the carrier for the show?

▮Section C Format Writing

Acquaint yourself with the following.Finish the exercises that ensue.

Bill of Lading 提單

CONSIGNOR: MERMAID CORPORATION 7955 COPENHAGEN, DENMARK		OUR BOOK No. :	B/L No. : EXY8774732
CONSIGNEE: SHANGHAI MACHINERY I/E CORP No. 12 RENMIN ROAD, SHANGHAI, CHINA		REMARKS:	
PORT OF LOADING: COPENHAGEN	VESSEL: EAST EXPRESS	VOYAGE No. : 121 A	FLAG DENMARK

PORT OF DISCHARGE: SHANGHAI CHINA via HONGKONG			PLACE OF DELIVERY		
MARK	No. OF PKGS	DESCRIPTION OF GOODS	GROSS WEIGHT	NET WEIGHT	MEASU-REMENT

1 ×20' SCZU 8774532 （3PACKAGES）   15, 025KGS

1×40' SCZU 8634721 （6PACKAGES）

SAID TO CONTAIN :

3 UNITS OF

00AGFF-7832DM   A80 FORKLIFT TRUCK

SHANGHAI CHINA

PACKING : SUITABLE FOR LONG DISTANCE OCEAN
TRANSPORTATION QUANTITY : 3 UNITS

MANUFACTURER : GEERLOFS TRUCK B.V., GERMANY

CONTRACT No. : 00AGFF-7832DM

TOTAL NUMBER OF CONTAINERS

OF PACKAGES （IN WORDS）

LADEN ON BOARD THE VESSEL DATE: May 16, 2003 BY _____	FLYEAGLE FERRY CO., LTD BY _____

Invoice 發票

CONSIGNEE: SHANGHAI MACHIERY I/E CORP No. 12 RENMIN ROAD, SHANGHAI, CHINA	No. : DATE: AD7832 MAY 14, 2003
	L/C No. : DATE: LC7843A837 JAN 19, 2003 BANK OF CHINA, SHANGHAI BRANCH, CHINA

PORT OF LOADING：COPENHAGEN	VESSEL：EAST EXPRESS	VOYAGE No. ：121 A	FLAG DENMARK
PORT OF DISCHARGE：SHANGHAI CHINA via HONGKONG		CONTRACT No. ：00AGFF-7832DM	
MARKS & No. OF PKGS	DESCRIPTION OF GOODS	QUANTITY/ UNIT	UNIT PRICE	AMOUNT

			DEM	DEM
	DELIVERY OF CIF SHANGHAI CHINA OF 3 UNITS & 6 P'KGS OF			
00AGFF-7832DM SHANGHAI CHINA	A80 FORKLIFT TRUCK			
	H. S. CODE：84271090			
	DETAILS AS PER THE ATTACHED SHEET			
	MANUFACTURER：GEERLOFS TRUCK B. V. ，GERMANY			
	CONTRACT No. ：00AGFF-7832DM			
	A80	17951. 00		53853. 00
	FREIGHT CHARGES			2050. 00
	INSURANCE			1346. 00
	TOTAL			57249. 00

MERMAID CORPORATION

P. O. BOX：7955 COPENHAGEN，DENMARK

TELEPHONE：

MERMAID CORPORATION

SIGNED BY _____

Application Form For Cargo Transportation Insurance 貨物運輸保險投保單

被保險人（INSURED）

發票號（INVOICE NO.）

合約號（CONTRACT NO.）

信用證號（L/C NO.）

發票金額（INVOICE AMOUNT）_____ 投保加成（PLUS）_____%

茲 有 下 列 貨 物 投 保。（INSURANCE IS REQUIRED ON THE FOLLOWING COMMODITIES.）

標 記 MARKS & NOS.	數量及包裝 QUANTITY	保險貨物項目 DESCRIPTION OF GOODS	保險金額 AMOUNT INSURED

起運日期：   裝載運輸工具：

（DATE OF COMMENCEMENT）_____（PER CONVEYANCE）_____

自（FROM）_____ 經（VIA）_____ 至（TO）_____

提單號（B/L NO.）_____ 賠款償付地點（CLAIM PAYABLE AT）

投保險別：（PLEASE INDICATE THE CONDITIONS&/OR SPECIAL COVERAGES：）

請如實告知下列情況：［如「是」在（）中打「√」「不是」打「×」（IF ANY, PLEASE MARK 「√」OR 「×」）］

1. 貨物種類：袋裝 （ ） 散裝 （ ） 冷藏 （ ） 液體 （ ）

GOODS：BAG/JUMBO BULK REEFER LIQUID

活動物 （ ） 機器/汽車 （ ） 危險品等級 （ ）

LIVE ANIMAL MACHINE/AUTO DANGEROUS CLASS

2. 集裝箱種類：普通 （ ）開頂 （ ）框架 （ ） 平板 （ ）

CONTAINER：ORDINARY　　OPEN　FRAME　　FLAT

冷藏（）

REFRIGERATOR

3. 轉運工具：海輪　（　）飛機　（　）　　駁船　（　）　　火車　（　）

BY TRANSIT：SHIP　　PLANE　　　　BARGE　　　　TRAIN

汽車（）

TRUCK

4. 船舶資料：　　　　　　　船籍　（　）　　船齡　（　）

PARTICULAR OF SHIP：REGISTRY　AGE

備註：被保險人確認已經完全瞭解本保險合約的條款和內容。投保人（簽名蓋章）APPLICANTS'SIGNATURE

THE ASSURED CONFIRMS HEREWITH THE

TERMS AND CONDITIONS OF THESE INSURANCE

CONTRACT FULLY UNDERSTOOD　　　　電話：（TEL）

投保日期：DATE _____ 地址：（ADD）

Useful words and phrases：

1.notify party 通知人

2.pre-carriage by 前程運輸

3.place of receipt 收貨地點

4.ocean vessel 船名

5.Voy.No. 航次

6.place of delivery 交貨地點

7.final destination 目的地

8.Container No. 集裝箱號

9.Seal No. 封條碼

10.No.of containers or pkgs 箱數或件數

11.kind of packages：description of goods 包裝種類與貨名

12.gross weight 毛重

13.measurement 尺碼

14.freight and charges 運費

15.prepaid at 預付地點

16.total prepaid 預付總額

17.place of issue 簽發地點

18.No.of Original B（s）/L 正本提單份數

19.booking approved by 訂艙確認

Declaration Form 報關單

U.S.Customs and Border protection

Customs Declaration （1）

Customs Declaration family member must provide the following information （only ONE, written declaration per family is required)

Each arriving traveler or responsible party

1.Family Name

First （Given）

Middle

2.Birth date

Day

Month Year

3.Number of family members traveling with you

4.（a）US street address （hotel name/destination)

（b）City （c）Street

5.Passport issued by （country）

6.Passport number

7.Country of residence

8.Countries visited on the trip prior to US arrival

9.Airline/Flight No.or Vessel Name

10.The primary purpose of this trip （business） Yes ☐ No ☐

11.I am （We are） bringing

（a）fruits, plants, food, or insects Yes ☐ No ☐

（b）meats, animals, or animal/wildlife products Yes ☐ No ☐

（c）disease agents, cell cultures, or snails Yes ☐ No ☐

（d）soil or have you visited a farm/ranch/pasture Yes ☐ No ☐

12.I have （We have） been in close proximity of （such as touching or handling) livestock Yes ☐ No ☐

13.I am （We are） carrying currency or monetary instruments over $10,000 U.S.or foreign equivalent. Yes ☐ No ☐

14.I have （We have） commercial merchandise. Yes ☐ N o ☐ (articles for sale, samples used for soliciting orders, or goods that are not considered personal effects)

15.Residents—the total value of all goods, including commercial merchandise.I/We have purchased or acquired abroad （including gifts for someone else, but not items mailed to the United States）and am/are bring to the U.S.is $_____

Visitors—the total value of all articles that will remain in the U.S.including commercial merchandise is $_____

Read the information on the back of this form.Space is provided to list all the items you must declare.

I HAVE READ THE IMPORTANT INFORMATION ON THE REVERSE SIDE OF THIS FORM AND HAVE MADE A TRUTHFUL DECLARATION.

U.S.Customs and Border Protection

Welcomes You to the United States

U.S.Customs and Border Protection is responsible for protecting the United States against the illegal importation of prohibited items. CBP officers have the authority to question you and to examine you and your personal property.If you are one of the travelers selected for an examination, you will be treated in a courteous, professional, and dignified manner.CBP Supervisors and Passenger Service Representatives are available to answer you questions.Comment cards are available to compliment or provide feedback.

Important Information

U.S.Residents—declare all articles that you have acquired abroad and are bringing into the United States.

Visitors （Non-Residents）—declare the value of all articles that will remain in the United States.

Declare all articles on this declaration form and show the value in U.S.dollars.For gifts, please indicate the retail value.

Duty—CBP officers will determine duty.U.S.residents are normally entitled to a duty-free exemption of $800 on items accompanying them.Visitor（non-residents）are normally entitled to an exemption of $100. Duty will be assessed at the current rate on the first $1,000 above the exemption.

Controlled substances, obscene articles, and toxic substances are generally prohibited entry.

Description of Articles

value

use only

Total

Customs Declaration（2）

Form 7525-V（7-18-2003）SHIPPER'S EXPORT DECLARATION

1a. U. S. PRINCIPAL PARTY IN INTEREST (USPPI) (Complete name and address) ZIP CODE			
1b. USPPI'S EIN (IRS) OR ID NO.	1c. PARTIES TO TRANSACTION ☐Related ☐ Non-related	2. DATE OF EXPORTATION	3. TRANSPORTATION REFERENCE NO.
4a. ULTIMATE CONSINGEE (Complete name and address)			
4b. INTERMEDIATE CONSIGNEE (Complete name and address)			
5a. FORWARDING AGENT (Complete name and address)			
5b. FORWARDING AGENT'S EIN (IRS) NO.		6. POINT (STATE) OF ORIGIN OR FIZ NO.	7. COUNTRY OF ULTIMATE DESTINATION
8. LOADING PIER (Vessel only)	9. METHOD OF TRANSPORTATION (Specify)	14. CARRIER IDENTIFICATION CODE	15. SHIPMENT REFERENCE NO.

10. EXPORTING CARRIER	11. PORT OF EXPORT	16. ENTRY NUMBER	17. HAZARDOUS MATERIALS ☐Yes ☐No
12. PORT OF UNLOADING (Vessel and air only)	13. CONTAINERI-ZED (Vessel only) ☐Yes ☐No	18. IN BOND CODE	19. ROUTED EXPORT TRANSACTION ☐Yes ☐No

20. SCHEDULE B DESCRIPTION OF COMMODITIES (Use columns 22-24)				
21. D/F or M	22. SCHEDULE B NUMBER	23. QUANTITY-SCHEDULE B UNIT(S)	24. SHIPPING WEIGHT (KILOGRAMS)	25. VIN/PRODUCT NUMBER/VEHICLE TITLE NUMBER

27. LICENSE NO/LICENSE EXCEPTION SYMBOL/ AUTHORIZATION	28. ECCN (When required)
29. Duly authorized officer or employee	The USPPI authorized the forwarder named above to act as forwarding agent for export control and customs purposes.	

30. I certify that all statements made and all information contained herein are true and correct and that I have read and understood the instructions for preparation of this document, set forth in the **"Correct Way to Fill Out the Shipper's Export Declaration."** I understand that civil and criminal penalties, including forfeiture and sale, may be imposed for making false or fraudulent statements herein, failing to provide the requested information or for violation of U. S. laws on exportation (13 U. S. C. Sec. 305; 22 U. S. C. Sec. 401; 18 U. S. C. Sec. 1001; 50 U. S. C. App. 2410)

Signature	**Confidential**—Shipper's Export declarations（or any successor document）wherever located, shall be exempt from public disclosure unless the secretary determines that such exemption would be contrary to the national interest［Title 13, Chapter 9, Section 301（g）］.
Title	
Date	31. AUTHENTICATION（When required）
Telephone No. （Include Area Code）	E-mail address

SHANGHAI IMPORT & EXPORT COMMODITY INSPECTION BUREAU OF THE PEOPLE'S REPUBLIC OF CHINA

Certificate of Origin 產地證明書

地址：   證書號

Address   No.

電報：   日期

Cable：   Date

電話：

Tel：

發貨人：

Consignor _____

收貨人：

Consignee：_____

標記及號碼 Marks & No.	品名 Commodity	數量 Quantity	毛重(總重量) Gross Weight

茲證明上述商品確係中華人民共和國出產或製造

THIS IS TO CERTIFY THAT THE ABOVE-MENTIONED COMMODITIES WERE PRODUCED OR MANUFACTURED IN THE PEOPLE'S REPUBLIC OF CHINA.

Notes of Format

Always bear in mind the following.

會展中很重要的一個項目就是展覽，或者也可以說是產品展示。展覽有時是會議的一個組成部分，有時是以一種獨立的活動形式出現，有的是在本國國內進行，有的是在境外進行。如果是在國外進行，大型展品需要透過海運或空運出入境。出境運輸中有幾個重要環節，除了必須申請報關外，還得租船訂艙、投保和裝運。貨物在裝船出運之前必須向海關辦理報關手續，填寫「出口報關單」，並附上發票、裝箱單、商檢證、產地證、出口許可證、合約和信用證副本等必要單證，一併交給海關。只有在海關核對審查無誤後，在裝貨單上蓋上「放行」印章後才能裝運。因此，單證必須準確無誤。有時出境展品回國時也會涉及運輸過程中的一些單據，如訂載單、裝貨單、提單、投保單等。

報關申請

報關申請是參展單位向展覽活動承辦單位所在的城市申請其產品入關的一種業務程序。擬定報關申請一般應注意以下幾項：

1. 必須明確說明報關申請單位。

2. 必須明確說明報關產品的性質。

3. 必須明確說明要求產品入境的具體時間、產品在展覽地停留的時間、出境的時間以及產品入境後停留的地點。

貨物的收發貨人或其代理人向海關辦理貨物進出口手續時，要填寫《進口貨物報關單》或《出口貨物報關單》，同時提供批准貨物進出口的證件和有關的貨運、商業票據，以便海關審查貨物的進出口是否合法，確定關稅的徵收或減免，編制海關統計。

報關單的正確性將直接影響到報關率，展品的及時到位和海關監督的各個工作環節。因此，作為會展從業人員應掌握報關單的基本常識。

報關單的一般要求：

1. 報關必須真實，要做到兩個相符：一是單證相符，即報關單與合約、批文、發票、裝箱單相符；二是單貨相符，即報關單中所報內容與實際進出口貨物情況相符。尤其是貨物的名稱、規格、數量、原產地、價格等內容必須真實，不能出錯，更不能偽報、瞞報或虛報。

2. 不同合約的貨物，不能填在同一份報關單上；同一批貨物中有不同貿易方式的貨物，也須用不同的報關單向海關申報。

3. 報關時填報的項目要準確齊全。報關單所列各欄要逐項詳細填寫，內容無誤，要求盡可能打字填報。如手寫，字跡須清楚端正。填報項目，若有更改，須在更改項目上加蓋校對章。

常用術語：

1.transaction 交易

2.USPPI （United States Principal Party in Interest） 貨主

3.ultimate consignee 收貨人

4.intermediate consignee 中轉人

5.forwarding agent 運輸代理人

6.loading pier 裝運碼頭

7.export carrier 出口承運人

8.port of unloading 卸貨港

9.containerized 集裝箱運輸

10.transportation reference No. 運輸編號

11.entry number 入境編號

12.hazardous materials 危險品

13.in bond code 扣關待完稅貨號

14.schedule B No. 商品標記號碼、封條、包裝數量、包裝種類等數據

15.license No. 出口許可證號碼

16.authorization 授權

17.ECCN （Export Control Classification Number） 出口貨物分類號碼

18.forwarder 運輸代理

19.violation 違反

20.authentication 真實性

提單

提單一般包括以下內容：發貨人、收貨人、運輸工具、航次、收發貨物港口、集裝箱號、箱數和件數、貨物種類和貨名、尺碼、運費交付方式等資訊。

常用術語：

1.FOB （free on board） 裝運港船上交貨價，離岸價

2.CIF （cost, insurance and freight） 成本、保險費加運費價，到岸價

3.CFR （cost and freight） 成本加運費

4.FCA （free carrier） 貨交承運人指定地點

5.CPT （carriage paid to） 運費付至

6.CIP （carriage and insurance paid to） 運費保險費付至

7.L/C （letter of credit） 信用證

8.B/L （bill of lading） 提單

9.packing list 裝箱單

10.consignor 託運人

11.consignee 收貨人

12.port of loading 裝運港

13.port of discharge 卸貨港

14.country of origin 原產國

15.place of delivery 交貨地點

16.gross weight 毛重

17.net weight 淨重

Chapter 7 Exhibit Space Preparation and Decoration 展臺搭建

Section A Reading Assignment

Warming-up Activity

Go over the following terms with your teacher.

stage 安排，舉辦展覽會	themed stands 主題展台	prop 道具	cut through 克服（困難）	turn upside down 完全改變
drap 用布裝飾	spotlit 燈光照射的	set up 布置	presto 立刻，剎那間	dress up 裝飾

Pre-reading Questions

Answer the following questions without referring to the text.

1.what purpose（s）are exhibitions expected to achieve?

2.What do you think is critical in the success of an exhibition?

3.What kind of exhibition is very popular nowadays?

4.What do you think the decorations of an exhibition are?

Text

Key Factors for Successful Events

The word "exhibition" is normally used to describe an organized public display of manufactured goods and works of art.Here the word is used to describe the temporary display of sample goods in a specialized exhibition.There is no question that exhibitions offer one great advantage over other more traditional communication techniques—the face-to-face contact of a niche market, something which has always been difficult to get.

"The normal rules of presentation turn upside-down at exhibitions.In the clamor of competing stands, nobody gives you undivided attention.When a buyer walks over your aisle, you only have a few seconds to grab their interest," says Ian Whitworth, marketing director of staging connections, Australia's largest event staging company, which stages over 20, 000 events every year.

You'll have to tell them your story in a way that cuts through the clutter.An effective stand must stand out.Themed stands use sets, props and theatrical lighting to transport the visitor to another place—a jungle, an outback town, a beach, or outer space.It is one of the fast-growing trends in exhibition stand design.

"It's not a question of how much money is spent, but rather of thinking outside the square and making an event fun," Whitworth says.If it's fun, people are far more likely to remember the event.

Some key factors for event success are :

· Start with a plan of what it is that you want to achieve and the message you want to send.

· One of the most inexpensive ways to dress up a stand is with draping.Add a spotlit logo, and presto, big show impact.

· If your space "feels" like you've made an effort, your visitors will naturally assume your information will be interesting.

· Effective communication calls for special tactics to be seen and heard above the crowd.

Ordering things

Read your exhibitor's manual carefully.You will find all the information you need to make ordering things easy.After you have defined your objectives and designed your stand, establish a list of your requirements.Ask questions.Talk to the preferred suppliers if you are not sure whether you need clarification or ideas.Ask for written confirmation of the things you have ordered from your supplier.Make sure your stand coordinator brings a copy of your order to the show during set-up.Get in early, at least four weeks prior to the show.Last minute orders can incur late fees and delays during set-up.You may also have to compromise due to shortages in supply.Use the official show contractor.They have been selected on their performance and will be there to help at the show if you need it.Keep it simple.Don't order too much for your floor space.As a rule, at 50%of your floor space should be left for visitors.

Booking a stand

Establish how much space you ideally require to display your products and/or services.Check whether this fits within your budget. Select a stand with high traffic flow, i.e.near entrance, adjacent to kiosk, or on a corner.Ideally your stand should have more frontage than depth, for better traffic exposure.Ask who is on the adjacent stands.Do you wish to be next to competitors? Book early to obtain the widest choice of stands, and to gain an "early booking" discount.Sign and return the "contract for space" promptly, with deposit, to confirm your preferred site.If you require special services e.g.gas, air, water, ensure your preferred stand has these.

The meeting area

Business meetings are one of the main ways that business people get things done.Though some people say business meetings are a waste of time, business people must meet to talk and negotiate buying, selling, and partnerships.To support them, hotels, conference centers, and meeting areas of all kinds must prepare the meeting area and be ready to serve the needs of business people while they are holding their meetings.One good point for organizations providing meeting services is that most businesses that have meetings don't have just one.They usually will go back again and again as long as the service is good.Repeat customers are the key to profitability, so it is important to make sure every customer is satisfied every time.

Preparing the meeting area is a key task.The meeting area should be clean with no distractions.If the area is dirty or the furniture is run down or broken, it will reflect badly on the side that chose you for the meeting.Most formal meetings have groups on both sides of a table, sitting in chairs and probably using presentation aids of some kind.The furniture arrangement will be determined by the customer. The table should be a standard height, with no distractions in the middle, like plants, that will stop people from seeing one another.One or both of the sides in a meeting may have printed agendas.They may need document services, like translation, print, copy, or distribution services.A calculator, a telephone, and stationery items like paper and pens should be in the meeting room as well.AV, computer, and presentation equipment should be on a meeting checklist that the staff have reviewed with customer.

Serving the needs of business people while they are holding their meetings is important.Staff should be within earshot, but far enough away so they do not hear every word that the sides in a meeting are saying.Reaction time when called is one of the main points for service people to remember.They should jump when called, not slowly get up and rub their eyes and yawn.Staff serving a meeting area should be ready to go get something that is needed by someone in the meeting, whether it is food, beverage, equipment of some kind, or to print and bring back an important document at a printer.Customers notice how fast things get done when service people are called.They remember this when they choose a meeting location the next time.

Check-in

Do you have any questions about the text? If any, ask your teacher.

Important Vocabulary

clutter	[ˈklʌtə]	n.	混亂
jungle	[ˈdʒʌŋgl]	n.	熱帶叢林
grab	[græb]	v.	（一把）抓住

hockey	[ˈhɒkɪ]	n.	曲棍球，冰球
specific	[spəˈsɪfɪk]	a.	特定的，具體的
consultation	[ˌkɒnsəlˈteɪʃən]	n.	商量，磋商
violation	[ˌvaɪəˈleɪʃən]	n.	違反，違背
banner	[ˈbænə]	n.	橫幅
pyrotechnics	[ˌpaɪərəuˈtekniks]	n.	煙火裝置
elevate	[ˈelɪveɪt]	v.	舉起，使升高
reputable	[ˈrepjutəbl]	a.	聲譽好的
flammable	[ˈflæməbl]	a.	易燃的
clarification	[ˌklærɪfɪˈkeɪʃən]	n.	簡明
confirmation	[ˌkɒnfəˈmeɪʃən]	n.	批准，證據
coordinator	[ˌkəuˈɔːdɪneɪtə]	n.	協調人
incur	[ɪnˈkəː]	v.	帶來，招致
compromise	[ˈkɒmpəmaɪz]	n.	妥協，讓步
contractor	[kənˈtræktə]	n.	承包人
adjacent	[əˈdʒeɪsənt]	a.	鄰近的
kiosk	[kiːɒsk]	n.	報亭，電話亭，售貨亭
profitability	[ˌprɒfɪtəˈbɪlɪtɪ]	n.	盈利
distraction	[dɪˈstrækʃən]	n.	分心，分散注意力的事情
agenda	[əˈdʒendə]	n.	議事日程
distribution	[dɪstrɪˈbjuːʃən]	n.	分發，分送
stationery	[ˈsteɪʃənərɪ]	n.	（總稱）文具

Useful Expressions

manufactured goods	商品
outback town	偏遠小鎮
call for	要求
works of art	藝術品
sample goods	樣品
specialized exhibition	專門展覽，專題展覽

within earshot	在聽力所及範圍內
prior to	先於，比......早，早於
due to	由於
traffic flow	（川流不息的）人流，車流

Language Focus

1.Special conditions should be in the contract, and the venue management company should insist approval rights and on seeing detailed drawings of each installation before they are started.

合約中應包括一些特殊條件，會場管理公司應堅持有審批權，並應堅持在所有安裝、裝飾工作開始之前看到所有細節圖示。

2.One good point for organizations providing meeting services is that most businesses that have meetings don't have just one.

有一點對提供會議服務的機構十分有利：大多數召開會議的公司都不只開一次會。

3.Staff serving a meeting area should be ready to go get something that is needed by someone in the meeting, whether it is food, beverage, equipment of some kind, or to print and bring back an important document at a printer.

會議區域的服務人員應為與會者提供他們所需的物品，無論是食物、飲料、某種設備，還是去影印和從影印機上取回重要的文件。

Group Discussion

Discuss the following topics in group.Select one on the team to make a presentation before the class.

1.How to have a successful exhibition ?

2.Suppose you are the exhibitor, what will you do to compete for attention? Guidelines for Discussion

▁ convey 傳達

▁ relevant 相關的

■ surround 圍繞

■ demonstration 展示

■ interactive 互動的

■ issue 議題

▁ dynamic 活力

▁ stage 舉辦

■ set 布景

■ theme 確定主題

■ lighting 燈光

■ flooring 鋪地材料

Writing Activity

Summarize the text by outlining major points.Write a few lines about the preparation and decoration for a stand.

Section B Case Study

Read the following passage before solving the problems that ensue.

Theme Building of the Event

The intuitive, all-encompassing nature of marketing messages conveyed at an exhibition can make them more relevant than ever, and therefore more likely to break through the clutter barrier. Take a product launch exhibition, for example.You have the ability to surround a (usually) highly qualified audience with your key messages.The fact that it is an "event" has also created the emotive effect of being involving and fun.

An exhibition can also allow a detailed product demonstration and a hands-on element, allowing people to see, hear and feel the product without having pressure to buy.Events are highly interactive. People can ask questions and seek reassurance on any issue.Finally, there's a group dynamic, a certain buzz which helps communicate the product's message.

A well executed theme can deliver a strong message to your audience.When the message surrounds them, it can be a far more involving experience and is far more likely to be remembered.Creative theming stimulates all the senses.The feel and smell of bark chips under foot with a soundtrack of chirruping crickets can be powerfully evocative.A well designed set will add a vital stamp of individuality to your stand, reinforce the theme of the event and draw visitors' attention.

Staging Connections lasr year put together its own exhibition stand at the AIME show in Melbourne.The stand looked more like something out of a Raiders of the Lost Ark movie than a traditional exhibition stand.The centerpiece, an Aztec temple, was surrounded by a seven-meter-high jungle, complete with monkeys swinging from trees, giant insects, bamboo, and the occasional tribal spear partially buried in the bark chip flooring.Guests had to "bush bash" their way to the center of the stand through tunnels of plants in order to meet friendly Indiana Jones-clone sales people.The $12,000 outlay generated more than $400,000 worth of work, according to Ian Whitworth, and even four months later was continuing to pull in business.

Problem Solving

How do you solve the following problems? Outline your assertion.

1.How to grab the buyer's interest in the first few seconds in a car show?

2.What can be done to control carefully the use of pyrotechnics and other flammable substances?

Section C Format Writing

Acquaint yourself with the following.Finish the exercises that ensue.

Part 1 Notice 通告

A.Notice for Lease

FOR LEASE

Prime exhibition space at the entrance

First Floor-50 sq.m.

AVAILABLE NOW

For rental information contact：

Exhibition Service Dept.

Tel：5525 7266

招 租

入口處絕佳展位

一樓 五十平方公尺

有關租賃事宜請與會展服務部聯繫

電話：5525 7266

B.Meeting Notice

National HR Management Association

Notice

All participants are requested to meet in the A1 Conference Hall on Friday （March 26）at 2 ： 00 p.m.to hold discussions on the problems of employment faced by the HR managers.

March 24, 2004

本星期五（3 月 26 日）下午兩點，全體人員在 A1 會議廳開會，討論人力資源經理面臨的員工僱用問題，請準時出席。

全國人力資源管理協會

2004 年 3 月 24 日

C.Exhibition Notice

EXHIBITION

Shanghai Art Gallery （Shanghai Meishuguan）Ancient Indian Art Exhibition, Nov.19-27, hours：8 ： 30a.m.-11 ： 30 a.m., 1 ： 00 p.m.-4 ： 30 p.m., closed on Mondays.Tel：63272829.

古印度藝術展於 11 月 19 日至 27 日在上海美術館舉辦。開放時間為：上午 8 ： 30-11 ： 30，下午 1 ： 00-4 ： 30。週一不對外開放。聯繫電話：63272829。

Questions about the Samples

Choose the best answers to the following questions based on your understanding of the format writing.

1.What is for lease in the first sample?

A.Exhibition Service Dept.   B.The first floor.

C.Prime exhibition space at the entrance.   D.50 sq.m.

2.Who wrote the meeting notice?

A.The national HR Management Association.   B.All participants.

C.The A1 conference Hall.   D.HR managers.

3.The exhibition is about_____.

A.Shanghai Art Gallery   B.Ancient Indian Art

C.Shanghai Meishuguan   D.Shanghai Ancient Art

Notes of Format

Always bear in mind the following.

通告撰寫時應注意做到以下六點：

1. 用詞精練簡潔。

2. 標題鮮明。

3. 正文部分可使用完整句子。

4. 段落清晰，讓觀者一目瞭然。

5. 必要時可使用黑體字，斜體字或下劃線等方式來強調某些重要訊息。

6. 儘量簡短，避免冗贅。

撰寫步驟：

1. 確定目標 Identify the task

2. 列出要點 List the points

3. 撰寫通知 Write the notice

4. 反覆檢查 Check the notice

Do It Yourself

Write a notice according to the following situation：

The third annual meeting of shareholders of Wisdom Holdings Limited is to be held at 1：30 p.m.May 5th, 2004, at the conference hall of Shanghai International Convention Center.As the conference coordinator of the hotel, you need to prepare the notice for the company.

Part 2 Leaflet 傳單

CHINA TRAVEL FAIR

Dates：June 10-23, 2003

Sponsored by：

China National Tourism Administration

Shanghai People's Municipal Government

Secretariat of Travel Fair

Add：Rm 2237 No.10 Jianguo St., Shanghai, China

Tel：55335533

Fax：66723350

Post Code：201435

Telex：54189901

The travel agents from _____ are welcomed to contact us to arrange for the setup of _____.

We recommend you travel routes that contain many well-known scenic spots.

We show you rich travel resources in _____.

We offer you _____.

Participants from _____ are welcomed.

Questions about the Samples

Choose the best answers to the following questions based on your understanding of the format writing.

1.The leaflet in sample 2 is about _____.

A.China National Tourism Administration

B.Shanghai People's Municipal Government

C.China Travel Fair

D.Jianguo st.Shanghai

2.The Fair is sponsored by _____.

A.Jianguo St., Shanghai, China

B.Shanghai People's Municiple Government

C.China National Tourism Administration

D.Both B and C

Notes of Format

Always bear in mind the following.

會展推廣是會展承辦者透過各種媒體向社會或者目標觀眾宣傳某次展會項目的一種市場營銷活動。會展推廣文書是以文字形式對展會活動進行促銷的一種方式，目的在於讓社會或者目標觀眾瞭解有關項目的內容、時間、地點以及聯繫方式等各種有關資訊。會展推廣文書屬於廣告文書的範疇，與一般廣告文書沒有太大區別。

編寫會展推廣文書應該注意：

1. 必須明確承辦會展的單位或公司名稱。

2. 必須明確舉辦會展的時間。

3. 必須明確舉辦會展的地點。

4. 必須明確聯繫方式。

5. 必須明確參加會展的目標觀眾。

6. 明確會展承辦者所提供的產品與服務類型。

7. 明確會展承辦者所提供的技術支持。

撰寫會展推廣宣傳資料應遵循 AIDA 原則：

1. 引起注意（draw Attention）

2. 引發興趣（arouse Interest）

3. 造成慾望（create Desire）

4. 導致行動（induce Action）

Do It Yourself

1.You are supposed to write a leaflet for the Shanghai World Travel Fair.The organizing committee is planning the large-scale event to popularize the World Travel Fair 2008, which will be held again in Shanghai New International Expo Center.The contact information is：

P.R.Dept., No.2525, Zhong Shan Road （W）.The telephone number is 6481 0699.You should provide other information that a leaflet requires.

2.Translate the following leaflet into Chinese：

Who else can guide you to a successful meeting?

Years of experience have taught us how important business meetings are.That's why we've developed a unique Meeting Guide.It offers a wealth of practical advice and useful tips to make organizing conference or meeting as simple as possible.It also has helpful worksheets so that you don't forget those important little details that make all the difference.So send off for our free Meeting Guide today.

Holiday Inn

STAY WITH SOMEONE YOU KNOW

Reference Answers

Answers to Questions about the Samples of Part 1 of Format Writing

1.C 2.A 3.B

Reference Answer to Do It Yourself of Part 1 of Format Writing

Wisdom Holdings Limited

Notice

All shareholders are requested to meet at the conference hall of Shanghai International Convention Center on Friday （May 5th）at 1：30 p.m.to have the third annual meeting.

April 28, 2004

Answers to Questions about the Samples of Part 2 of Format Writing

1.C 2.D

Reference Answer to Do It Yourself of Part 2 of Format Writing

1.

Shanghai World Travel Fair

Venue：Shanghai New International Expo Center

Dates：October 10-23, 2005

Sponsored by：

China National Tourism Administration

Shanghai People's Municipal Government

Secretariat of Travel Fair

Add：P.R.Dept., No.2525, Zhong Shan Road （W）

Tel：6481 0699.

Fax：6481 0699.

Post Code：201103.

The travel agents from _____ are welcomed to contact us to arrange for the setup of _____.

We recommend you travel routes that contain many well-known scenic spots.

We show you rich travel resources in _____.

We offer you _____.

Participants from _____are welcomed.

2. 引導成功會議，非我莫屬！

多年的經驗告訴我們，商務會議至關重要。為此，我們開發了獨特的會議指南。它包含大量實用且行之有效的建議，使會議的組織不再煩瑣。同時，它還包含有工作流程表，幫助您記住重要細節，它將是您的得力助手。寫信索取我們為您免費提供的會議指南，今天就行動吧。

假日酒店

與朋友相約

Chapter 8 Event Information Management 會展資訊管理

Section A Reading Assignment

Warming-up Activity

Go over the following terms with your teacher.

information network 訊息網路	information technology 訊息技術	information linkages 訊息鏈接
time and cost-saving 時間與成本節約型	convention hotel information development 會議酒店訊息研發	computerization 電腦化
convention file data 會議文件資料	information bank 訊息庫	online exhibition 在線展覽

Pre-reading Questions

Answer the following questions without referring to the text.

1. Do you think online convention and exhibition will squeeze the traditional off-line conventions and exhibitions out of the market?

2. What role does the Internet play in the convention and exhibition industry?

3. Can IT surely guarantee you a successful convention or exhibition?

Text

The Guest Package System

The convention and exhibition industry is a dynamic information network and the proliferation of information technology has revolutionized information linkages and blurred boundaries among industry members.

Information is the essential element in every part of the convention and exhibition venues' activities.Use of information technology enables them to promote their services and effectively communicate with meeting planners, exhibitors, attendees and visitors.Information technology also permits them to improve business processes, more efficiently conduct marketing research, provide customer service, and facilitate performance management and planning.

There is no doubt that technology has changed the face of the exhibition industry and will continue to do so.One advance was the development of virtual exhibitions.Virtual exhibitions created storefronts on the Internet, allowing exhibitors to provide on-line demonstrations and collateral to buyers.

Exhibition organizers quickly tried to develop their own virtual exhibitions to compete with this new type of technology.Virtual exhibition is becoming more and more popular, due to its time-saving and cost-saving advantages.Many convention centers are moving from paper questionnaires to online evaluation to solicit customers' reactions.More and more associations have logged their meeting calendars on their websites, which contain rich information concerning their conventions and meetings, such as show information about exhibits, attendees, organizers, schedule, cost of booths, participation, procedures, online service, hall layout, cooperation media, and photo albums.

Let's take convention hotel information development as an example.In today's convention hotel environment, there is an increasing need to ensure guest packages are received, stored, and delivered carefully, quickly and accurately.Our Guest Package System guarantees your success in achieving that goal by recording all incoming package information, whether the package is for a hotel guest, convention group, or hotel employee.

With the network version of Guest Package System, once data is correctly entered into the program, that information on the package is quickly accessible by other users, shortening employees'response time and increasing customers' satisfaction.

Package information can be retrieved using virtually any query combination in our unique Versatile Query Technology.

However, it soon became apparent that the virtual exhibition would not take the place of traditional model of face-to-face exhibitions.In fact, a study conducted by Exhibit Surveys, Inc., for the center for Exhibition Industry Research, substantiates that all forms of face-to-face marketing are still important.Therefore traditional ways of information management are still seen as effective.

Computerization

Many organizations have gone into computerization, which is supposed to act as a panacea for all front desk ills.They are only as good as the human beings who operate them, and, like humans, they seem to have their good and bad days.Just last week, I had a meeting in New Orleans and after 3 phone calls, we settled on a 2 bedroom and parlor arrangement for one of our directors and the chairman of the committee meeting there.The director and chairman arrived at the front desk to find that the computer knew nothing about their arrival. It was after 7：00 in the evening.No sales department or convention service personnel were available, and the hotel was fully occupied.The city was tight, the hotel was locked in, and 4 people, 2 of whom were on cots, occupied the parlor we were supposed to have.The director and the chairman got 2 broom closets for the night.

Result：I got a phone call the next morning and my ears are still burning from that conversation.Evidently the communication link slipped between the front desk and the sales office.Hopefully, those hotels switching to computerization will also put in back-up equipment.

Information bank

Most of the chains have national sales meetings and it would seem to me there should be an opportunity at these meetings to pass along the information on the needs or all their customers.If they don't have it or keep updating it, they are not doing their job.It is a waste of valuable time and money when sales director of Sheraton, Hyatt or Marriott calls and just solicits the next available meeting.I classify these as the cold calls and there is really nothing I can give them except for the fact that I will contact the regional office when I have a request for a meeting in their particular area.

I have two other favorite things that happen to me and I would like to again blame individuals not doing their homework or not checking their records.You know there is a certain tendency in the hotel business to move about.In fact, I have been tempted to put a big board on my wall and get darts with your names on them so I could throw them around the board as often as you move around the country.

Use your records

When you get this great opportunity to move to another property, whether with the same hotel operation or another, I would guess that the first thing you do is to get to know every nook and cranny in the hotel.Included in one of these little corners are files which, if your predecessor's secretary is not Phyllis Diller, are in order by corporate or trade association name.

Convention file data

Such files should also include as much information on organizing and promoting conventions as possible.There are many who are responsible for putting on conventions every year and you are in need of their assistance in these areas as well.Your convention liaison director can build up a really substantial file on this phase of convention planning alone merely by speaking with convention organizers, obtaining copies of their promotional literature, post convention critiques, etc.This is all a part of the total package of ensuring a successful convention.

I am also aware that some hotels have over the years issued printed "Meeting Planner Guidebooks" and those that have are to be congratulated for doing so.Unfortunately, however, I am afraid that in a number of cases, the hotel sales representative who hands these guides out to a prospective client, with great deal of pride in what a great thing his hotel is doing for the convention industry, has not actually read them himself.When you engage him in a conversation on certain recommendations contained in these "Meeting Planner Guidebooks," he is at a loss.

I realize that you cannot be out making important sales calls and at the same time be poking your nose into the meeting rooms of every convention being held in your hotel.There are, however, a number of sources right on the staff of every hotel from which you, as a sales representative, can garner all the data you needed to build up a substantial reference file.

There are banquet captains and head waiters who probably listen to more speakers addressing more groups on a wider variety of subjects in one month than most of us do in a lifetime.So don't overlook the opportunity to tap this valuable source.

Everything has its drawbacks, including IT.

Check-in

Do you have any questions about the text? If any, ask your teacher.

Important Vocabulary

dynamic	[daɪˈnæmɪk]	v.	動態的
proliferation	[prəˈlɪfəreɪʃən]	v.	激增、擴散
linkage	[ˈlɪŋkɪdʒ]	a.	鏈接
facilitate	[fəˈsɪlɪteɪt]	a.	簡化
retrieve	[rɪˈtriːv]	n.	提取
computerization	[kəmˌpjuːtəraɪˈzeɪʃən]	n.	電腦化

Useful Expressions

online exhibition and trade show	網上展覽與工業展覽
convention and exhibition information management system	會展資訊管理系統
convention and Exhibition data bank	會展數據庫

Language Focus

1.The convention and exhibition industry is a dynamic information network and the proliferation of information technology has revolutionized information linkages and blurred boundaries among industry members.

會展業是一個活躍的資訊網絡，資訊技術的擴展使資訊連結發生了革命性的變化，而且也使行業各成員之間的界線模糊化。

2.Online exhibition is becoming more and more popular with its time-saving and cost-saving edges.

線上展覽因其省時省成本的優勢而越來越受歡迎。

Group Discussion

Discuss the following topic in group.Select one on the team to make a presentation before the class.

What should be concerned when developing a convention or exhibition information system?

Guidelines for Discussion

▬ easy access

▬ convenient information linkage

▬ customer supporting

▬ market research

Writing Activity

Summarize the text by outlining major points.Write a few lines about online exhibitions.

▎Section B Case Study

Read the following passage before solving the problems that ensue.

Stages of IT Implementation

IT implementation in American convention and visitor bureau has gone through 4 stages：

Stage 1：substitution

In the initial stage, bureaus recognized that the Internet provided an important alternative format for communication and promotion. However, substitution does not mean that traditional communication channels are completely replaced.While keeping other means of communication intact, the bureaus improved the depth and breadth of information on their site.Yet, most of the websites created by those bureaus in this stage were still "passive websites" with limited functions.The most basic on-line tool—the inclusion of hyperlinks— was employed.

Stage 2：enlargement

The bureaus became more sophisticated in using websites as communication and marketing tools and their confidence in them increased.Consequently, they were able to use the Internet to do more of the same tasks.At the same time, increasing hits and requests on the website sent out strong signals that encouraged almost every bureau to revamp its websites.More functions and information were added to meet the needs of customers and, as this process occurred, bureau directors realized a sense of need to consider the Internet as an essential information channel.Thus, visible efforts were made to promote website addresses.

Stage 3：gestation

Enlargement came with a price.As bureau directors were experiencing the advantages of the Internet, they also quickly started struggling with its negative side effects related to management and control issues, such as pressure on financial and human resources.As bureaus continued to experience the growth of on-line visitation and requests, more work and more staff time were required； however, while the technology within the bureau had evolved considerably, the organizational aspects of the bureau had not.Thus, the lack of development in OC gradually pressured bureau directors to learn more about the technology and orchestrate staff to handle the growing amount of work.Indeed, some bureau directors indicated that they spent all their time in learning, staff retaining, and data entering. They, in turn, began to question their investment and the value of the Internet.

Stage 4：reconfiguration

IT does more than merely change the means by which information is delivered and presented.The more profound impact of IT implementation is to facilitate the new development of products and services.At this stage, some bureau directors began to realize that the value of IT went beyond passive information provision and communication； that is, they began to think about how to use IT in order to do things differently.They started using IT to collaborate with industry partners in order to develop various itineraries and travel packages, using E-mails to broadcast time-sensitive information to attract the attention of potential visitors with on-line visitors' permission, investing virtual exhibitions, and developing on-line registration systems for annual marathons.Actually, the reconfiguration led to a change of the bureau leaders' vision of the role of IT within its overall marketing efforts.

Problem Solving

How do you solve the following problems? Outline your assertion.

1.What does the implementation of IT in American Convention and Visitor Bureau imply?

2.How can an exhibition enterprise get most from IT?

Section C Format Writing

Acquaint yourself with the following.Finish the exercises that ensue.

E-mail 電子郵件

Receiver：mrowers @ meetingplanner.on.ca

CC：hwger @ hotmail.sh.cn

Subject：The proposal

Date：

Attachment：

Dear Ms.Ferguson：

It is our pleasure to present for the consideration of the HULA ASSOCIATION FOR A HEALTHIER AMERICA, a detailed proposal of the services that ADAMS &ASSOCIATES TRAVEL will provide for you 2006 Annual Meeting in Honolulu, Hawaii.

This proposal is divided into three sections that are attached to this mail.

When you have had a chance to look over the enclosed, we would very much appreciate the opportunity to discuss these arrangements with you and sincerely hope that you will choose ADAMS & ASSOCIATES TRAVEL to coordinate arrangements for this important meeting.

I will call you next week and hope to set up an appointment at your convenience to discuss this with you.With kind regards,

Sincerely,

ADAMS & ASSOCIATES TRAVEL

Ralph Philips

Sales Manager

Questions about the Samples

Answer the following questions based on your understanding of the format writing.

1.What is the E-mail address of the receiver?

2.What is the address of the sender?

3.What is the mail about?

Notes of Format

Always bear in mind the following.

電子郵件是一種更加快捷的信郵方式。郵件的主要部分與傳統的商務信函並無二異。只是日期一般不用寫出來，因為電腦會自動顯示日期。

Do It Yourself

Work out an E-mail with the English prompts.

Suppose you, Jessie Liu of Phoenix Co-operation, are to send an E-mail message to powerbitz @ netexcutive.com, the E-mail address of a travel agency, asking for advice and hotel arrangement for a one-week tour in Thailand.

Reference Answers

Answers to Questions about the Samples

1.mrowers @ meetingplanner.on.ca

2.hwger @ hotmail.sh.cn

3.A proposal of a pre-post meeting tour arrangement

Reference Answer to Do It Yourself

To：powerbitz @ netexcutive.com

CC：

Subject：Inquiry

Dear Sir or Madam,

We are going to make a one-week tour in Thailand.Would you give us some advice about the trip and arrange two double rooms from Oct.7 for us?

Look forward to your reply.

Sincerely,

Jessie Liu

Phoenix Co-operation

Chapter 9 Food and Beverage Service 會展餐飲服務

▌Section A Reading Assignment

Warming-up Activity

Go over the following terms with your teacher.

setup 準備·布置	accommodate 安排食宿	linen 檯布(亞麻布)	first aid kit 急救箱
catering executive 餐飲主管	sit-down banquet 就座式宴會	pepper shaker 胡椒瓶	guest count 客人人數
confirmation letter 確認函	theater style 劇院型	flatware 餐具	napery 餐巾
head table 主桌	runway 通道	stirrer 攪拌器	hallway 門廳·走廊
bandstand 樂隊演奏台	easel 畫架	lighter 打火機	layout 布局·陳列
display table 陳列台	seating chart 就餐座位表	fire escape 消防通道	elaborate banquet 豪華宴會

Pre-reading Questions

Answer the following questions without referring to the text.

1.What is the space reserved for banquet viewed as?

2.Does unused space represent lost profit?

3.What's the use of function room diary?

4.What serves as official authorization for an event?

5.What factors should be considered in banquet room assignments?

6.Can a room hold more people for a sit-down banquet than a stand-up reception?

7.What should be taken into consideration when the function room is set up?

8.Does a function room accommodate more people when it is placed theater-style?

9.What should a manager in charge do before the event begins?

Text

Banquet Room Reservation, Assignment and Setup

The space reserved for a banquet is very important to both the facility and the guests.The facility views this space as a product to be sold.Unused space represents lost profits.

Banquet Room Reservation—Function room diary plays a vital role in banquet room reservation.Catering executives use a daily function room diary to determine if space is available for a particular banquet.They also use the diary to reserve the room after they sell an event so that no one else will commit it for another function.

The daily function room diary lists all the function space a property has available for sale and divides it into various intervals throughout the day for the sale of different events.The diary varies, according to the size of the operation and the number of available function rooms.Some facilities require less information in their daily function room diaries than others do.

Catering executives may make a tentative entry in the diary to hold space for a potential client until the client has made a definite commitment for a particular room on a particular day.

When the catering executive confirms an entry, the diary's coordinator will officially enter the event into the appropriate time slot.An actual copy of the guest-signed confirmation letter or a function room diary entry form may serve as official authorization for the event.Again, remember that facilities vary their procedures considerably according to what best suits their needs.Banquet room assignment—In making banquet room assignments, the following factors should be considered :

▶ Is space available for all the support services, entertainment, and other equipment? Besides space for a specific number of guests, it may be necessary to provide space for head tables, portable bars, buffet tables, entertainment bandstands, dance floors, and other items.

▶ Does the event require the seating of guests? The room may easily accommodate many more people for a stand-up reception than a sit-down banquet. (A rule of thumb is 10 square feet per person if guests sit, 9 square feet if they stand.)

▶ Are any events planned for the space immediately before and/ or after the special function under consideration? For example, if you must tear down a room that held a meeting with exhibits before you can set up the next activity, you will need much more time to prepare the room for the next function than if the room were set up for a theater-style meeting or a stand-up reception.

▶ What type of function is planned in rooms adjacent to the room being considered for assignment? Many after-dinner programs have been spoiled by a loud rock band performing on the other side of a "soundproof" wall.

▶ What municipal codes and ordinances affect room assignments? Fire or other codes may limit the number of people that can occupy a room.Moreover, you must never block fire escape doors.

▶ Is the room easily accessible to both the guests and the service staff?Rooms accessible only by stairs might be undesirable ; you should use them only when no other appropriate space is available.

▶ What are the sizes of the tables, chairs, and other equipment that you plan to use for the event? While this may seem like a minor point, tables or chairs that are just a few inches larger than others can significantly reduce the number of guests that you can accommodate. For example, 900 chairs arranged theater style, which are just two inches wider than necessary, will require 25 square feet more than their smaller counterparts.

▶ If a reception is scheduled to be held outdoors, have the convention service manager and meeting planner provided for indoor backup space in case of inclement weather?

Setting up function rooms—Getting ready for service for banquets and catered events includes setting up the function room (s) , scheduling staff members and preparing, plating, and storing banquet food.The design and decor of function rooms, like the food and beverages that are served in them, can take many forms.A simple coffee break may be served in an undecorated themeless room, while an elaborate reception featuring foods from around the world may be held in a function room that has complex decorations to fit the theme. The type of function room chosen and how it is decorated are largely dictated by the needs and expectations of the client.

Frequently, managers come up with creative layouts for function rooms to help setup crews carry out instructions on the function sheet.Some clients have strong preferences about the layout of function rooms, and those might be expressed in unusual or creative layouts as well.Managers should carefully plan the location of room elements such as, bars, food buffet stations, ice carvings, garden and tree decorations, and stages for speakers or entertainers.The location of these elements affects the guests' experiences in the room.The need for staff members to pay close attention to the details listed on the function sheet and illustrated on the layout is just as important for small events as it is for large, elaborate events.

Adequate space for display tables, guest tables, and other room elements （for example, stages and lecterns） is an important setup consideration for banquets and catered events.Crowded, hot rooms make for an unpleasant dining experience.Adequate space also allows for more efficient movement of inventory and people.

The client is usually responsible for reviewing any seating charts that the event may require.However, the manager can assist the client with that task and indicate the staff's preferences regarding seating arrangements.

Procedures for setting up function rooms vary according to the needs of the client and his or her group.The following is a partial list of activities and items that might be involved in setting up a function room：

▶ Placing runways, carpets and pianos

▶ Placing dinner tables, meeting tables and head tables

▶ Placing chairs, sofas and other seats

▶ Placing bars, buffets and cake tables

▶ Placing the registration, gift and display tables

▶ Placing the video/movie screen, projector table, projector and exten-sion cords

▶ Placing chalkboards, easels and any other display equipment

▶ Placing microphones, lecterns and flags

▶ Placing linens, ashtrays, sugar bowls, salt and pepper shakers and other table items

▶ Placing cakes, candle holders, fountains, flowers and decorations

▶ Placing table numbers on each table, if necessary

Because guests at banquets and catered events must be served quickly, service stations should be set up to allow for maximum staff efficiency.Equipment requirements vary with type of function and the menu, but function-room service stations may have the following :

▶ Microwave ovens

▶ Flatware

▶ Glassware

▶ Water, coffee and tea

▶ Cream, sugar and stirrers

▶ Placemats and napery

▶ Candles, flowers or other table decorations

▶ Matches or lighters

▶ First aid kits

▶ Salt, pepper and other condiments

Prior to opening the function room's doors and allowing guests to enter, the manager overseeing service for the event must ensure that the room setup is complete.Whenever practical, the manager should meet with the client immediately before the event to inquire about the latest guest count or any last-minute changes to the plan for the event. The manager should walk through the function room (or assign someone else to do so) to make a safety check.No cords should be positioned where someone could trip on them ; supports for platform panels, acoustical shells, table leaves and risers should all be secure ; chairs and tables should not wobble, and all their legs should be sturdy ; and doorways and hallways (especially fire exits) should not be obstructed.

The manager in charge usually holds a brief meeting with all service staff (and sometimes kitchen staff) to review details and give final updates just before the event begins.

Check-in

Do you have any questions about the text? If any, ask your teacher.

More Terms

宴會廳日誌 function room diary	站立式招待會 stand-up reception	菸灰缸 ashtray	調味品，佐料 condiment
時間段 time slot	撤．拆除 tear down	微波爐 microwave oven	面板，接線板 panel
正式授權 official authorization	搖滾樂隊 rock band	玻璃器具 glassware	出入口 doorway
餐具台 buffet table	接線 extension cord	餐具墊 placemat	消防通道 fire exit

Important Vocabulary

facility	[fəˈsɪlətɪ]	n.	設施，專用設備（場所）
represent	[ˌreprɪˈzent]	v.	代表，表示
property	[ˈprɒpətɪ]	n.	地產，房產
interval	[ˈɪntəvl]	n.	間隔，間隙
vary	[ˈveərɪ]	v.	變化，改變
tentative	[ˈtentətɪv]	a.	試探性的，暫時的
entry	[ˈentrɪ]	n.	登記，條目
potential	[pəˈtenʃl]	a.	潛在的
definite	[ˈdefɪnət]	a.	明確的，確定的
commitment	[kəˈmɪtmənt]	n.	承諾
confirm	[kənˈfɜːm]	v.	確認
coordinator	[ˌkəʊˌɔːdɪˈneɪtə]	n.	協調人
procedure	[prəˈsiːdʒə]	n.	步驟
considerably	[kənˈsɪdərəbl]	adv.	相當大地，……得多
factor	[ˈfæktə]	n.	因素
portable	[ˈpɔːtəbl]	a.	便攜式的，手提式的
spoil	[spɔɪl]	v.	損壞，破壞
soundproof	[ˈsaundpruːf]	a.	隔音的
municipal	[mjuːˈnɪsɪpl]	a.	市政的
ordinance	[ˈɔːdɪnəns]	n.	法令，條例
block	[blɒk]	v.	堵塞，把……堵住
accessible	[əkˈsesəbl]	a.	可接近的，可到達的
undesirable	[ˌʌndɪˈzaɪərəbl]	a.	不受歡迎的，不想要的
significantly	[sɪɡˈnɪfɪkəntlɪ]	adv.	重大地，顯著地
counterpart	[ˈkauntəpɑːt]	n.	對等的物或人
backup	[ˈbækʌp]	a.	備用的，替代的
inclement	[ɪnˈklemənt]	a.	惡劣的，狂風暴雨的
plate	[pleɪt]	v.	裝盤
undecorated	[ʌnˈdekəreɪtɪd]	a.	未經裝飾的

themeless	[ˈθiːmlɪs]	a.	無主題的
elaborate	[ɪˈlæbəreɪt]	a.	精心設計的，詳盡的；複雜的
feature	[ˈfiːtʃə]	v.	以......為特色，以......為主
dictate	[dɪkˈteɪt]	v.	口述，發號施令
layout	[ˈleɪaut]	n.	布局，陳列設計
preference	[ˈprefrəns]	n.	偏好
entertainer	[ˌentəˈteɪnə]	n.	請客者，賓客者
illustrate	[ˈɪləstreɪt]	v.	表明，顯示；給......配圖
lectern	[ˈlektən]	n.	（講話者放講稿的）講台
inventory	[ˈɪnvəntrɪ]	n.	存貨
regarding	[rɪˈgɑːdɪŋ]	prep.	關於，在......方面
partial	[ˈpɑːʃl]	a.	部分的
maximum	[ˈmæksɪməm]	a. /n.	最大（的），最大限度（的）
efficiency	[ɪˈfɪʃnsɪ]	n.	效率
oversee	[ˌəuvəˈsiː]	v.	監督，監管
ensure	[ɪnˈʃɔː]	v.	保證，確保
practical	[ˈpræktɪkəl]	a.	可行的，切合實際的
last-minute	[ˈlɑːstmɪnɪt]	a.	最後的一分鐘的，緊急關頭的
position	[pəˈzɪʃən]	v.	放置，確定......的位置
trip	[trɪp]	v.	絆，絆倒
acoustical	[əˈkuːstɪkl]	a.	聽覺的，聲學的
wobble	[ˈwɒbl]	v.	（使）搖晃，（使）顫抖
sturdy	[ˈstɜːdɪ]	a.	結實的，牢固的
obstruct	[əbˈstrʌkt]	v.	堵塞，阻塞
update	[ˌʌpˈdeɪt]	n. /v.	更新，變更

Useful Expressions

play a role	起......作用	divide. . . into. . .	把......分成......
hold space for. . .	給......留出空間	a particular day	某一天
official authorization	正式授權	rule of thumb	經驗法則

under consideration	考慮中	municipal codes	市政法規
fire escape	消防通道	be scheduled to	安排
in case of	以防，萬一	take many forms	有許多種形式
come up with	想出，提出，找到	carry out	實施，完成
in charge	負責	pay close attention to	密切注意
make for	導致，促成	allow for	考慮到
be involved in	涉及，參與	prior to	在……之前
safety check	安檢	trip on	被……絆倒
have strong preferences	特別偏愛		

Language Focus

1.The daily function room diary lists all the function space a property has available for sale and divides it into various intervals throughout the day for the sale of different events.

功能廳使用日誌每天列出場館或飯店可用於銷售的場地，並且把它分成不同的時間段推銷給不同的活動。

「a property has available for sale」是省略了連接詞「that」的定語從句，在句中作「all the function space」的定語；省略的「that」在從句中相當於「has」後的賓語。

2.For example, if you must tear down a room that held a meeting with exhibits before you can set up the next activity, you will need much more time to prepare the room for the next function than if the room were set up for a theater-style meeting or a stand-up reception.

比如，如果你必須先撤除放有展品的會議室，而不是撤除劇院式布置的會議室或是站立式招待會的布置，那麼你準備下一個活動所花的時間要多得多。

本句結構較複雜，「if」條件句中又帶有一個「that」引導的定語從句以及「before」引導的時間狀語從句；主句中帶有「than」引導的比較狀語從句；此句翻譯時語序需要調整。

The various meeting room setups include theater, senate, V-shaped, U-shaped, T-shaped, hollow square, schoolroom, herringbone, board of directors, and banquet.

會場場地布置有劇院形、半圓形、V形、U形、T形、中空方形、教室形、鯡骨形、董事會會議形式以及宴會圓桌形。他們的具體要求是：

（1）Theater-Chairs are set up in straight rows （with aisles） parallel to the head table, stage, or speaker's podium.

（2）Senate-Same as a theater setup, except chairs are placed in semicircle rather than in rows.

（3）V-shaped-Same as a theater setup, except chairs are placed in a V.

（4）U-shaped （or horseshoe）-Tables are set up in the shape of a block-letter U；chairs are placed outside the closed end and on both sides of each leg.

（5）T-shaped-Tables are set up in the shape of a block-letter T and chairs are placed around the outside.

（6）Hollow Square-A series of tables forms a square with a hollow middle；chairs are placed around the outside.

（7）Schoolroom （or classroom）-The most common setup. Tables are lined up in rows （one behind the other） on each side of an aisle.There are usually three to four chairs to a table （depending on table size）, and all tables and chairs face the head table, stage, or speaker's podium.

(8) Herringbone-Similar to a schoolroom setup, with tables and chairs arranged in a V.

(9) Board-of-Directors-This is a popular arrangement for small meetings.It calls for a single column of double tables with seating all the way around.

(10) Banquet-A meal setup that generally uses round tables.

3.A simple coffee break may be served in an undecorated themeless room while an elaborate reception featuring foods from around the world may be served in a function room that has complex decorations to fit the theme.

簡單的咖啡時間可能會選擇一個未經布置的、無特定主題的房間進行，而一個豪華型、以世界各地美食為主的招待會則會在裝飾齊全的宴會廳舉行以切合它的主題。

「while」意思是「然而，而」。如：She is hard-working, while he is very lazy. 她能吃苦耐勞，而他卻很懶惰。

4.The need for staff members to pay close attention to the details listed on the function sheet and illustrated on the layout is just as important for small events as it is for large, elaborate events.

員工需要密切注意宴會任務單上列出的每個細節以及宴會廳布置設計的說明，在這一點上小型活動和大型會展一樣重要。本句的主語是「The need」；謂語動詞是「is」；「listed on the function sheet and illustrated on the layout」是過去分詞短語作後置定語，修飾「the details」。

5.Prior to opening the function room's doors and allowing guests to enter, the manager overseeing service for the event must ensure that the room setup is complete.

在功能廳（宴會廳）開門迎客之前，監管此活動的經理必須確保房間已布置完畢。

「overseeing service for the event」是現在分詞，作後置定語，修飾「the manager」。「ensure」意為「確保」。如：Please ensure all the dishes are sanitary before they are served. 要確保食物衛生，然後再上菜。

6.Whenever practical, the manager should meet with the client immediately before the event to inquire about the latest guest count or any last-minute changes to the plan for the event.

在活動舉辦之前，只要可行，經理要馬上與客戶見面瞭解最新的客人人數或者活動最新的變化。

「Whenever practical」相當於「Whenever it is practical」，在句中作讓步狀語。

Group Discussion

Discuss the following topic in group.Select one on the team to make a presentation before the class.

1.What documents play a primary role in booking and planning banquet and catering events? Why?

Guidelines for Discussion

__ function book

__ contracts or letters of agreement

__ function sheets

Reference：

（1）The function book, sometimes called the daily function room diary； （2）the contract or letter of agreement； （3）the function sheet, which is sometimes called a banquet event order (BEO) .

2.What does getting ready for service for banquets and catered events include?

Guidelines for Discussion

— setting up the function room

— scheduling staff members

— preparing, plating, and storing banquet food

3.What factors should be considered in making banquet room assignments?Guidelines for Discussion

— space available

— the seating of guests

— function planned in rooms adjacent to the room

— inclement weather ; indoor backup space

Writing Activity

Summarize the last section of the text by outlining major points. Write a few lines about the function room setup.

Translating Activity

Complete the following by translating the Chinese given in the brackets.

1.Most banquet departments have two main responsibilities : to sell food and beverage functions to business and individuals in the local community and to service _____ （現場會議和大型宴會） sold by the property's sales office.

2.The five elements of _____ （ 婚 宴 ） sold by the banquet department are menu and beverages, disposables, equipment, décor, and service.

3._____（對於傳統的自助早餐）, you might include two or three types of breakfast meats, three to six varieties of pastries, two styles of eggs, one potato dish, and several selections of cereals, juice, and fresh fruits.

4.While buffets are used quite often at dinner, _____ （跟其他用餐時間相比，晚餐時，就座、裝盤式用餐的需求量更大）.Even when buffets are used at night, most groups expect to receive greater service than at the daytime meals.

5.After the catering executive and client have agreed on the exact terms of the special function, _____ （他們應該用合約的形式確認這些條款）.

6._____ （ 會 議 策 劃 者 和 餐 飲 主 管 ） agree that the traditional locations-in the hall outside the meeting or in the rear of the meeting room-are in many instances the worst places for the refreshment break.

Section B Case Study

Read the following passage before solving the problems that ensue.

Dining Service Styles and Procedures

There are many variations in the procedures and techniques food service operations use to serve food to guests, but most can be categorized under the following main styles of table service：plate service, cart service, platter service, family-style service.

Plate service （also called American service） follows these basic procedures：

1.Servers take guests' orders in the dining area.

2.Kitchen staff produce food orders, portion them, and place them on plate.

3.Servers take the orders to the guest.

4.Bus persons assist servers and clear tables.

Cart service （also called French service） is an elaborate service style in which menu items are prepared beside guest tables by specially trained staff members.Menu items are cooked in front of the guests.The impact that cart service has on facility design, staffing, and guest satisfaction is profound.

Platter service （also called Russian service） requires servers to deliver platters of fully cooked food to the dining room, present the platters to guests for approval, and then serve the food.This type of service is featured many of the best international restaurants and hotel.

Family-style service （also called English service） requires food to be placed on large platters or in large bowls that are delivered to the guests' tables by severs.It is relatively easy to implement, for service staff members do not need to be highly skilled.In fact, with family-style service, they generally put more effort into clearing tables than into presenting and serving the food.

In addition to the four table-service styles, buffet service is being used by an increasing number of properties, often in combination with a table-service style.Buffets display food on counters or tables and guests help themselves to as many and as much of the items as they wish to eat.Food is usually placed on buffets in the following order：salads and other chilled meal accompaniments, hot vegetables, meats, poultry, fish, and other hot entrees.

Problem Solving

How do you solve the following problems? Outline your assertion.

1.Give as many food service styles as possible.

2.What are the disadvantages of cart service?

3.What are the advantages of family-style service?

Section C Format Writing

Acquaint yourself with the following. Finish the exercises that ensue.

Function Sheet 餐飲服務訂單

Great Wall Hotel

Name of the client：Jonas Lee	Master No. ：633 820 6639 Telex：／ Telephone：57100000 Reservation No. ：366
Function：Farewell Reception	Location：Lotus Function Room
Day：Friday	Date：June 23
Time：7：00 p. m.	Attendance：80 persons
Room to be Ready by：6：30 p. m.	Billing：Master Account
Price：RMB 200 plus 15% surcharge per person	

Menu

Mixed Salad

Seafood Minestrone Soup

Seasonal Fresh Fruit Plate

Grilled Steak

Deluxe Cold Dish Combination

Shark's Fin with Crab Meat

Steamed Fresh Pomfret

Pan-fried Diced Beef with Black Pepper

Sautéed Prawns with Celery

Sautéed Corn with Pine Nuts

Fried Seasonal Vegetable

Pastries

Wine

Champagne

Setup	
Cover tables with jade linen, white napkins. Floral bud vases on each table.	
Service requirements:	Plate Service
Other requirements:	A dance floor
Audiovisual requirements:	(n/a)

Questions about the Samples

Answer the following questions based on your understanding of the format writing.

1.Who makes the function reservation?

2.What type of function is it?

3.How many people are expected to attend the function?

4.How would the client like to make his payment?

5.How would he like the table to be set up?

6.What is the expected dining service style?

Notes of Format

Always bear in mind the following.

餐飲訂單應列出所有與之相關的細節。其中包括：（1）用餐類型（function）；（2）用餐地點（location）；（3）星期幾用餐（day）；（4）用餐日期（date）；（5）具體時間（time）；（6）參加人數（attendance）；（7）希望場地在何時準備好（room be ready by）；（8）如何結帳（billing）；（9）收費標準（price）；（10）菜單（menu）；（11）場地布置（setup）；（12）服務要求（service requirements）；（13）其他要求（other requirements）；（14）音像設備要求（audio/visual requirements）。其他細節，如：客戶姓名（name of the client）；客戶具體聯繫方式等（telephone），也可在此表中列出。

Do It Yourself

Work out a function sheet with the Chinese prompts.

路易斯先生要預訂長城飯店鑽石多功能廳歐陸式早餐。他們一行共 30 人。他要求在 6 月 26 日星期五早上 7：00 用餐，並且希望飯店能在早上 6：30 布置完畢。他們每人的用餐標準是 60 元人民幣，另加 15% 服務費，到時費用計入總帳。菜單中包括冰柳橙汁（chilled orange juice）、冰葡萄柚汁（chilled grapefruit juice）、新鮮草莓（fresh strawberries）、新鮮無子葡萄（seedless grapes）、新鮮切片鳳梨（sliced pineapple）、新鮮西瓜（melon）、新鮮奇異果（kiwi）、各式早餐麵包和小糕點（pastries）、黃油、果醬、咖啡、茶。所有咖啡用品放置在帶裙邊的餐桌上。

Meal Requirements	
Function:	**Location**:
Day:	**Date**:
Time:	**Attendance**:
Room to be ready by:	**Billing**:
Price:	
Menu	
_____	
_____	
_____	
Setup	
_____	
_____	
Service requirements:	
Other requirements:	
Audiovisual requirements:	

Reference Answers

Reference Answers to Translating Activity

1.in-house convention and group functions

2.a wedding reception

3.For a traditional breakfast buffet

4.there is a greater demand for sit-down plated dinners at the evening meal than at other meal periods

5.they should confirm the terms in a contract

6.Meeting planners and catering directors

Answers to Questions about the Samples

1.Jonas Lee.

2.It is a farewell reception.

3.80.

4.He would like to put it onto the master account.

5.He would like tables covered with jade linen and white napkins and floral bud vases on each table.

6.Plate service

Reference Answer to Do It Yourself

Meal Requirements	
Function：Continental Breakfast	**Location**：Diamond Function Room
Day：Friday	**Date**：June 26
Time：7:00 a. m.	**Attendance**：30
Room to be ready by：6:30 a. m.	**Billing**：Master Account
Price：RMB 60 plus 15% surcharge per person	

Menu
Assorted Chilled Juices（Orange, Grapefruit）
Fresh Fruit Platter（Strawberries, Seedless Grapes, Sliced Pineapple, Melon, Kiwi）
Assorted Breakfast Breads and Miniature Pastries
Butter, Jams
Coffee, Tea

Setup	
Display all coffee service materials on a skirted table station.	
Service requirements：	/
Other requirements：	（n/a）
Audiovisual requirements：	（n/a）

Chapter 10 Event Finance 會展財務

▌Section A Reading Assignment

Warming-up Activity

Go over the following terms with your teacher.

budget 預算	one-off 一次性事物	time-limited 受時間限制的	forecast 預測
surplus 盈餘‧順差	profit 利潤	expense 費用	mission 佣金
vision 前景	analysis 分析	transaction 交易	adjustment 調整
meeting planner 會議策劃者	registration 報名‧註冊	postage 郵資	insurance 保險

Pre-reading Questions

Answer the following questions without referring to the text.

1.How do you prepare a budget for an event?

2.The first step to successful budgeting for an event is developing an expense event, isn't it? Why?

Text

Successful Budgeting

Budget control represents the heart of all fiscal management in that it provides a financial check point on a month-by-month, a week-by-week, and even a day-by-day basis.A budget is a forecast or plan that helps to regulate the operation of an event （or any business） over a given period of time.In the case of a business, such as a hotel, the budget might be an annual one.In the case of an event, because events are one-off and time-limited, the budget will normally be for the time period of that event.A budget is also a management tool by which responsibility for various activities （e.g.sales or the control of costs） can be seen in much the same way as the general event plan. The budget, as it is both a forecast of what is intended to happen and a record of what is happening （or, after the event, of what had happened）, acts as a means of comparing the forecast with the reality and setting targets which the organizers can strive to achieve. Establishing budgetary philosophies.

The budget, because it is helping the planning process, should also seek to ensure that resources that the organizer has are most economically used, thus helping to keep costs in control or helping to ensure that a profit or surplus is made.For example, there is no point hiring twenty ushers all day if they are only going to be needed for the first ten minutes.Costs like this might well show up in the forecast, as being out of line with the rest of the budget.

The first step to successful budgeting is to determine the financial philosophy for a meeting.Should it simply break even.or should it produce a profit? It is no good setting a budget, in which a large profit is forecast, if the event is supposed to be for public entertainment and only intended to generate a small surplus or break even.In the case of these events, making a large profit might result in having to charge too high a ticket price.So what is the objective financially? Is the event intended to make money or simply cover its costs? If it is to cover costs only, what is the headline amount which can be spent, specified by either the clients or the organizing committee?

In its most basic form, a budget is your cash plan.It is how you are going to develop your mission and financially turn vision statements and your goals and objectives into reality.Don't let the budget become a burden.A budget should never be etched in stone ; it is the final bottom line that counts.That being said, never attempt to manipulate your budget to cover expense overages or revenue shortfalls.A budget is fluid, but the adjustments should be made after careful analysis of the entire project.

To help in this analysis and in developing specific budget points, there are some basic ideas that must be kept in mind initially.First and foremost, everything has a price attached.Although this premise may sound elementary, it is often the small financial details that are overlooked that will have a huge impact on your marketing activities. Forgetting the price of postage to mail your 5, 000 invitations can quickly erode any profit margin.Price doesn't necessarily have to be a monetary outlay ; it could be an in-kind contribution or a barter/ trade-off.Regardless of the type of transaction, the price has a value associated with it that impacts your budget on both the revenue and the expense sides.

The other two basic ideas to keep in mind while developing a budget are equally important to one another : price and cost.As you develop your budget, remember that price is the value placed on goods or service, while cost is what you sacrifice in the future by paying the price for goods or services today.An example would be an organization that pays $5,000.00 (the price) for a one-time print advertisement for an event.This organization may then lack funds to pay for radio spots in the future.

Finally, when developing a budget plan, there are three areas that are frequently overlooked：contingency reserve plans, indirect costs （overhead）, and profit.Options differ on the amount of the overall budget needed to be set aside for a contingency plan, although between 10 and 20 percent is customary.You may ask, "If I have done my research and thought through the marketing strategy, why do I need a contingency plan?" The answer is simple.Unless you have a psychic on staff, you can't possibly know what will happen in the 10 or 18 months leading up to the event.

Developing the expense budget

As a budgeting philosophy usually dictates a profit, the process begins with developing the expense budget.Once the expenses have been determined, the income needed to meet costs can be identified and the fees set accordingly.

Mostly meeting planners find that a functional budget facilitates a more accurate comparison of expenses and income for each area of the budget.

Categories that could be included in a functional expense budget for a typical medical meeting, for example, are given in the following table：Sample functional expense budget

Program development and production Program committee expense

Abstract printing, distribution, selection

Speaker honoraria, travel, lodging

Program production

Board and committees

Travel, lodging

Meeting expenses

Promotion

Exhibits

Promotion, prospectus

Decorator, drayage

Poster boards

Security

Exhibit space rental

Registration

Badges, forms

Personnel

Computer analysis

Audio-visual

Social functions

Tickets

Opening reception

Banquet

Awards luncheon

Coffee breaks

Operations and overhead

Staffing and overhead

Telephone

Duplication

General postage

Insurance

Staff travel, lodging

Meeting room rental, setups

Extra microphones Contingency

TOTAL

Developing the income budget

Again, the philosophy must be considered.Is a considerable profit expected from the exhibit space rental, or will most of the revenue come from registration fees? Should the social functions break even or are they designed to produce income? Will the organization depend on outside funding or grant for a portion of the revenue?

The following table gives an example of the meeting income budget, listing each of the revenue areas separately.Major revenue items include registration fees, exhibit space rental, social function fees, and investment income.

Sample functional income budget

Income

Registration fees

Member

Non-member

One-day

Exhibit functions

Opening reception

Banquet

Awards luncheon

Investment income

TOTAL

Setting up a spreadsheet control

After the final budget has been approved, it can be used on a month-to-month basis for control of actual income and expense.To set up this mechanism, divide the total budget into monthly increments that indicate the best estimate of when the income for a specific budgeted item will be received and when the expenditure must be paid.This "spreadsheet calculation" provides two important kinds of information : an indication of expected revenues and expenses at any time during the meeting planning process, and an indication of monthly positive or negative cash flow.

Check-in

Do you have any questions about the text? If any, ask your teacher.

More Terms

break even 得失相當，不賠不賺	outlay 費用	overhead 企業一般管理費用	barter 實物交易
honoraria 謝禮	social function 社交活動	luncheon 午宴，正式的午餐	coffee break 休息時間

Important Vocabulary

regulate	[ˈreɡjuːleɪt]	v.	控制，調節
headline	[ˈhedlaɪn]	n.	大字標題
manipulate	[məˈnɪpjuleɪt]	v.	操作，利用

overage	[ˈəuvərɪdʒ]	n.	過剩，過多
shortfall	[ˈʃɔːtfɔːl]	n.	不足
fluid	[ˈfluːɪd]	a.	不固定的，可改變的
premise	[ˈpremɪs]	n.	前提
render	[ˈrendə]	v.	致使
contingency	[kənˈtɪndʒənsɪ]	n.	意外事件
psychic	[ˈsaɪkɪk]	n.	通靈的人
dictate	[dɪkˈteɪt]	v.	命令，支配
facilitate	[fəˈsɪlɪteɪt]	v.	推動，幫助
prospectus	[prəˈspektəs]	n.	內容說明書
drayage	[ˈdreɪdʒ]	n.	運輸
duplication	[ˌdjuːplɪˈkeɪʃən]	n.	副本，複製
show up	[ˈʃəu ʌp]	v.	揭露，露出，露面
out of line	[ˈaut əv ˌlaɪn]		不成直線，不協調
set aside	[ˌset əˈsaid]	v.	留出

Language Focus

1.The budget, as it is both a forecast of what is intended to happen and a record of what is happening（or, after the event, of what had happened）, acts as a means of comparing the forecast with the reality and setting targets which the organizers can strive to achieve.

由於預算既是對未來情況的預測，也是對當前情況的記錄（或者，是在活動之後，對已發生情況的記錄），因此，它就成為一種工具，可以將預測與實際情況進行比較，以及確定活動組織者爭取實現的目標。

2.The budget, because it is helping the planning process, should also seek to ensure that resources that the organizer has are most economically used, thus helping to keep costs in control or helping to ensure a profit or surplus is made.

制訂預算有助於活動策劃，因此，它應該盡力確保組織者擁有的資源得到最經濟的利用，從而幫助控制成本，或是獲取利潤。

3.As you develop your budget, remember that price is the value placed on goods or services, while cost is what you sacrifice in the future by paying the price for goods or services today.

在制訂預算時，應該牢記，價格體現了產品或服務的價值，而成本則是由於現在購買產品或服務給未來帶來的損失。

Group Discussion

Discuss the following topic in group.Select one on the team to make a presentation before the class.

What are the basic factors to take into consideration while developing a budget for an event ?

Guidelines for Discussion

▬ financial philosophy

▬ objectives of events

▬ fluid budget

■ price and cost

■ expense and revenue

■ contingency reserve plan, overhead, profit

Writing Activity

Summarize the text by outlining major points.Write a few lines about successful budgeting using the following expressions.

· A budget is a forecast or plan that helps to regulate the operation of an event （or any business） over a given period of time.

· The first step to successful budgeting is to determine the financial philosophy for a meeting.

· To help in this analysis and in developing specific budget points, there are some basic ideas that must be kept in mind initially.

· When developing a budget plan, there are three areas that are frequently overlooked : contingency reserve plans, indirect costs （overhead）, and profit.

▌Section B Case Study

Read the following passage before solving the problems that ensue.

The Budget for the ASEM 2000 Conference

ASEM is a major professional organization dedicated to the science and art of engineering management.The goal of ASEM 2000 conference was to bring together the nation's leading engineering managers, with a special emphasis on the evaluation of technical leadership in the Washington metropolitan area's vibrant information systems technology sector.This annual conference in Washington, D.C.is highly respected among technical professionals in the United States.

ASEM 2000 was held from October 4 to October 7 in Washington's Marriott Hotel.The main stakeholders included ASEM, the conference management service at one large metropolitan university, engineering managers from high-tech organizations, and other organizations interested in the electronic communication's development.

The annual budget for the conference is close to $100,000 and the organization committee traditionally raised these funds by soliciting contributions from sponsors and by charging participants an attendance fee.The conference organizers had several contracts in place with major vendors : a conference facility, caterers, and a transportation company.These vendor contracts, signed five years ago and not revised since, were fixed-fee contracts.

Approximately ten months before holding the event, the conference committee faced a serious problem.There was a serious deficit of funds to complete the conference organization.Due to a sales decline, one of the conference's sponsors was not able to contribute a pledge this year, and others made clear that they would not be able to cover the gap.During a special meeting held by the organizers, two possible solutions were identified :

1.Generate more revenues by attracting additional sponsorship funds ;

2.Reduce the costs of the event by better expense management.

One of the possible solutions is to renegotiate the vendors' contracts.However, the organizers are not sure how to start the negotiations.It is very unlikely that the vendors will agree simply to cut their prices without strong reasoning from the conference organizers' side.

Problem Solving

How do you solve the following problems? Outline your assertion.

1.Do you agree with the possible solutions put forward in the case?

2.what are your recommendations to the organization committee on how to turn around the finances of the conference?

Section C Format Writing

Acquaint yourself with the following.Finish the exercises that ensue.

Financial Statements—Balance Sheet 財務報表——收支平衡表

Sample 1 Reporting Format

Sofia Wise Service Company

Balance Sheet

December 31 , 20 × 5

Assets

Cash	$ 9 000
Accounts Receivable(. net)	8 600
Accrued Revenue	1 000

Prepaid Insurance		450
Office Supplies		3 060
Office Equipment		$ 2 000
less Accumulated Depreciation	360	1 640
Total Assets		$ 23 750

Liabilities

Accounts Payable	$ 2 240
Precollected Revenue	410
Accrued Salaries Payable	100
Total liabilities	$ 2 750

Owner' s Equity

S. Wise , Capital	21 000
Total liabilities and Owner's Equity	$ 23 750

Sample 2 T-account Format

Sofia Wise Service Company

Balance Sheet

December 31 , 20 × 5

Assets			**Liabilities**	
Cash		$ 9 000	Accounts Payable	$ 2 240
Accounts Receivable (net)		8 600	Precollected Revenue	410
Accrued Revenue		1 000	Accrued Salaries Payable	100
Prepaid Insurance		450		
Office Supplies		3 060	Total Liabilities	$ 2 750
Office Equipment		$ 2 000	**Owner' s Equity**	
Less Accumulated Depredation	360	1 640	S. Wise , Capital	21 000
Total Assets		$ 23 750	Total Liabilities and Owner's Equity	
				$ 23 750

Questions about the Samples

Decide whether the following statements are True or False.

1.Balance Sheet is a statement of reporting the financial position of a business at a specific point of time.

2.The body of Balance Sheet contains two major sections：assets and liabilities.

3.Balance Sheet can be prepared in a T-account format or a reporting format.

4.Equality of total assets with total liabilities and owner's equity must always be maintained in a balance sheet.

5.The business financial position will be reflected in a balance sheet.

Notes of Format

Always bear in mind the following.

財務報表（Financial Statements）可以將財務資訊傳達給使用者，基本的財務報表包括資產負債表（Balance Sheet），收益表（Income Statement）和現金流量表（Statement of Cash Flows）。

資產負債表是用於報告企業某一時期的財務狀況的報表。表體由資產（assets）、負債（liabilities）和業主權益（owner's equity）三大部分組成，與會計恆等式相同。資產負債表可按兩種格式編制：一種為帳戶式（T-account format），另一種為報告式（reporting format）。

Do It Yourself

Put the following Profit & Loss Statement into English.

總經理月報——損益表			
酒店名稱：Claude Hotell		月份：May	
月份：　　　May			
實際　%	預算　%	去年　%	貨幣：人民幣
A	B	C	客房間數:

						310
51.0%		67.0%		63.0%		總出租率%
395.81		416.00		392.39		酒店日均房價
201.86		278.72		247.21		可供出租房收入（REVPAR）
						總結
2,961	100	3,664	100	3,358	100	主營業務收入
1,560	53	1,137	31	1,432	43	總人工成本
1,191	40	1,447	39	1,343	40	其他相關直接費用（包含營業成本、主營業務稅金及附加和其他相關費用）
210	7	1,080	29	583	17	經營利潤（GOP）
						房務部
1,959	66	2,678	73	2,418	72	房務部收入
238	12	174	6	229	9	人工成本
230	12	333	12	273	11	其他直接費用（其他費用＋主營業務稅金及附加）
1,491	76	2,171	81	1,916	79	房務部利潤
						餐飲部
493	87	482	88	446	88	食品收入
54	10	52	9	36	7	飲料收入
18	3	16	3	22	4	其他收入
0	0	0	0	0	0	服務費
565	19	550	15	504	15	餐飲收入合計
221	45	284	59	214	48	食品成本
22	40	24	46	20	56	飲料成本
10	54	14	88	7	32	其他成本
252	45	322	58	241	48	餐飲成本合計
268	47	222	40	334	66	人工成本
65	12	68	12	84	17	其他直接費用（其他費用＋主營業務稅金及附加）
(20)	(4)	(62)	(11)	(155)	(31)	餐飲部利潤

						其他小部門
124	4	164	4	191	6	其他小部門收入合計
61	49	108	66	96	50	其他小部門成本合計
15	12	27	16	28	15	人工成本
2	2	3	2	0	0	其他直接費用（其他費用＋主營業務稅金及附加）
46	37	26	16	67	35	其他小部門利潤
						其他收入、租金
313	11	272	7	245	7	其他收入
0	0	0	0	0	0	其他成本
0	0	0	0	0	0	人工成本
17	5	16	6	16	7	其他直接費用（其他費用＋主營業務稅金及附加）
296	95	256	94	229	93	部門利潤
1,813	61	2,391	65	2,057	61	部門毛利
						不分配費用
857	28.9	534	14.6	601	17.9	行政管理部門 - 人工成本
120	4.1	86	2.3	132	3.9	行政管理部門 - 其他費用
49	1.7	85	2.3	117	3.5	市場營銷部 - 人工成本
15	0.5	20	0.5	7	0.2	市場營銷部 - 其他費用
133	4.5	95	2.6	123	3.7	工程部 - 人工成本
14	0.5	18	0.5	23	0.7	工程部 - 其他費用
356	12.0	400	10.9	403	12.0	能源費用
59	2.0	73	2.0	68	2.0	基本管理費
1,603	54	1,311	36	1,474	44	不分配費用合計
210	7	1,080	29	583	17	經營利潤
8	0	43	1	12	0	效益管理費
50	2	0	0	50	1	房產稅
0	0	0	0	0	0	保險
265	9	300	8	309	9	折舊／攤銷
9	0	41	1	13	0	其他增加／扣除項目

0	0	0	0	0	0	租賃
332	11	384	10	384	11	GOP 後相關費用小計
(122)	(4)	696	19	199	6	息前利潤總額
107	4	150	4	92	3	淨利息（利息收入-利息支出）
(229)	(8)	546	15	107	3	利潤總額
(229)	(8)	546	15	107	3	稅前利潤（利潤總額）
(154)	(5)	0	0	72	2	淨利潤
143	5	996	27	508	15	稅前息前折舊前攤銷前利潤
67	2	116	3	80	2	管理費合計

Reference Answers

Answers to Questions about the Samples

1.T 2.F 3.T 4.T 5.T

Reference Answer to Do It Yourself

Hotel：Claude Hotel　　　　Month：May

Actual	%	Budget	%	L Year	%	Currency RMB - '000	
A		B		C		# Rooms：	
						310	
51.0%		67.0%		63.0%		Rooms Occupancy	%
395.81		416.00		392.39		Average Daily Rate	
201.86		278.72		247.21		REVPAR	
						Summary	
2,961	100	3,664	100	3,358	100	Total Revenue	

1,560	53	1,137	31	1,432	43	Total Payroll
1,191	40	1,447	39	1,343	40	Total Expenses (above GOP)
210	**7**	**1,080**	**29**	**583**	**17**	**Gross Operating Profit**
						ROOMS DEPARTMENT
1,959	66	2,678	73	2,418	72	Sales
238	12	174	6	229	9	Payroll & Related Expenses
230	12	333	12	273	11	Other Direct Expenses
1,491	**76**	**2,171**	**81**	**1,916**	**79**	**DEPARTMENTAL PROFIT**
						FOOD & BEVERAGE DEPARTMENT
493	87	482	88	446	88	Food Sales
54	10	52	9	36	7	Beverage Sales
18	3	16	3	22	4	Other F&B Revenue
0	0	0	0	0	0	Service Charge
565	**19**	**550**	**15**	**504**	**15**	**Total F&B Sales**
221	45	284	59	214	48	Food cost
22	40	24	46	20	56	Beverage cost
10	54	14	88	7	32	Other F&B cost
252	**45**	**322**	**58**	**241**	**48**	**Total F&B cost**
268	47	222	40	334	66	Payroll & Related Expenses
65	12	68	12	84	17	Other Direct Expenses
(20)	**(4)**	**(62)**	**(11)**	**(155)**	**(31)**	**DEPARTMENTAL PROFIT**
						MINOR OPERATING DEPTS
124	4	164	4	191	6	Sales
61	49	108	66	96	50	Cost of Sales
15	12	27	16	28	15	Payroll & Related Expenses
2	2	3	2	0	0	Other Direct Expenses
46	**37**	**26**	**16**	**67**	**35**	**DEPARTMENTAL PROFIT**
						OTHER INCOME / RENTALS
313	11	272	7	245	7	Sales
0	0	0	0	0	0	Cost of Sales
0	0	0	0	0	0	Payroll & Related Expenses
17	5	16	6	16	7	Other Direct Expenses

	95		94		93	
296	95	256	94	229	93	DEPARTMENTAL PROFIT
1,813	61	2,391	65	2,057	61	GROSS DEPARTMENTAL PROFIT
						UNDISTRIBUTED EXPENSES & PAYROLL
857	28.9	534	14.6	601	17.9	A&G-Payroll & related
120	4.1	86	2.3	132	3.9	A&G-Expenses
49	1.7	85	2.3	117	3.5	S&M-Payroll & related
15	0.5	20	0.5	7	0.2	S&M-Expenses
133	4.5	95	2.6	123	3.7	R&M-Payroll & related
14	0.5	18	0.5	23	0.7	R&M-Expenses
356	12.0	400	10.9	03	12.0	Energy-Expenses
59	2.0	73	2.0	68	2.0	Management Fee-Basic
1,603	54.1	1,311	35.8	1,474	43.9	TOTAL UNDISTRIBUTED EXPENSES
210	7	1,080	29	583	17	GROSS OPERATING PROFIT
8	0	43	1	12	0	Management Fee -Incentive
50	2	0	0	50	1	Property Taxes
0	0	0	0	0	0	Insurance
265	9	300	8	309	9	Depreciation/Amortisation
9	0	41	1	13	0	Other（Additions）/Deductions
0	0	0	0	0	0	Rent
332	11	384	10	384	11	TOTAL "BELOW GOP" COSTS
(122)	(4)	696	19	199	6	NET PROFIT/(LOSS) B I & T
107	4	150	4	92	3	Net Interest
(229)	(8)	546	15	107	3	NET OPERATING PROFIT
(229)	(8)	546	15	107	3	NET PROFIT /(LOSS) Before Tax
(154)	(5)	0	0	72	2	NET PROFIT /(LOSS) After Tax
143	5	996	27	508	15	E B I T D A
67	2	116	3	80	2	Total Management Fee

Chapter 11 Overseas Exhibition 出展管理

▊Section A Reading Assignment

Warming-up Activity

Go over the following terms with your teacher.

insurance	保險	expand	擴展	corporate	公司的	outbound	出境的
shipment	運輸	FOB	離岸價	CIF	到岸價	measurement	尺寸
gross weight	毛重量	net weight	淨重量	carrier	運貨人	trade show	貿易展覽
freight	貨物	consign	委托	booth	貨攤	claim	索賠
negligence	疏忽	sublease	轉租	licensed	獲准經營的‧有資質的		

Pre-reading Questions

Answer the following questions without referring to the text.

1. How does the exhibitor arrange for the shipment of the exhibits?

2. What are the benefits the organizer can get from the insured exhibits?

3. What factors should the exhibitor consider in reserving a stand?

Text

Shipment, Insurance and Stand

Travel agents have expanded their traditional role of selling package tours, transportation and guest room services to offer meeting planning services. This transition came naturally, as travel agents were able to keep abreast of changing airline price structures and routes, and many corporate meeting planners are now turning to travel agents to arrange everything from transportation to meeting space.Since not all travel agents are experienced in meeting planning, professional convention and exhibition organizations will inevitably replace travel agencies and play an important role in the overseas convention and exhibition service.

Convention and exhibition agencies have a wide variety of services in the outbound convention and exhibition field, ranging from outbound exhibition inquiry, passport application, outbound exhibition application to exhibit shipment and insurance.Outbound exhibition inquiry covers stand reservation and decoration, exhibit's FOB price and CIF price, exhibit shipment, etc.Of all these services, outbound exhibit shipment and insurance are the most complicated.

Secure outbound exhibit shipment weighs on the shipping agent. As required, convention and exhibition agent must help the exhibitor with the exhibit-related material, covering show site, consignee, exhibition date, exhibition management, measurement, gross weight, net weight and so on.

Outbound exhibition agent should also help his/her clients （exhibitors） select their own exhibit transportation carrier wisely. This would include checking the background of their carrier to make sure they are adequately qualified, equipped, licensed, and prepared to handle trade show freight.The definitive mechanism for an exhibitor, or their designated agent, to indicate their choice of exhibit transportation carrier is to list the carrier and sign the official contractor's （general service contractor） shipping instructions form.Once the exhibit transportation carrier has been selected, the exhibitor, or his agent, has the responsibility to inform the chosen carrier of the rules and regulations of the show in question.

Convention and exhibition center agents musts also be good at communicating and negotiating so that he/she can help his/her client (exhibitor) set up the liability insurance agreements that they must carry.The vast majority of convention and exhibition organizations stipulate that the meeting or exhibition group must agree to carry adequate liability insurance protecting the convention and exhibition center against claims arising from the group's activities conducted in the convention and exhibition center during the convention or exhibition.In doing business with associations and trade shows, a convention and exhibition organization incurs special liability in its relationship with trade show exhibitors.Exhibitors may sublease the floor space, so the convention and exhibition center should require the exhibitor to sign a liability agreement confirming that the convention and exhibition center is not responsible for damages or theft of material or equipment.Convention and exhibition centers also request that a contract be submitted to ensure that the meeting group and the convention and exhibition center should be responsible for its own negligence and that each party agree to hold the other party harmless if the actions of one party cause the other party to suffer a loss.

If an exhibitor desires to make a change in its outbound shipment, the agent must help do so in writing on a new official contractor's shipping instructions form, or by initiating the changes on the original form.These changes can be delivered to the service desk in person, or by fax or email if they are available.When it comes to official carrier status, show management must communicate internally to show management staff, as well as all appropriate parties within their service network, who the official carriers are. Then they must further specify the manner in which they want these authorized parties to be represented in the service kit, on the show floor, and at the service desk.Once show management has clarified these relationships it is incumbent upon all trade show service organizations, official and non-official, to collaborate and abide by show management decisions.

Having decided on the trade show or exhibition to participate in, the exhibitor and its agent should reserve a stand or a space at the exhibition center to show its exhibits.Organizers usually hire a venue and subdivide it into stands—separate portions of space.Depending on their size and location, the stands vary in cost.A stand that is large and located directly opposite the entrance would be very expensive. If the stand is small and is in a block away from the main entrance, it would be considerably less expensive.As well as simply selling stand space, organizers may sell modular stand packages, which will include floor space plus, typically, walls and ceilings, lighting, and so on.Sometimes the modular stand is just a shell, but at other times it can be a fully developed stand.If it is just a shell, then the organizers will provide an opportunity, at extra cost, for exhibitors to purchase their needs from the appointed contractor.The exhibitor has to consider the cost involved, covering such factors as labor charges, electricians' and carpenters' services, electrical, power, steam, gas, water and waste lines.

Check-in

Do you have any questions about the text? If any, ask your teacher.

Important Vocabulary

transition	[trænˈzɪʃən]	n.	轉變
corporate	[ˈkɔːpərət]	n.	公司
outbound	[ˈautbaund]	a.	外向的，出境的
inquiry	[ɪnˈkwaɪərɪ]	n.	詢問
shipment	[ˈʃɪpmənt]	n.	運輸
stand	[stænd]	n.	展位
FOB	[ˌef əu ˈbiː]	n.	free on Board離岸價
CIF	[ˌsiː aɪ ˈef]	n.	cost, Insurance and freight 到岸價
measurement	[ˈmeʒəmənt]	n.	規格，尺寸
consign	[kənˈsaɪn]	v.	委託，交付
mechanism	[ˈmekənɪzəm]	n.	技巧，方法
carrier	[ˈkærɪə]	n.	承運商

license	[ˈlaɪsns]	n.	證照
freight	[freɪt]	n.	貨物
designated	[ˈdezɪgneɪtɪd]	a.	指定的
notifications	[ˌnotəfəˈkeʃən]	n.	通知，告示
liability	[ˌlaɪəˈbɪlɪtɪ]	n.	責任
stipulate	[ˈstɪpjuleɪt]	v.	規定
claim	[kleɪm]	n.	索賠
incur	[ɪnˈkɚ]	v.	遭受，獲得
sublease	[ˌsʌbˈliːs]	v.	分租
confirm	[kənˈfɚːm]	v.	確認
damage	[ˈdæmɪdʒ]	n.	損壞
submit	[səbˈmɪt]	v.	提交
negligence	[ˈneglɪdʒəns]	n.	疏忽
parties	[ˈpɑːtɪz]	n.	（合同）各方
authorized	[ˈɔːθəraɪz]	a.	被授權的，有權的
incumbent	[ɪnˈkʌmbənt]	a.	必須履行的，有責任的
collaborate	[kəˈlæbəreɪt]	v.	合作
modular	[ˈmɒdjulə]	a.	組合式的，模塊化的
shell	[ʃel]	n.	空殼，（房屋的）骨架

Useful Expressions

keep abreast of	隨時了解
turn to	求助於
range from. . . to	從……到……的範圍
weigh on	依靠，是負擔
gross weight	毛重量
service kit	全套服務
net weight	淨重
in question	正在討論的
fulfill one's responsibility	履行職責
inform sb. of sth.	通知（某人）某事

arise from	由……引起
hand off	轉運，轉交
official contractor	官方承辦者，指定承辦人
abide by	遵守
at extra cost	額外成本

Language Focus

1.This transition came naturally, as travel agents were able to keep abreast of changing airline price structures and routes.

旅行代理人的業務轉變是自然而然形成的，因為旅行代理人瞭解航空票價和航線的即時變化。

2.Secure outbound exhibit shipment weighs on the shipping agent.

可靠的出境參展的展品運輸主要由運輸代理商承擔。

3.As required, convention and exhibition agent must help the exhibitor with the exhibit-related material, covering show site...

按照要求，展會代理人要協助參展商提供展品相關資料，包括參展地……

4.Once the exhibit transportation carrier has been selected, show management should insure that the exhibitor has the right to access their carrier.

一旦確定了展品承運商，展會管理者要保證參展商與承運商取得聯繫。

5.In doing business with associations and trade shows, a convention and exhibition organization incurs special liability in its relationship with trade show exhibitors.

在展銷會上，展會承辦方（組織者）對參展商負有特別責任。

6.The final rewards will more than compensate for any loss you may incur.

最後的結果將不只是彌補你所遭受的損失。

7.Initiate the changes on the original form.

在原始表單上註明變更事項。

8.They must further specify the manner in which they want these authorized parties to be represented in the service kit.

他們必須進一步明確被授權方在服務中以何種方式代表授權方。

9.It is incumbent on me to attend.

我有責任參加。

Group Discussion

Discuss the following topic in group.Select one on the team to make a presentation before the class.

How do you manage exhibits for an upcoming overseas exhibition?

Guidelines for Discussion

▬ How to choose exhibits?

▬ How to decide on the amount of exhibits for exhibition?

▬ What activities to take to ship the exhibits to the venue?

▬ What to insure?

▬ What formalities to go through?

▬ What problems to be warned of?

Writing Activity

Summarize the text by outlining major points.Write a few lines about overseas exhibition management using the following expressions.

Important Vocabulary

insurance	保險	indemnity	賠償
travel agents	旅行代理人	meeting planners	會議策劃者
trade show freight	展會貨物	loading dock	裝卸碼頭
special liability	特別責任	damages or theft	損壞與偷竊
negligence	疏忽大意		

Useful Expressions

a wide variety of services
outbound exhibition inquiry
passport application
outbound exhibition application
exhibit shipment
insurance
the exhibit-related material
exhibit transportation carrier

the liability insurance agreements
make a change in its outbound shipment
stand reservation

Language Focus

· It is incumbent upon all trade show service organizations, official, and non-official, to collaborate and abide by show management decisions.

· When it comes to official carrier status, show management must communicate internally to show management staff, and to all appropriate parties within their service network who the official carriers are.

· In doing business with associations and trade shows, a convention and exhibition organization incurs special liability in its relationship with trade show exhibitors.

· Fulfill the required notifications and show site rules and regulations.

· Protect the convention and exhibition center against claims arising from the group's activities.

Section B Case Study

Read the following passage before solving the problems that ensue.

Show Rules and Regulations Concerning the Exhibitors

FLOOR PLAN

Floor plans shall be submitted with a Special Event Permit Application available from your Event Manager.Six copies of the exhibit floor plans for your event should be submitted to the Corporation at least six （6） months prior to your official move-in date.It is recommended that the general service contractor generate the floor plans and send them to us directly.Please note these basic rules：

· Aisles between display areas are ten （10） feet.

· Nothing may intrude into the aisle space.

· One hundred （100） linear feet of continuous display space are allowable before a cross aisle must be present.

· Aisles must be configured to provide clear access to exit ways.

· There must be twenty (20) feet of clearance in front of all exits.

· The travel distance within any booth or exhibit enclosure to an exit access may not be greater than fifty (50) feet.

The following items must be designated on your floor plans :

· Booth spaces and what is in the booths (i.e., exhibit booths) .

· Bulk spaces.

· Enclosed areas in a booth or bulk space (Enclosed areas, i.e., closets, offices, etc., need to be equipped with an approved battery-operated smoke detector and a stipulated fire extinguisher) .

· Proposed crate storage areas.

· Multi-level booths.All multi-level booth must be designated on your floor plan.Please note the following rules that apply to multi-level booths :

· A certified structural drawing of a multi-level booth must be submitted to our Fire Marshal at least ninety (90) days in advance of the first move-in day to allow sufficient time for any needed corrections.

· One 2A10BC-type fire extinguishers must be on each level of the display, easily available and unobstructed from view.

· All areas under multi-level booths must be equipped with an approved battery operated smoke detector attached to the ceiling or understructure.

· No ceilings are allowed on the top most level.

· If any deck is designed to hold over 10 people, a second staircase is required for emergency evacuations.

· All stairways must be at least three （3）feet in width and must be equipped with a handrail on at least one side.

CARPET & WALL COVERINGS

Show management is responsible for all damage to carpets and wall coverings during an event.Understanding that temporary stains will occasionally occur, show management will be responsible for cleaning costs associated with the removal.If carpet/wall coverings cannot be sufficiently cleaned or if the damage is severe （cuts, rips or tears）, show management will be responsible for the cost of the carpet or wall covering replacement.

As a general policy, exhibitors are responsible for providing or arranging for their own carpeting in the booth area.Tabletop displays may be allowed in a carpeted area without additional treatments. However, any carpeted area used for commercial exhibits or substantial displays must have additional protective carpet laid over the Center's carpet to protect it from inordinate wear and tear or damage.

For safety reasons, motorized carts are not allowed in any public areas including the lobby.Wheel coverings are required on the tires when traveling in carpeted areas.To reduce the risk of accidents, please exercise due caution when operating motorized carts in approved areas.

Vehicles on display must follow the following rules：

· No more than 1/4 tank of gas.

· A locking gas cap or tape over the gas cap.

· Batteries shall be disconnected in an approved manner.

· A drip pan under the vehicle's drive train （motor to differential）.

· Keys delivered to event security.

· Vehicles shall not be moved during show hours.

· Refueling is prohibited in the facility.

· Floor plans must indicate where vehicles are to be located.

Food and beverage product exhibitors who are germane to events and are lawful manufacturers or distributors of food and/or beverage products may distribute samples.Samples must be distributed from those specific exhibitor booth locations only.Samples may not exceed two （2） ounces by weight of a solid product, and four （4） ounces by volume of a non-alcoholic beverage product.All alcoholic beverage sampling must be serviced by the Convention Center's Food and Beverage Department.Approval for distribution of samples must be obtained prior to an event.

Check-in

Do you have any questions about the case study? If any, ask your teacher.

Important Vacabulary

| permit | [pə'mɪt] | n. | 許可、許可證 |

move-in	[ˈmuːv ˈɪn]	n.	進場
aisle	[aɪl]	n.	通道
linear	[ˈlɪnɪə]	a.	長度的，線狀的
configure	[kənˈfɪgə]	v.	描畫，構圖
clearance	[ˈklɪərəns]	n.	空隙，出入港許可證，清倉大拍賣
booth	[buːð]	n.	（隔開的）小房間，展攤
enclosure	[ɪnˈkləuʒə]	n.	圍場，活動場地，觀眾席
proposed	[prəˈpəuzd]	a.	計劃的，建議的
crate	[kreɪt]	n.	貨物箱
certified	[ˈsəːtɪfaɪd]	a.	取得證照的
unobstructed	[ʌnəbˈstrʌktɪd]	a.	開闊，無障礙的
approved	[əˈpruːvd]	a.	獲得認證的，獲得許可的
understructure	[ˈʌndəstrʌktʃə]	n.	下層結構，基礎
rip	[rɪp]	v.	綻開，撕破
replacement	[rɪˈpleɪsmənt]	n.	替換，替代物
substantial	[səbˈstænʃl]	a.	相當多的
motorized	[ˈməutəraɪzd]	a.	裝上發動機的
germane	[dʒəˈmeɪn]	a.	恰當的，相關的
distributor	[dɪˈstrɪbjutə]	n.	銷售者

Useful Expressions

bulk space	大空間，大面積
be equipped with	有......設施
smoke detector	煙霧探測器
fire extinguisher	滅火器
apply to	適用於
be submitted to	提交
Fire Marshal	消防署長
attached to	附屬於，附加
emergency evacuation	緊急疏散
wear and tear	磨損
exercise due caution	給予適當告誡

Language Focus

1.It is recommended that the general service contractor generate the floor plans and send them to us directly.

建議總承包商設計展位平面圖並直接交給我們。

2.Understanding that temporary stains will occasionally occur, show management will be responsible for cleaning costs associated with the removal.

考慮到意外的汙染物時有發生，展覽管理方將負責清場時的清潔費用。

Problem Solving

How do you solve the following problems? Outline your assertion.

1.Vehicles are moved during the show hours.

2.Food and beverage product exhibitors distribute samples.

Section C Format Writing

Acquaint yourself with the following. Finish the exercises that ensue.

Reservation Fax 預訂傳真

<table>
<tr><td colspan="2" align="center">Four Season Convention Corporation
Shanghai, China Fax: 0086-021-58198666</td></tr>
<tr><td>To:</td><td>New York Convention and Exhibition Center, NY, USA</td></tr>
<tr><td>From:</td><td>Mr. Jeffery Johnson, Customer Affairs Manager</td></tr>
<tr><td>Date:</td><td>June 18, 2005</td></tr>
<tr><td>Subject:</td><td>Room Reservation</td></tr>
<tr><td>Message:</td><td>Pls reserve 5 standard rooms for 5 nights from July 16 to July 20. Please guarantee—Master card No. 6638 77902 8669.

Sincerely yours,
Jeffery Johnson</td></tr>
</table>

Fax on Ticket Booking

<table>
<tr><td colspan="2" align="center">Four Season Convention Corporation
Shanghai, China Fax: 0086-021-58198666</td></tr>
<tr><td>To:</td><td>American Airlines</td></tr>
<tr><td>From:</td><td>Mr. Jeffery Johnson, Customer Affairs Manager</td></tr>
<tr><td>Date:</td><td>June 18, 2005</td></tr>
<tr><td>Subject:</td><td>Booking Flight Tickets</td></tr>
<tr><td>Message:</td><td>Pls reserve 3 tickets for July 21 from New York to Shanghai, China. Business class. The tickets should be under the name of Liu Hui, Fang Hua and Xing Bin. Please guarantee—Master card No. 7790 6349 28669. Please send the tickets to the following address: No. A106, New York Convention and Exhibition Center, NY, 32058 USA.

Sincerely yours,
Jeffery Johnson</td></tr>
</table>

Questions about Format Writing

Complete the following statements based on the texts.

1.Mr Jeffery Johnson is working at _____.

2.Payments would be made _____.

3.The flight tickets would be delivered to _____.

4.Pls is the short form for _____.

5.The reservation is made _____in advance.

Notes of Format

Always bear in mind the following.

會展服務機構可以給客戶提供出展服務，海外訂房、訂票為其所提供的服務之一。就海外訂房、訂票而言，除了電話直接預訂外，個人和團體還可以透過書信、電子郵件、網路及傳真等方式完成。運用現代通訊方式進行預訂既方便又快捷，現已成為常用的預訂方式。下面是海外訂房、機票預訂傳真寫作的要點。

1.To 後寫收件人或單位；

2.From 後寫發件人或單位；

3.Subject 後簡要寫明事由；

4.Date 後寫發傳真的日期；

5.Message 後寫清具體預訂的房型、房間數量、停留天數、具體到達以及離開時間。若希望對方提供有保證預訂則還須給出信用卡卡號或其他保證方式；若是機票預訂則需寫清具體離港時間、數量、機票持有人姓名等資訊。若希望對方提供有保證預訂也需給出信用卡卡號或其他保證方式。

Do It Yourself

Work out a Room Reservation Fax with the Chinese prompts.

請以會展服務公司 Johnson Convention and Exhibition Agency 的名義為你的客戶 Brian Hans 在 Las Vegas Convention and Exhibition Center 預訂兩間標準房。用房時間為十月八日到十二日。

To：
From：
Date：
Subject：
Message：

Reference Answers

Answers to Questions about Format Writing

1.Four Season Convention Corporation

2.with Master card

3.No.A106, New York Convention and Exhibition Center, NY, 32058 USA

4.Please

5.about a month

Reference Answer to Do It Yourself

To：	Las Vegas Convention and Exhibition Center
From：	Johnson Convention and Exhibition Agency
Date：	September 10, 2004
Subject：	Room Reservation
Message：	Pls reserve 2 standard rooms for 5 nights from October 8 to 12 under the name of Mr. Brian Hans.
	Sincerely yours,
	（Signature）

Chapter 12 Event Management 展覽現場管理

Section A Reading Assignment

Warming-up Activity

Go over the following terms with your teacher.

variability 變化	delegate 代表(n.)；授權(v.)	Variance 差異	Maintenance 保持，維持
approach 方法，途徑	resort 求助	exercise 行使	disposal 處理
undertake 進行，從事	performance 業績	trust-worthiness 可靠	routine 常規
framework 框架	contingency 應急	emergencies 緊急情況	coordinator 協調者
implementation 執行	back-up 後備，補充	flexible 靈活的	operation 運作
promptness 迅速	pinch point 問題點	overwhelming 巨大的，極富挑戰性的	

Pre-reading Questions

Answer the following questions without referring to the text.

1.What is the nature of running an event?

2.How would you cope with the possible emergencies arising at the event?

3.What homework would you do to ensure a successful event?

Text

All for the Big Day

The big day is almost upon us.We have done as much planning as was needed, and we have organized all the various people, parts, organizations, suppliers and equipment that we planned for.For all the considerable effort that goes into planning an event, running it on the day can still prove a challenge.The coordination of a wide range of different and even unusual activities, facilities and services can be overwhelming.Event management has to be effective and event managers must be good communicators and good delegates in situations that may be constantly changing.The importance of having done the planning for this situation is that it reduces the variability and uncertainty of what is taking place and allows the event coordinator to concentrate on those things which require immediate or constant attention.

The nature of the event business is such that each occasion is unique and a production line approach can rarely be adopted.The activities undertaken to make one event proceed effectively may not necessarily work for another event, euen if these events share common features.Thus the recurrence of routine tends to be in the framework—the approach, the organization and the management— rather than in the implementation or the operation.It is this uniqueness that systems and staff must be sufficiently flexible to cope with.Systems and staff are intended to work hand in hand. If an operation can be systematized or automated to reduce costs, especially labor costs, then it should be.And in fact, some event-related activities, such as food production, can be systematized.

The maintenance of standards in non-routine service activities is also a significant concern of management in a business such as events management.The non-routine and non-systematized nature of anything, from site layout to variances in individual audience requirements, needs to be accommodated by allowing flexibility of operations, while adequate supervision and control are maintained. Simple managerial control may be exercised by detailed supervision and the use of checklists, by techniques such as "management by exception," or by improving the quality of staff and staff training to the level at which quality control can largely be placed in the hands of the staff themselves.In events, quality can mean error-free performance, safety, promptness, efficiency, problem solving, courtesy, reliability, and trust-worthiness.In attempting to deliver high-quality programs and service, the event manager faces a number of operational challenges.No event or service can ever be truly perfected, so constant innovations and improvements are essential.This can be difficult in short-lived organizations putting on events, because there is limited time to train staff and limited time to get to know what abilities they have.

Time is the most precious resource when an event is underway. Making sure that procedures and plans in place can help to identify the potential emergencies, enable the planners to make essential changes, and keep all the parties involved aware of what is required. Event planners will have more time to make informed decisions and can avoid panic responses.In today's complex event environment, this has never been more important.

Perhaps one of the most common management techniques used by events coordinators is management by wandering around.Draw up a checklist of things you need to keep an eye on and give yourself a route to go round, preferably covering your main department leaders and those places you regard as "pinch points." Pinch points are where things are likeliest to go wrong, or be busiest, or need support at crucial times.

Above all, communicate actively and frequently as you do your rounds.It is important you delegate wherever you can, so that your regular staff learn to handle and solve problems for themselves.Step in if you have to, but remember you are the last resort and should not try to sort out minor problems, particularly when your staff could do so on their own.

When you are making decisions and solving problems, it is vital to be aware of the factors which have led to the problem and to be able to take the correct action.It may be that you have to take action first and ask questions later, but it is essential to ask questions, as otherwise you might fail again.If you fail to identify the source and origin of a problem correctly, it will occur again, and you may not be able to get yourself and the event out of it next time.Therefore a good decision is dependent on the recognition of the right problem.So in your efforts to solve problems and make decisions, keep a notebook in your pocket and take a minute to write the problem down, as well as what you did to sort it out.In this way you can help to avoid problems happening again or concentrate resources in places where you think they might recur.Walk steadily through the event, take breaks when you can, sit down when you can and take drinks when you can.It is important that you make a good decision which is dependent on the recognition of the right problem.

Checklist 1

▶ Contingency plan check—Go through the contingency plan with all involved suppliers.

▶ Event pocket handbook—Receive confirmed information that all involved suppliers have the same up-dated version of the event program.

▶ Contact list—Make sure that all involved staff have an updated (with date of most recent update) contact list with those responsible for key areas and their back-up persons, specifying decision makers and areas of responsibility.

▶ Waste material control—Obtain a confirmation that the implemented waste material disposal procedure is in place.

▶ Pre-con meeting—Make sure that, prior to each day's activities, a pre-con meeting takes place with the involved suppliers and your team leaders.

▶ Daily re-cap—A re-cap meeting between your PCO, suppliers and sub-suppliers daily to evaluate mistakes and accidents and to adjust for enhanced performance the following day.

▶ Reports on amendments in program—Receive a report on all amendments and performance changes that have been agreed.

▶ Reported deviations from the amendments—Request a report on all major deviations/errors/damages that have occurred during the day or event.

▶ Operational function check—Request a report daily that all departments and responsible persons are aware of the up-dated program.

▶ VIP information program—Establish a specific updated VIP treatment document.Specify the VIP procedures and VIP delegate name list.Include photos of VIPs to avoid misunderstandings.

▶ VIP list confidentiality—Have all person receiving information on VIP to sign the confidentiality agreement.

▶ Media responsible—Update the appointed media representative regarding information that can be published, and allocated media spokespersons.

Checklist 2

1.Communication procedures during the event : Confirm there is a written communication plan involving all relevant parties, and that all parties have been informed about the plan.

2.Event time plan checklist : Set out each activity, time and duration of activity, person responsible, reporting needs.

3.Report on amendments : Produce a communication plan that covers all type of amendments that need to be reported.Identify what needs to be reported immediately and what can be reported after the event.

4.Report on errors and deviations : Produce a communication plan that covers all errors and deviations from plan that happened during each element of the event.

5.Report on damages/injuries : Produce a communication plan that covers all damages/injuries that occurred during each element of the event.

Check-in

Do you have any questions about the text? If any, ask your teacher.

Important Vacabulary

overwhelming	[ˌəʊvəˈwelmɪŋ]	adj.	巨大的，極富挑戰性的
variability	[veərɪəˈbɪlɪtɪ]	n.	變化
approach	[əˈprəʊtʃ]	n.	方法，途經
undertake	[ˌʌndəˈteɪk]	v.	進行，從事
framework	[ˈfreɪmwɜːk]	n.	框架
implementation	[ˌɪmplɪmenˈteɪʃən]	n.	實施
maintenance	[ˌmeɪntənəns]	n.	保持，維持
variance	[ˈveərɪəns]	n.	差異，不同
exercise	[ˈeksəsaɪz]	v.	行使
trust-worthiness	[ˈtrʌstˈwɜːθɪnɪs]	n.	可靠
emergency	[ɪˈmɜːdʒənsɪ]	n.	突發事件
panic	[ˈpænɪk]	adj.	恐慌
crucial	[ˈkruːʃl]	adj.	重要的，關鍵的
delegate	[ˈdelɪˌgeɪt]	v.	授權
resort	[rɪˈzɔːt]	n.	求助
pace	[ˈpeɪs]	v.	合理安排，使有規律
contingency	[kənˈtɪndʒənsɪ]	n.	偶發事件
back-up	[ˈbæk ʌp]	adj.	後備，相關的
disposal	[dɪˈspəʊzl]	n.	處理
pre-con	[prɪ kɒn]	n.	會前會議
enhanced	[ɪnˈhɑːnst]	adj.	提高的
amendment	[əˈmendmənt]	n.	修正，修改
deviation	[ˌdiːvɪˈeɪʃən]	n.	變化，差異
confidentiality	[ˌkɒnfɪˌdenʃɪˈælətɪ]	n.	保密
allocate	[ˈæləkeɪt]	v.	分配，分派

Useful Exprssions

big day	盛大活動日
be intended to	目的，意圖是
site layout	場地佈局
keep an eye on	注意，留心
pinch point	問題點，易出問題的事物
step in	插手，干預
sort out	分類，弄清楚
get out of it	擺脫，消除
contingency plan	應急預案

Language Focus

1.We have done as much planning as was needed.

我們應該做的計劃都做了。

2.The nature of the event business is such that each occasion is unique and a production line approach can rarely be adopted.

會展活動的特點是每一次活動都與前一次不一樣，按照流水線生產的方法來組織會展活動往往難以奏效。

3.Thus the recurrence of routine tends to be in the framework—the approach, the organization and the management—rather than in the implementation or the operation.

所謂的常規程序的重複只是理念上的，指的是方式、組織與管理，而不是實施過程中或者操作層面的。

4.It is vital to be aware of the factors which have led to the problem and to be able to take the correct action.

關鍵是要明白造成問題的因素是什麼，以及能採取哪種正確的改正措施。

Group Discussion

Discuss the following topic in group.Select one on the team to make a presentation before the class.

How to cope with the non-routine work in event business?

Guidelines for Discussion

— define the non-routine work or illustrate the non-routine work

■ organizational approach

■ managerial approach

■ training

■ other approaches

Writing Activity

Summarize the text by outlining major points.Write a few lines about event management using the following expressions.

overwhelming	艱巨的	constantly changing	不斷變化的
coordination	協調	operational challenges	操作難題
flexible	靈活的	management technique	管理技術
do your rounds	巡視	checklist	工作要點‧檢查單
potential emergencies	潛在的問題‧可能發生的問題	systemize	系統化

Expressions

‧ For all the considerable effort that goes into planning an event, running it on the day it is actually held can still prove a challenge.

‧ It is this uniqueness that systems and staff must be sufficiently flexible to cope with. ‧ Step in if you have to, but remember, you are the last resort, and you should not be trying to sort out minor problems when your staff could do so on their own.

‧ In this way you can help to avoid problems happening again or concentrate resources in places where you think they might recur.

Section B Case Study

Read the following passage before solving the problems that ensue.

Wi-Fi Success at a Film Festival

Movie star Robert Redford's Sundance Film Festival has always pushed both the artistic and technical envelope.For example, the event, held every January in Park City, Utah, a ski town near Redford's ranch, now includes a parallel online festival of short digital films.

This year, in a project that could serve as model and inspiration for Wireless LAN （WLAN）, systems integrators and conference planners, the festival and its technology sponsors went one step further.

Using some very up-to-the-minute Wi-Fi technology, they established a temporary hotspot network to distribute festival information and get participants "communicating digitally in new ways," as Ian Calderon, the Sundance Institute's director of digital initiatives, puts it.

Hewlett-Packard Company provided 500 Jornada PocketPCs, which the festival distributed to VIP attendees—film makers, producers, journalists—as well as key staff.

Symbol Technologies, a Holtsville New York maker of WLAN equipment, contributed access points and CF （Compact Flash） Wi-Fi cards—the Wireless Networker product, which the company introduced last October.

And FluxNetwork Inc., a Santa Cruz, CA （Computer Assistance）, software developer specializing in "rich media" applications for wirelessly-enabled Personal Digital Assistants (PDAs) and smartphones, implemented a Wi-Fi network using the Symbol gear.

There were five hotspots : three at film venues, one at festival headquarter and one at the festival's Digital Center, where hardware and software vendors like Sony and Avid show off their digital film making gear.

FluxNetwork's primary contribution was the proprietary software platform it built to support online multimedia services for what company CEO Kurt Thywissen likes to call "captive consumer environments."

Using the software, it loaded the PocketPCs with easy-to-use schedules, interactive maps, information about the films and film makers, and samples of the short films in the online festival.Each day, participants could update their PDAs content at one of the Wi-Fi hotspots, including downloading a new batch of digital shorts.

The PocketPCs replaced a phone-book-size festival catalog and reams of collateral material.It also became an on-the-go film theater.

Like other PocketPCs based on Microsoft's Windows CE operating system, the HP Jornadas have slightly larger, higher-resolution color screens than standard Palm PDAs and more processing power.So viewing clear, sharp, albeit still small, digital videos was still perfectly viable.

The project was so successful that Calderon, a Sundance Institute co-founder, says that the festival hopes to be able to expand the program next year to include as many as 1, 500 participants all connected wirelessly.

"The goal for Sundance," says Calderon, "was to create a platform for artists and creative people, to build digital community."

Calderon envisions participants viewing the online films on the PDAs, communicating with each other about them online, and about other festival events, and generally creating a dialog.

It's not clear how much of that actually happened at this year's event.But the PDAs and the wireless network were certainly the talk of the festival, Calderon and other participants say.

"We're really looking at a modest, crude version of what this will become," Calderon says."I believe it will evolve into something very sophisticated." He's talking more about the way participants used the technology than the technology itself.

The goal of the sponsors was of course somewhat different, namely to show off their technology to potential paying customers. But both sides clearly won in the process, as did attendees.

"I've got to say, I was very impressed," says San Francisco Examiner and Variety magazine film critic Joe Leydon who received one of the PocketPCs. "It came in very handy throughout the festival."

Leydon says he "religiously" updated the content of his PocketPC wirelessly every day to make sure he had an up-to-the-minute schedule showing all the late changes to when and where films would play.This was especially important given the packed schedules film festival reporters have to maintain, he says, juggling interviews and film showings from morning to evening.

If a publicist called him on his cell phone while he was out and about—as happened several times—to request a changed time for an interview, Leydon could consult his PocketPC to figure out a way to re-jig his schedule.With a few taps, he could find out if there was another later showing of the film he had originally planned to see during that time slot.

Finding a hotspot from which to update was not a problem, he says.The network did not cover the whole town, but access points were placed strategically where he had to be anyway, such as at the theaters.It was simple to update while he waited to get into the auditorium. (This was exactly what organizers intended, says Thywissen.)

Leydon was most impressed with the wirelessly updated schedules and instant access to other festival information.In particular, the biographies of film makers came in handy when he was called in to last-minute and impromptu interviews.And not having to carry around the weighty festival catalog was also very appealing.

Leydon did look at all the digital short films—often while riding in the shuttle bus between venues—and was impressed by the way new films appeared each day.But it was clearly the practical benefits that impressed most.

Best of all, says Leydon, a self-confessed technophobe, the system was easy to learn and use.Connecting to the network for updates took a couple of taps on the PocketPC's touch screen and a few minutes."If I can do it," he says, "believe me, anybody can do it."

FluxNetwork acted as the systems integrator on the project. "Because we have a focus on rich media," explains Thywissen, "we wanted to find a high-profile event where we could roll it out and demo those capabilities. Sundance was ideal."

The software was designed to work seamlessly in 802.11b networks.The company originally set out to build services, for 3G networks, but Wi-Fi happened first.And now Thywissen believes 3G will probably never be used for delivering rich media content.

Thywissen also believes there is a business providing services, similar to the one at Sundance, to profit-making conferences and trade shows.Participants would use their own PDAs or rent them, or rent just the Wi-Fi cards.They might even pay for some content.

The value of the FluxNetwork software license and systems integration services at Sundance was about $100,000. Costs for a similar system for other events could be anywhere from $30,000 to $200,000, Thywissen says.

There are already signs the Sundance experiment may provide a glimpse of the future of conferences and trade shows.

Accenture and Compaq joined forces to provide a similar service for the World Economic Forum in New York at the end of January, distributing 2, 000 Compaq iPaq PocketPCs.Thywissen says the service was not as well received, mainly because the integrators did not pay enough attention to making it easy to use.

FluxNetwork is currently evaluating the possibility of developing a business providing turn-key services for event managers—providing Wi-Fi network, content and PDA/Wi-Fi card rental.It's also interested in working with other systems integrators, which is what it's doing in Japan.

There would of course be other costs to setting up such a service. The PocketPCs sell at retail for close to$600. The Wireless Networker Wi-Fi CF product lists for $180.

Is this a bona fide opportunity for WLAN systems integrators? We think it might be.

Check-in

Do you have any questions about the case study? If any, ask your teacher.

Vacabulary

ranch	[rɑːntʃ]	n.	大牧場
implement	['ɪmplɪment]	v.	執行．實現
proprietary	[prə'praɪətrɪ]	n.	獨家製造的．專利的
captive	['kæptɪv]	adj.	被迷住的
re-jig	[rɪ'dʒɪg]	v.	重新調整
impromptu	[ɪm'prɒmptju]	adj.	即席的
demo	['deməu]	v. & n.	演示
seamlessly	['siːmlɪslɪ]	adv.	天衣無縫地

put it	解釋
access points	接入點
reams of	大量的
on-the-go	（口語）忙個不停
came in handy	派上用途．使用便捷
shuttle bus	定時定點班車
roll it out	大顯身手
turn-key service	全方位服務

Language Focus

1.Wi-Fi：wireless fidelity 無線傳真

　　該詞由兩個詞的首音節拼成，故稱為混成詞（Blending）。同時該詞也是由 Hi-Fi（高傳真）類比（analogy）而來。會展英文名稱多由此構詞法衍生而來。

　　2.up-to-the-minute：up-to-the-date 包含最新訊息的

　　它是由 up-to-the-date 的結構類比而來。英語詞彙日新月異，許多新詞產生的初期都以臨時語的形式出現。再如：smartphone ＝ smart ＋ telephone（智慧電話）、easy-to-use（傻瓜型的）、phone-book-size（電話本大小的）、technophobe ＝ technology ＋ phobia（技術進步恐懼症）、high-profile（資質好的），等等。

　　3.albeit：儘管，但是

　　如：

A useful, albeit complex device

一個結構複雜但很有用的裝置

They are still waiting, albeit with growing impatience.

他們還等著，儘管越來越不耐煩。

　　這是一個古英文詞，近年來該詞多見於英美報刊文字，一般用來連接短語，不連接句子。

　　4.Calderon envisioned participants viewing the online films on the PDAs...Calderon

陷入遐想，猶見觀眾手執掌上電腦觀看線上電影……

　　5.time slot：interval 休息時間

　　6.self-confessed：自認的

　　7.Costs for a similar system for other events could be anywhere from$30,000 to $200,000...

在其他一些會展活動中，類似的系統成本可能在 3 萬至 20 萬之間。

8.bona fide：真誠的（地），真正的（地），守信的（地）

Problem Solving

How do you solve the following problems? Outline your assertion.

1.How can you arrange a meeting or exposition through Wi-Fi?

2.What services are needed for a modern exposition of conference?

Section C Format Writing

Acquaint yourself with the following. Finish the exercises that ensue.

Opening Address 開幕致辭

Sample 1

Opening Night Speech—Tom Byrne's one man show "Coast to Coast" at the Tonic

The great Irish painter Markey Robinson once said that a painter has either got it or he hasn't got it.Tom Byrne has got it.When you look at Tom Byrne's paintings, you know he has got it and when you meet Tom Byrne, the man, you know he has got it.

I would like to thank Pam for organizing this wonderful exhibition.Over the years she has nurtured many new talents.

I would also like to thank John and Thelma for providing this wonderful exhibition space.In a short time Tonic has become an important cultural centre in Blackrock.

Finally, I would like to thank the artist for his presence here tonight with his partner Chloe.

We will all look back on this evening as an important cultural event.Again, thank you for coming.

Sample 2

Mr.Chairman,

Ladies and gentlemen,

It gives me great pleasure to officiate at this opening ceremony today.

Former president of the General Electric Group Mr.Jack Welch once said, "I want General Electric to develop a big-company body with a small-company soul." This remark brings out the key to success in Small and Medium Enterprises （SMEs）, namely flexibility, proactive management, innovation and a venturous spirit.

SMEs have always been a major pillar of Hong Kong's economy. Over the years, they have played an essential role in stimulating economic growth, creating jobs, promoting entrepreneurship, nurturing business leaders, and introducing into Hong Kong new products and service culture.Many successful international business giants we now have in Hong Kong started as SMEs years ago.

Today, we have about 300, 000 SMEs in various trades, accounting for 98% of the total number of businesses in the territory.They hire as many as 1.4 million people, representing 60% of all employees in the private sector.It has been the Special Administrative Region （SAR） Government's policy to support the development of SMEs, enabling them to bring full play to their strengths and sharpen their competitive edge, so as to open up new economic scopes and job opportunities for Hong Kong.

Globalization, the emergence of knowledge-based economy, and China's accession to the World Trade Organization pose new challenges and opportunities to us.To harness these opportunities, we must restructure our economy and head for a high value-added direction.To be successful in our economic restructuring, SMEs will have a vital part to play.We must encourage all local SMEs to make good use of innovative technology to enhance efficiency, to invest more in product research and marketing, and to develop their own brand names.I hope our SMEs can develop a vision to move beyond the territory to establish a footing in the world.

I once pledged to set up four funding schemes totaling $1.9 billion, namely the SME Business Installations and Equipment Loan Guarantee Scheme, the SME Export Marketing Fund, the SME Development Fund and the SME Training Fund.These schemes aim at helping SMEs to secure loans for the purchase of business installations and equipment, to help proprietors and staff to get appropriate training, to encourage businesses to strive for higher efficiency, to develop new brand names and products and to explore markets outside Hong Kong, so as to boost our overall competitiveness.

As Joshua just said, our SMEs have responded positively to the funding schemes.I extend my appreciation to the Small and Medium Enterprises Committee for recommending to us last June these four schemes and many other measures in support of SMEs.These recommendations are constructive and useful.I would also like to take this opportunity to call upon SMEs to make the best use of the funding schemes as well as the Support and Consultation Centre for Small and Medium Enterprises opened today.

The Trade and Industry Department also launched a Pilot Mentorship Programme for SMEs last year, which won accolades from the participating mentors and SMEs.The Department is about to fully implement the programme.I earnestly hope that more accomplished entrepreneurs will join the mentorship, sparing a little time to share their valuable experience with our SMEs to help them strengthen their foothold.Indeed, I told Joshua that if possible, I would also like to be one of the mentors to share with at least some of our SMEs my experience in corporate management.

Ladies and gentlemen, the opening of this Centre today illustrates the Government's determination and commitment to the further development of the sector.Let's wish all our SMEs a prosperous future.

Thank you very much!

Questions about the Samples

Complete the following statements based on the passages.

Based on Sample 1

1.The exhibition is held in honor of the artist named _____.

2.The organizer of the exhibition is _____.

3.The exhibition space is provided by _____.

4.Tonic is the name of _____.

Based on Sample 2

1.The speech focuses on the importance of _____ in Hong Kong and their development.

2.The speech is delivered on the special occasion of _____.

3.The aim of the four funding schemes is _____.

4.The function of the Pilot Mentorship Programme is _____.

Notes of Format

Always bear in mind the following.

會議、展覽會致辭主要內容通常包括：

1. 向與會者致意；

2. 表達對參加會議或展覽的喜悅與榮幸；

3. 對東道國的稱讚；

4. 對會議組織者的感謝；

5. 對展會的成功祝願。

Do It Yourself

Work out an opening speech to be addressed on the anniversary of the Silver Jubilee of a university.

Your speech may begin like this：

Ladies and Gentlemen,

It is a very great pleasure indeed for me to be able to attend this…

Reference Answers

Answers to Questions about the Samples

Based on Sample 1

1.Tom Byrne

2.Pam

3.John and Thelma

4.the exhibition center

Based on Sample 2

1.SMEs（small and medium enterprises）

2.the opening of the Support and Consultation Centre for Small and Medium Enterprises

3.helping SMEs to secure loans for the purchase of business installations and equipment, to help proprietors and staff to get appropriate training, to encourage businesses to strive for higher efficiency, to develop new brand names and products and to explore markets outside Hong Kong, so as to boost our overall competitiveness

4.to let accomplished entrepreneurs share their valuable experience with SMEs to help them strengthen their foothold

Reference Answer to Do It Yourself

Ladies and Gentlemen,

It is a very great pleasure indeed for me to be able to attend this Silver Jubilee celebration of the university.

Congratulations to the university on its 25th anniversary!

The SHTM has made a very significant contribution to Hong Kong.You can be very proud of what you have achieved over the last 25 years.You have produced some 10,000 graduates who have been the forefront of the tourism industry.The university's success is important for the region—it is by far the largest institute of its kind in Asia as well as being the leader in this field.

I want to congratulate Professor Wang and all the staff for their dedication and commitment to Tourism Education in Hong Kong.It is also a time to honor the graduates of the school and we wish them every success in their careers in our industry.

Chapter 13 Security，Safety and Risk Management 安保與風險管理

▌Section A Reading Assignment

Warming-up Activity

Go over the following terms with your teacher.

valuable item 貴重物品	threats or risk assessment 威脅風險評估	computer crimes/hacking 電腦犯罪/駭客	monitor screen 監視器
silicon-vidicon camera 矽光導攝像管攝像機	concealed article 囊中之物	staff entrance 員工入口	microwave fence 微波柵欄
closed-circuit television system 閉路電視	junction box 接線盒	anti-intrusion system 反侵入系統	identity badge 身份牌
fire-fighting equipment 滅火器	walk-through screening 經過監視器	escape route 逃生路線	statutory obligation 法律責任

Pre-reading Questions

Answer the following questions without referring to the text.

1.Do you think security and safety control is necessary for a successful meeting?

2.What should be done to secure a meeting or exhibition?

Text

Handling Hazards that Might Arise

By bringing together groups of people who may represent valuable business interests, professional expertise, political authority and other sectors of influence, congresses and meetings and exhibitions present a degree of risk.Security must be provided for delegates, speakers and other visitors, valuable items of equipment （including exhibits）, information, and for the premises generally.

The assessment of threats or hazards will depend to a large extent on the subjects of the meeting, the host organization, attendees, publicity, extent of press and public entry （including other events at the same time）and access for vehicles.

Threats or risk assessment should be part of a wider provision to deal with all types of hazards that may arise, such as computer crimes/hacking, failure of IT or some other essential system, industrial action by staff or external services, failure of suppliers to meet deadlines, terrorism, sabotage, accidents, fire and other natural disasters.

Remote observation and monitoring of areas inside and outside the building is an essential part of security and management operations.Closed-circuit television systems used for this purpose are made up from a number of cameras strategically located and linked to junction boxes （for transmission and power supply）, then relayed to monitor screens with adjustment and switch-over controls housed in the security office.

Closed-circuit television （CCTV）cameras fall into several categories, depending on the location （indoors or outdoors, light conditions, angles of views）, lens requirements （remote iris adjustment, focusing and zooming) and head operation (pan and tilt) .Positions of nearby lamps that could shine into the lens, causing glare, must be considered.For night vision, silicon-vidicon cameras used in parallel with infrared beams may be installed.

Typical locations for cameras are :

· Vehicle entrance/exit ;

· Staff entrance, including security check ;

· Inside lobby towards main entrance and above reception desk ;

· Foyers—towards entrance doors ;

· Emergency and secondary exits.

Other anti-intrusion systems include :

· Infrared beams across specific paths ;

· Microwave fences to detect crossing ;

· Electrical continuity—to indicate opening of doors, etc. ;

· Security lighting, with illumination of car parks, paths, grounds and buildings.

Concealed articles can also represent a threat to security and control.Guest's luggage, visitor's bags, and posted or deposited parcels may conceal weapons, explosives or items stolen from the premises. Theft by staff and service personnel is also a matter for concern. Search operations must be carried out quickly and as discreetly as possible to avoid causing innocent people inconvenience and invasion of privacy and to minimize delay and congestion on arrival or departure.

Portable equipment used for search and detection includes：low dosage X-ray inspection of hand luggage placed in an inspection chamber, a walk-through screening unit with remote electronics console to detect metal objects and fluoroscopic cabinets for inspection of unopened letters, packages and luggage.

Stringent safety requirements apply to the use of such equipment, and security services are normally hired for particular situations that could involve security risks.Identification systems are commonly installed in the staff entrance area, together with time-recording equipment.Similar identity badges may be issued to visitors and delegates.

Safety is a major consideration in all aspects of meeting, exhibition and hotel operation.Meetings and other events impose obligations on both the owners and organizers of venues.

Statutory obligations for safety cover fire protections and means of escape, as well as workplaces, hygiene, engineering equipment, and the premises generally.A system of regular inspection, reporting, recorded attention to defects, and planned maintenance and replacements must be introduced.

Protection against danger from fires in buildings is covered by legislation and includes：

· Fire resistance of walls, partitions, floors, staircases, lift shafts and doors to delay the spread of fire and retain structural integrity for specified periods to allow evacuation and fire control measures to be carried out；

· Limitations on the use of combustible materials in areas of high risk and of lining materials which may create hazard to occupants from high rates of surface flame spread, smoke or toxic fume emission or by melting and shattering ;

· Installation of fire alarms, appropriate fire-fighting equipment and systems, emergency signs, lighting and ventilation of escape routes together with training of staff to deal with emergencies.

Fire escape provisions are based on an evacuation time of 2-3 minutes from any occupied part of the building, and are subject to specific requirements in local codes and regulations.

As a rule, at least two alternative exits must be provided from a hall, sited more than 45m apart from any position in the room and within a direct distance of 30m and maximum travel distance round furniture of 45m.

Exits must be kept clear, protected from fire and smoke with self-closing doors opening in the directions of travel, fitted with emergency signs and lighting and must lead to a safe final exit and place of assembly in the open.

Where the hall is above or below ground level, the hall exits must allow for 10 percent greater occupancy and lead to the final exits via fire-protected lobbies and staircases.Regular checking of appliances, exit routes and procedures is essential.

Food and Beverage safety and sanitation is also essential to the success of a convention or exhibition.Convention facility and exhibition venues should be responsible for ensuring the safety of people within the establishment at any given time.Whenever a service function is performed, a concerted effort should always be made to assure the personal safety of everyone in the facility, including guests and fellow workers alike.Accidents do not just happen.They are caused by neglect, carelessness, thoughtlessness, and ignorance. Consumers today have a much-increased awareness of safety and sanitation issues.Safety and sanitation can be two critical factors if a venue is to maintain customers' confidence in and satisfaction with its food and service （and, not incidentally, maximize repeat business and participation rates）.

Accidents may result from a number of causes—physical, psychological or environmental leading to falls, cuts, shocks, burns, collision at work and many more.These can be classified into eight main categories：structural inadequacy, improper equipment placement and installation, improper working habits, the nature and behavior of people, and improper maintenance and storage.

The materials used in stand construction must not present a fire hazard within a hall—essentially, materials must be incombustible, inherently non-flammable or flame-proofed by impregnation or proofing.Plastics must be self-extinguishing in addition to having acceptable flame resistance.

Satisfactory security service doesn't just happen.You should always try to make everything ensured in advance.The best way to fight accidents is to prevent them from happening.The following are some tips for you：

· Ensure that your insurance policies are extended to cover the show.

· Whilst thefts rarely occur at exhibitions, be particularly alert during move in and move out.

· Always have a lockable cupboard or storage area on your stand, for personal valuables, i.e.wallets, and phones, and handbags.

· Co-operate with security guards employed by the organizer, as they are there to protect your property.

· Report any thefts immediately to the organizer.

· Never leave small, portable, valuable items unattended on your stand, i.e.laptop, and handbags.

· During move out, station somebody on your stand until all product is removed.

· Don't leave commercially sensitive material on your stand, i.e.pricing folders, and client lists.

Check-in

Do you have any questions about the text? If any, ask your teacher.

Important Vocabulary

premises	[ˈpremɪsɪz]	n.	房屋
sabotage	[ˈsæbətɑːʒ]	v.	陰謀破壞
strategically	[strəˈtiːdʒɪklɪ]	adv.	頗為策略地
relay	[ˈriːleɪ]	v.	轉播
lens	[lenz]	n.	鏡頭
iris	[ˈaɪərɪs]	n.	虹膜
tilt	[tɪlt]	a.	傾斜的
silicon	[ˈsɪlɪkən]	n.	矽
vidicon	[ˈvɪdɪkɒn]	n.	光導攝像管
infrared	[ˌɪnfrəˈred]	a.	紅外線的
foyer	[ˈfɔɪeɪ]	n.	灶·爐
continuity	[ˌkɒntɪˈnjuːətɪ]	n.	連續性
illumination	[ɪˌluːmɪˈneɪʃən]	n.	照明
discreetly	[dɪˈskriːtlɪ]	ad.	謹慎地
congestion	[kənˈdʒestʃən]	n.	擁擠
stringent	[ˈstrɪndʒənt]	a.	周密的
statutory	[ˈstætjuːtərɪ]	a.	法令的
combustible	[kəmˈbʌstəbl]	a.	易燃的
evacuation	[ɪˌvækjuˈeɪʃən]	n.	疏散
sanitation	[ˌsænɪˈteɪʃən]	n.	衛生

Useful Expressions

security office	保安辦公室
safety and security requirements	安保規定
forbidden exhibit	禁展品

Language Focus

1.By bringing together groups of people who may represent valuable business interests, professional expertise, political authority and other sectors of influence, congresses and meetings and exhibitions present a degree of risk.

代表大會、會議和展覽把一批人聚集在一起。這些人可能代表著有價值的商機、專業造詣、政治權威和其他領域的影響力，故而也就存在某種程度的風險。

2.Search operations must be carried out quickly and as discreetly as possible to avoid causing innocent people inconvenience and invasion of privacy and to minimize delay and congestion on arrival or departure.

檢查工作必須迅速而且要盡可能地謹慎。這樣不但可以避免給無辜的人帶來不便或侵犯隱私，而且還可以把進場或散場時的延遲和擁擠現象降低到最小的程度。

3.Exits must be kept clear, protected from fire and smoke with self-closing doors opening in the directions of travel, fitted with emergency signs and lighting and must lead to a safe final exit and place of assembly in the open.

出口通道應該保持暢通無阻，可防煙火，並安裝有朝外開放的自動門，還必須備有緊急出口標誌和燈光。這些通道必須通往最終的安全出口以及露天的集合場地。

Group Discussion

Discuss the following topic in group.Select one on the team to make a presentation before the class.

What security and safety issues should be considered when a convention or exhibition is held?

Guidelines for Discussion

— fire safety

— exhibit safety

— construction safety

■ security equipment

■ security service

■ security and safety inspection

Writing Activity

Summarize the text by outlining major considerations about safety and security.Write a few lines about the importance of security and safety service.

Section B Case Study

Read the following passage before solving the problems that ensue.

The First Theft at the Kongju National Museum

The first ever theft occurred at the Kongju National Museum.One National Treasure artifact and three undesignated, but highly valued cultural properties, 4 pieces in total, were removed on May 15.

Police asked for cooperation at airports, seaports and customs to prevent the artifacts from being smuggled out of the country.The two burglars, both in their 30s, broke through the entrance of the duty office at Kongju National Museum in Joong-dong, Kongju-si, Chungcheongnam-do, at about 10：25pm on May 15.They threatened Mr.Park（35, researcher）, who was on duty at the time with high-voltage stun guns and the other deadly weapons, tying his hands together with duct tape.One of them stood guard while the other broke glass displays on the first floor with the heavy stick.He also broke the door lock leading to the display room from the duty office and took National Treasure No.247, a bronze statue of Bodhi-sattva.He broke the glass display in another room and stole two other artifacts. These were a Koryo celadon dish with inlaid patterns excavated from the Sea in front of Boryong in 1986, and a Koryo celadon inlaid with chrysanthemums, excavated from Hadae-ri, Gyaeryong-myeon, Kongju-si in the same year.Park stated, "The burglars suddenly assaulted me while I was reading a book in the duty office". That same day, two police officers were on duty in the office (ticketing office) 20 meters away from the duty office in the museum.However, they did not notice anything unusual.It took only 15 minutes for the burglars to get away with their prizes.

Police suspect that the crime was committed by a contract thief who secured an outlet in advance, because any cultural property designated as a National Treasure is impossible to sell on the open market.Considering the fact that the thieves did not enter the second floor exhibition area in which a closed-circuit TV (CCTV) was installed, it is presumed that they planned their crime in a professional manner.Park stated that the buglers were both about 170 centimeters tall, in their mid 30s, of slender build, and spoke in Gyeongsang province dialects.According to Park's statement, police have made a composite photo of the thief who was not wearing a mask and distributed it around the nation.Police also offered 20 million won for any leads as to the whereabouts of the criminals.

Problem Solving

How do you solve the following problems? Outline your assertion.

1.How did the two burglars attack the museum?

2.What can we do to ensure the security of a convention or exhibition premises?

Section C Format Writing

Acquaint yourself with the following. Finish the exercises that ensue.

Safety Requirements of Science Fair Rules 科技展覽會安全規章

It is essential that safety of the public be a prime consideration. Suitable precautions must be taken to help ensure that serious consequences do not result in terms of personal injury, property damage, or legal action.All exhibits MUST conform to the following standards which will be rigidly enforced by the Safety Officer.

General Safety

（a）Remove or otherwise shield all sharp edges or corners on prisms, mirrors, enclosures, glass and metal plates.

（b）Enclose hazardous exhibits with screens or shields.

（c）Hazardous exhibits must never be left unattended by the exhibitor.

（d）Lengths of hose or extension cords are to be kept to a minimum and out of the way to eliminate tripping hazards.Use tape to secure hoses and cords.

Fire Safety

（a）Heat sources must not be used near combustible materials.

（b）Open flames and heat sources must not be used unless protected and previously approved by the Science Fair Safety Officer.

Chemical Safety

(a) No toxic, corrosive or flammable chemicals or gasses are allowed unless approved by the Science Fair Safety Officer.In general, dangerous chemicals should be avoided.

(b) For exhibition, we recommend that substitutes be displayed in place of hazardous (toxic or flammable) chemicals actually used in the project.

For example, water can be substituted for flammable solvents and molasses can represent heavy petroleum products.

(c) When chemicals are simulated, they should be labelled with the names of the substances they represent followed by the word "simulated" in brackets.

i.e.ETHER (simulated) .

Electrical Safety

In general, all electrical circuits, fittings, cords, switches, etc. must conform to Canadian Standards Association regulations.In particular, please observe the following guidelines.

(a) Use only extension cords and appliance cords that are in good repair and have CSA approval.The Safety Officer will disallow use of unsafe cords.

(b) Use the lowest possible voltage.

(c) Where practical and necessary, it is recommended that pilot lights be used to indicate that voltage is on.

(d) An insulating grommet is required at the point where the electrical cord enters the enclosure.

(e) Electrical devices must be protectively enclosed where practical and the enclosure should be non-combustible.

(f) All non-current carrying metal parts of an electrical apparatus must be grounded. (g) No exposed live parts over 36 volts are allowed.

(h) Disconnect the power connection to your apparatus at the end of the day or the viewing period.

Structural and Mechanical Safety

(a) Construction of frame work, exhibits, displays, etc.must be of a safe design with adequate stability to keep them from tipping.

(b) Dangerous moving parts such as belts, gears, pulleys or fan blades must be suitably guarded.

Compressed Gasses

Exhibits using compressed gasses must have facilities for securing gas cylinders.Free standing cylinders or cylinders lying unsecured on the floor will not be allowed.

Lasers

All lasers used must have a power of 1 milliwatt or less. Precautions must be taken to ensure that the direct beam never reaches the eye of the observer.

THE SCIENCE FAIR SAFETY OFFICER WILL INSPECT EACH EXHIBIT AND DETERMINE WHETHER OR NOT AN EXHIBIT MAY BE DISPLAYED WITH OR WITHOUT FURTHER MODIFICATION.THE DECISION OF THE SAFETY OFFICER IS FINAL.

Questions about the Samples

Choose the best answers to the following questions based on your understanding of the format writing.

1.How many safety issues are mentioned?

A.Four

B.Two

C.Three

D.Five

2.Which of the following is not a general safety concern?

A.The physical appearance of the exhibits

B.Hazardous exhibits packaging

C.Hazardous exhibits storage

D.Safety consideration of hoses and cords

3.According to the safety requirements, what kind of exhibits will not be accepted?

A.Fireworks and paints

B.Computer monitor screens

C.Lawn lamps

D.Nutrition substitutes

Notes of Format

Always bear in mind the following.

安全規章是會展活動順利進行的基本保證。它是會展組織方尋找評估挑選承辦方的重要考慮因素之一。安全規章一般由會展承辦方起草。

撰寫安全規章應該主要考慮以下幾個方面：

1. 以條目的形式羅列注意事項。

2. 條目清楚，一條一事，分開羅列。

3. 句子段落寧短勿長，應儘量做到清晰簡潔。

4. 通俗易懂，一看便知。

5. 必須以大寫的形式明確授權安全保衛部門的最終否決權。

Do It Yourself

Work out a safety requirements for 2010 Shanghai Expo with the Chinese prompts.

Suppose you are to draft safety requirements for the 2010 Shanghai Expo, considering the following articles and items given in Chinese.

防火安全

1. 易燃、易爆物品必須有人照看。

2. 參展商必須熟悉會展中心滅火器具的位置。

3. 會展中心禁止明火。

展品安全

1. 所有參展品在保存時必須使用會展中心統一保存箱。

2. 參展商必須對自己展位上的展品負責。

所有展品都必須經過上海世博保安辦公室的檢查批准方可進入展區。上海世博保安辦公室的決定是最終決定。

Reference Answers

Reference Answers to My Solutions

Solution to problem 1 The two burglars suddenly assaulted the security guard while he was reading a book in the duty office.

Solution to problem 2 I think the security of premises can be ensured by providing alert security guards and anti-intrusion systems.

Answers to Questions about the Samples

1.D 2.C 3.A

Reference Answer to Do It Yourself

Fire Safety

1.Flammable and explosive items should not be left unattended.

2.Exhibitors must be familiar with the location of fire-fighting equipments at the venue.

3.Fire-making is forbidden at the venue.

Exhibit Safety

4.All exhibits should be stored within packing boxes provided by the venue.

5.Exhibitors should be responsible for the safety of items on their own stands or booths.

THE SHANGHAI 2010 EXPO SAFETY OFFICER WILL INSPECT EACH EXHIBIT AND DETERMINE WHETHER OR NOT AN EXHIBIT MAY BE DISPLAYED WITH OR WITHOUT FURTHER MODIFICATION. THE DECISION OF THE SAFETY OFFICER IS FINAL.

Chapter 14 Pre-Post Convention Tours 會前會後旅遊

▌Section A Reading Assignment

Warming-up Activity

Go over the following terms with your teacher.

professional association 專業協會	proposal 提議	online registration form 網上登記表	background information 背景訊息
travel arrangements 旅行安排	travel agency 旅行代理商	hotel reservations 飯店預訂	the letter of appointment 任命書

Pre-reading Questions

Answer the following questions without referring to the text.

1.Should there be any entertainment activities before or after a convention?

2.What kind of activities can you arrange for attendees before or after the convention?

3.How can you arrange a successful pre-or post-convention tour?

Text

Tour Proposals

There are thousands of associations, many being trade or professional associations, whose members meet periodically to keep abreast of developments in their fields.

A characteristic of conventions and meetings is that they lend themselves to be combined with a vacation trip before or after the convention.If individuals who attend a convention or meeting add the expense of this travel to what they would normally spend on a vacation, they can visit places usually too far from their regular vacation budget.

Conventions and meetings involving over 1,000 participants should probably be left to agencies specializing in this type of group because they have the necessary staff and computers required to efficiently handle this volume.

The meeting organizer should first of all send a proposal to the meeting planner in the hope of selling the services of the agency.A proposal consists basically three parts :

1.An introduction or background information about the travel agency.In this section, mention is made as to the qualifications of the travel agency proposing to handle the group in question.Usually this involves indicating what other groups the agency handled in the past, how long the agency has been in operation, a brief description of the experience of the persons that would be involved in the processing, etc.

2.An outline of the specific services that the agency proposes to provide for the group, such as travel arrangements, hotel reservations, etc.

3.An itemized list of the advantages of dealing through a travel agency versus dealing directly with the airlines, hotels, etc.It could be said that this part is both a teaching and selling tool.

It is an easy matter to customize this sample proposal for any potential group sponsor.The proposal usually takes the form of a letter sent to those in charge of clubs, associations, or other groups.As in all sales efforts, the letter is usually followed up by telephone calls requesting the opportunity to elaborate personally on the proposal.

Based on this proposal and many other requests for services, the agreement is reached and the sponsor sends an official letter to the meeting organizer appointing the travel agency the sole agent.This letter is essential in that it gives the agency the authority to approach airlines, hotels, and ground operators as the exclusive representative of the group.

An agency should contact the airlines, hotels, etc., even before sending out a proposal to determine if space is available and what the approximate costs will be.

Once the letter of appointment is received, the agency will immediately inform the airlines, hotels, etc.establishing itself as the sole agent for the group, in order to secure definite block space and obtain firm price commitment, if possible.

And the most important thing that should be done is to make a preliminary tour arrangement which contains an itinerary, rate as well as ways of registration.The following is a sample of a suggested pre-and post-meeting optional tours.

Please book your optional tours via the online registration form

Please note that tours will depart and return from/to the Palais de Congrés Convention Center.

PANORAMIC CITY TOUR OF PARIS

Tuesday April 12, 2005

13：30-17：30

Discover the main highlights of Paris! Visit the bustling Opera Square, the rue de la Paix, the majestic Place vendôme, the Grands Boulevards, where the major department stores are situated, the Madeleine church and the spectacular Concorde Square with its famous obelisk.Continue to the Champs Elysées, crowned by the Arch of Triumph with the tomb of the Unknown Soldier.From there, on to the residential Avenue Foch to the Trocadero for a spectacular view of the Eiffel Tower before going on to the imposing memorial of Les Invalides with the tombs of Napoleon and his son l'Aiglon.

Return to the Right Bank of the Seine via the Alexander III Bridge and continue along the Seine passing the French Academy, the Mint and the Conciergerie, the prison where Marie-Antoinette was held.

The tour then continues on the Left Bank of the Seine and through the Latin Quarter, traditionally the student area of the city. See the historical University of Paris, the Sorbonne, the Luxembourg Gardens of Italian influence, the Pantheon, where many of the great men of France are buried.Then on to the Bastille with the new Opera House and the Notre-Dame, the impressive masterpiece of Gothic architecture, impregnated with the history of Paris since its construction in 1163.

Drive through the Carrousel square and see the Louvre Museum with its new glass Pyramid surging gracefully in the middle of eight centuries of architecture.

Rate per person：Euro 22

VERSAILLES PALACE TOUR

Tuesday April 12, 2005

13：30-17：30

The present palace was established by the Sun King Louis XIV in 1668 during the golden age of French royalty.The palace was the government headquarters and the political center of France from 1682 to 1789 except during the Regency period.Versailles was the largest Palace in Europe and housed up to 20,000 people.

The guided tour includes the sumptuous main State Apartments and the Hall of Mirrors, where 17 great mirrors face the tall arched windows overlooking the gardens.Guests will have free time to wander in the magnificent formal gardens, designed by Le Nôtre, who broke the monotony of the original symmetrical layout with expanses of water and creative use of uneven ground.

Rate per person：Euro 58

FLEA MARKET TOUR

Sunday April 17, 2005

14：00-17：00

Enjoy a bustling and exhilarating tour to experience the true flavor of Parisian life, with time for a good browse around and a bargain hunt at the Flea market.Here, dealers sell everything from used kitchen utensils to vintage jeans, from Art Deco clocks to signed eighteenth-century Secretars—as the saying goes "everything but the kitchen sink"! Why spend a fortune on souvenirs when this kind of treasure hunt can be so much fun?

Rate per person：Euro 30

THE PICASSO MUSEUM & WALKING TOUR OF THE MARAIS

Monday April 18, 2005

09：00-13：30

Once an area of marshland as its name suggests, the Marais grew steadily in importance from the 14th century by virtue of its proximity to the Louvre, the preferred residence of Charles V. Its heyday was in the 17th century, when it became the fashionable area for the richer classes.They built many grand and sumptuous mansions as well as the "hotels" that still dot the Marais today.By the beginning of the 17th Century, the then Place Royale, now the famous Place des Vosges built by Henri IV, had become the focal point of the Marais. A walk under the remarkable arcades will allow you to discover its exceptional beauty.Strolling along the narrow streets of the Marais is a must during your stay in Paris.Several private mansions host famous museums, such as Carnavalet （whose exhibits trace the history of Paris from Roman times） and the Hotel Sale housing the Muse Picasso.

Visit the Picasso Museum.

Rate per person：EURO （） 43

NOTE：

All tours include entrance fees as per itinerary and touring in an air-conditioned bus with service of an English-speaking guide.

Rates for all tours are based on minimum 30 participants per tour.

Tour rates are subject to change in the event of statutory increase of VAT or museum entrance fees.

Changes in routes, departure/arrival times may occur for reasons beyond our control.

Comfortable walking shoes are recommended.

Group Discussion

Discuss the following topic in group.Select one on the team to make a presentation before the class.

What market concepts can be enhanced by online tools?

Guidelines for Discussion

— brand building

— direct marketing

— online commerce

— customer supporting

— market research

— product/service development and testing

Writing Activity

Summarize the text by outlining major points.Write a few lines about online marketing tools.

Section B Case Study

Read the following passage before solving the problems that ensue.

Tour 1.EXPO 2000-Excursion to Hannover （3 day tour） 11-13 October 2000

Registration Deadline：14 April 2000

The World Exposition EXPO 2000is probably the single most important event in Germany at the turn of the millennium.Between 1 June and 31 October 2000 more than 40 million visitors from all over the world are expected to come to Hannover.The motto of the EXPO 2000 "Humanity—Nature—Technology" promises a stimulating event.

Day 1 （Wednesday 11 October）

Transfer in the early afternoon from Frankfurt to the Hotel Pannonia in Hannover.

Dinner and overnight stay at the hotel.

Day 2 （Thursday 12 October）

Morning departure by coach to the EXPO where you will have the entire day at your disposal to discover the whole world of new ideas.

170 countries are expected to participate.Dinner and overnight stay at the hotel.

Day 3 （Friday 13 October）

Return to Frankfurt airport in the morning.

Price：EURO （€）620 per person （sharing twin/double room）

Single room supplement：EURO （ € ）141 per person for the entire stay （limited number available）

Minimum number of participants：25 persons

Check-in

Do you have any questions about the case study? If any, ask your teacher.

Important Vacabulary

excursion	[ɪkˈskɜːʃən]	n.	遠足
motto	[ˈmɒtəu]	n.	格言
stimulating	[ˈstɪmjuːleɪtɪŋ]	adj.	刺激的

Useful Expressions

at one's disposal	任由某人擺布（使用）

Problem Solving

How do you solve the following problems? Outline your assertion.

1.What information is missed in the brochure?

2.How can you solve the problem?

Section C Format Writing

Acquaint yourself with the following. Finish the exercises that ensue.

Post-meeting Tours Itinerary 會後旅遊路線

"Pearls of the Aegean"：Pergamon-Assos-Troy-Gallipoli

Date：01-03 July 2005

DAY 1.Transfer from your hotel to Istanbul Atatürk Airport for an evening flight to Izmir, birthplace of Homer.Meeting at Izmir airport and transfer to the hotel.Dinner and overnight.

DAY 2.After breakfast, drive to Pergamon.Visit the Aesculapium, the medical center built in the name of Aesculapius "God of Medicine". After lunch, continue to Pergamon Acropolis.Proceed to the antique city of Assos, where first human settlements go back to 4, 000 years ago.Visit the Temple of Athena, Agora and the Theatre. Overnight in Assos.

DAY 3.After breakfast, drive to Troy, famous for the legendary Trojan Horse and the first mythological beauty contest between the goddesses Aphrodite, Hera, and Athena that caused the Trojan War. Then on the way to Istanbul, visit the battle fields, the Anzac Cove, Cemeteries of the World War I, and other memorials at Gallipoli. Arrive at Istanbul and transfer to your hotel.

Price：

Per Person in a Double：$267

Single Room：　　　　$283

"Pearls of the Mediterranean"

Olympos（Chimera）-Phaselis-Termessos

Date：01-03 July 2005

DAY 1.Transfer from your hotel to Istanbul Atatürk Airport for the flight to Antalya.Meeting at Antalya Airport and transfer to the Türkmen Pension, "Tree House & Bungalows," at Olympos.Lunch at Ulupýnar Botanic Restaurant.After lunch, visit the remains of the ancient city of Olympos.After dinner at Türkmen Pension, Wine Party at Mt.Olympos（Chimera）.Overnight at Türkmen Pension.

DAY 2.After breakfast, tour to Phaselis, a harbour city and once a major commercial centre of the Mediterranean region.After lunch, tour to Termessos within the grounds of Termessos National Park near Antalya at a height of 1, 050 meters on the Taurus Mountains.Due to its strategic location like an eagle's nest, Alexander the Great failed to conquer it in 333 BC.Return to Olympos.Dinner and overnight at Türkmen Pension.

DAY 3.After breakfast, transfer to Antalya airport.

Price：

Per Person in a Double：$336

Single Room： $370

"Zümrüt" Village at the Küre Mountains

National Park, SGP Project Site

Date：01-03 July 2005

DAY 1.Early morning departure by minibus from Istanbul to Pýnarbapý via Safranbolu.Check-in and lunch at the Konak in Pýnarbapý.Afternoon visit the Ilýca Waterfalls and Valla Canyon. Dinner and overnight at the Konak, a 200 years old, wooden mansion, recently renovated for conservation and touristic purposes.

DAY 2.After breakfast, drive through a lush greenery uphill to Zümrüt Village.Meet the local people and enjoy the beauty of the Küre Mountains.Trekking with guidance is possible.Lunch at Zümrüt Village.Late afternoon return to Pýnarbapý.Dinner and overnight at the Konak.

DAY 3.After breakfast drive to Istanbul.Transfer to your hotel in Istanbul.

Price：

Per Person：$250 （on sharing a twin bedded room basis only）

Single rooms are not available and the tour price is valid for minimum 8 people.If the number of participants is less than 8, DER-TUR keeps the right to alter the tour price accordingly.

Tour prices include：

· Hotel accommodation, all breakfasts, meals and tours as specified in the programs

· English-speaking professional guide

· Airport-hotel-airport transfers as specified in the programs

· All entrance fees during the tours

· Air-conditioned private buses for the transfers and tours

Tour prices do not include：

· Istanbul-Izmir and Istanbul-Antalya-Istanbul domestic air tickets

(If you could make up your mind to join one of these tours early, please consult your travel agent before purchasing your international air ticket.You may save a considerable amount of money by including the domestic portion into your international air ticket instead of buying a separate one here)．

· Alcoholic and non-alcoholic drinks.

· Any personal expenses or those not mentioned in the programs.

Notes：

AC/WC：AC ＝ Air-conditioning 空調

WC ＝ water closet 廁所

Do It Yourself

Create a summary itinerary for the Detailed Passenger Itinerary given below.

Detailed Passenger Itinerary

08：00 AM Board your coach for a garden trip in Suzhou.Today, two garden tours and a lunch will be provided in addition to a guided tour of the area.

10：00 AM Arrive at the Humble Administrator's Garden. Here you will have a tour and enjoy the traditional Chinese art of gardening.Plenty of time will be given for picture taking.

11：30 AM A Chinese style lunch will be provided at a cozy lakeside restaurant.

01：00 PM Arrive at Liu Yuan garden.

02：00 PM Arrive at Lion's grove.

03：30 PM Get back home to Shanghai! We hope you will enjoy your garden tour!

Reference Answers

Reference Answers to Problem Solving

1.It failed to provide the information about the services included in each price.

2.I can solve the problem by listing out services which can be available in the price as：

The price per person includes the following services：

· travel in modern coach with AC/WC as per itinerary

· accommodation for two nights in a four-star hotel—double room, incl.breakfast

· three course dinner at the hotel on 11 and 12 October 2000, excl.beverages

· English-speaking tour guide for the entire tour

· entrance fee to EXPO 2000

· service charges and V.A.T.

Reference Answer to Do It Yourself

Enjoy a wonderful day of garden tours in Suzhou! Enjoy your scenic ride and guided tour of the city before you tour and appreciate the traditional Chinese art of Garden building. Have lunch at a lakeside Chinese restaurant, and return home with a cherished memory of the finest gardens in China.

Chapter 15 Event Evaluation 會展評估

Section A Reading Assignment

Warming-up Activity

Go over the following terms with your teacher.

convention management 會議管理	post-convention critique 會後鑑定	face-to-face meeting 面對面的會晤	pre-convention meeting 預備會
convention coordinator 會議協調員	departmental executive 部門主管	positive and negative reaction 積極和消極反應	post-convention meeting 總結會
after-the-fact review 紀實性審查	convention performance 會議	evaluation meeting 評估會	off-site visitor survey 場外參觀者調查

Pre-reading Questions

Answer the following questions without referring to the text.

1.How do you know whether your convention or exhibition is a success or failure?

2.What should be considered when doing a post-convention evaluation?

3.How can you get to know whether the attendees are satisfied or not?

Text

Event Evaluation Approaches

Following the philosophy that the buyer and seller are partners in successful convention management, there are an increasing number of convention buyers who wish to provide a post-convention critique to executives of the headquarters facility.

In some instances, the convention buyers will review in writing, point by point, his or her appraisal of the performance of the staff at the headquarters hotel/motor inn.This will also include a detailed analysis of the property's physical equipment, conditions of the function rooms, etc., and, most importantly, the buyer can evaluate the ability of the hotel's or motor inn's personnel to cope with any unforeseen emergencies that may have arisen during the convention.

While the written analysis is beneficial, a face-to-face meeting with the same department heads who attended the pre-convention meeting is infinitely more advantageous.Rather than having the convention coordinator, sales director, or general manager serve as a catalyst to advise the department heads of the customer's reaction—both negative and positive—the department heads are afforded the opportunity to hear the report directly from the buyer.

Within the spirit of positive cooperation, the key departmental executives should also have the opportunity to advise the meeting planner of the property's positive and negative reactions to the convention.Obviously, since the buyer is the buyer, negative criticism must be tinted with diplomacy.However, intelligent professional meeting planners are appreciative of learning ways and means by which they can conduct better meetings in the future.

Post-convention meetings can be most helpful to both buyer and seller when the information exchanged is factual rather than emotional, when both sides endeavor to avoid dealing in individual personalities, and when the attitude of mutual cooperation and mutual improvement is present.

The post convention meeting described above serves as an excellent after-the-fact review of the positive and negatives of the convention performance.While the review of the negatives of the convention can be an educational experience and hopefully eliminate problems in the future, it normally has little, if any, effect in our ability to rebook a group if they have had a significant number of complaints.

Visitor satisfaction is the essential factor influencing the possibility of rebooking.Therefore having a clear view of the visitor's reaction is fairly important.Follow-up letters and questionnaires are the most popularly used tool to solicit visitors' responses.

Questionnaires can also be helpful in pinpointing areas where improvements may be needed—particularly with respect to staff attitudes, courtesy and all around service.

When problems arise during a convention, the delegates do not—and should not—be concerned with who is at fault.Too often, valuable time that could be used to correct the problem is spent in discussing who is at fault.Professional meeting planners, working together equally with professional hotel or motor inn sales executives, can operate as a team to eliminate the problem as expeditiously as possible.Hopefully, they can resolve the difficulty before the general membership even knew a problem existed.

Whether by self-completed questionnaire or direct interview, on-site or off-site visitor surveys provide the most useful information for evaluating a convention.They are relatively easy and inexpensive to take and analyze, at least at a basic level ; however, they do present challenges of design, sampling and interpretation.There are some essential requirements for visitor surveys, and if they can't be met it is better not to attempt one.

Evaluators can have a lot of fun playing with various measures of customer satisfaction, preference, and problems experienced.These questions must be adapted to the particular needs of your convention. At the simplest level, are open-ended questions asking visitors to state likes, dislikes, problems and suggestions.Some generally applied in a questionnaire may include the following :

Please tell us about any problems you have experienced at the convention.

What did you particularly like about the convention?

What did you particularly dislike about the convention?

Do you have any suggestions for improving the event?

What else would you like the event offer in the future?

An evaluation meeting is another very popular and effective way to get information exchanged about future improvement.The members of an evaluation meeting should be the same people who attended the pre-convention meeting.The following mistakes should be avoided when conducting an appraisal of an employee :

· Don't focus on one specific incident—review the entire cycle that the appraisal covers.

· Don't rely solely on memory—base the review on accurate and factual data.Use TOOL 7 （Incident Report） often for documenting good and poor behavior during the evaluation cycle.

· Avoid the "halo" and "horns" effects.Just because the employee performs badly in one area does not make their overall performance bad.The same goes for good performance.

· Length of service or job grade does not necessarily mean better performance.Look carefully at the individual's performance within that job.

· Avoid bias about an employee based on your personal feelings for that individual.

· Don't base current performance on past performance.Look at the cycle currently being reviewed.

· Don't overrate a poor performer as a motivational tool.

· Not all individuals are the same.Analyze each employee carefully ; each employee should be rated without consideration of any other employee.

· Don't rush through the appraisal.Take time to record accurate information, which truly reflects the individual's performance.

· Don't be afraid to provide truthful information.

A post convention meeting should be held with the same people who attended the pre-convention meeting.The purpose of a post-convention meeting is to evaluate what worked and what did not, review the bills and solicit feedback immediately from the facility. The following should be considered when doing an evaluation of a convention :

· Ask your attendees to provide feedback about the program content and format, meeting facility, speakers, meal functions and other special activities.

· Administer evaluations immediately after the meeting, while opinions are still fresh and your staff can be present to collect the information.Otherwise, mail surveys or evaluations from the meeting so they are on participants' desks when they return to work.

· Solicit feedback from the meeting sponsor.Determine if meeting goals were met, the financial implications of the meeting and steps to be taken to follow up on the results.Consider a more formal measurement tool to measure a meeting's return on investment.Some ways to approach this：

· Consider the unique goals of individual meetings that could be measured.

· Test attendees before and after training sessions to document how much and what was learned.

· Provide a written report of the meeting for the files and to senior management.

· File contracts for future meetings.

· Write thank-you letters to staff, speakers, hotel staff and other vendors.

· Share Return on Investment （ROI） information with senior.

Check-in

Do you have any questions about the text? If any, ask your teacher.

Important Vocabulary

critique	[krɪˈtiːk]	n.	審定，評論
appraisal	[əˈpreɪzl]	n.	評價，評估
unforeseen	[ˌʌnfɔːˈsiːn]	adj.	未預見到的
advantageous	[ˌædvənˈteɪdʒəs]	adj.	具有優勢的
coordinator	[kəʊˈɔːdɪneɪtə]	n.	協調員
catalyst	[ˈkætəlɪst]	n.	有感染力的人
diplomacy	[dɪˈpləʊməsɪ]	n.	外交手段
appreciative	[əˈpriːʃɪətɪv]	adj.	有鑑賞力的
endeavor	[ɪnˈdevə]	v.	努力，盡力
eliminate	[ɪˈlɪmɪneɪt]	v.	消去，淘汰
pinpoint	[ˈpɪnˌpɒɪnt]	v.	找出，找到
expeditiously	[ˌekspɪˈdɪʃəslɪ]	ad.	迅速地，敏捷地

Useful Expressions

evaluation questionnaire	評估調查問卷
online evaluation	網上評估
evaluation method	評估方法

Language Focus

1.While the written analysis is beneficial, a face-to-face meeting with the same department heads who attended the pre-convention meeting is infinitely more advantageous.

雖然書面分析很有用，但是與參加預備會的部門主管們舉行一次見面會卻更有好處。

2.When problems arise during a convention the delegates do not—and should not—be concerned with who is at fault.

會議在舉辦的過程中如果出現什麼問題，代表不會而且也不應該考慮是誰的過失。

3.The purpose of a post-convention meeting is to evaluate what worked and what did not, review the bills and solicit feedback immediately from the facility.

總結會的目的是為了評估會議舉辦過程中哪些起作用了、哪些沒有，審查帳目以及立即瞭解承辦單位的回饋意見。

Group Discussion

Discuss the following topic in group.Select one on the team to make a presentation before the class.

What should be discussed at an evaluation meeting?

Guidelines for Discussion

▬ what worked and what did not work

▬ evaluating bills

▬ convention facility

▬ coordination

▬ equipment renting

▬ reception

▬ reservation

▬ security and safety

▬ food and beverage

Writing Activity

Summarize the text by outlining major points.Write a few lines about convention evaluation tools.

Section B Case Study

Read the following passage before solving the problems that ensue.

Follow up on the Japanese Propaganda Exhibition in Perkins

Hello Community member, yesterday, Zhao Wei, Luo Jun and I went to the library to represent the deep concerns on the Japanese propaganda piece in the perkins hallway exhibition.The librarians explained their purpose and allowed to change the description a little bit.While we wholeheartedly agree with the value of library archives, we are still deeply concerned that lack of accompanying historical information with this part of the exhibit will in fact mislead the viewer and thereby compromise its original educational purpose.

As the elected president of DCSSA, I submitted a letter to Chronicle to express our concerns and also to provide the necessary historical background of the exhibition for further education purpose. Besides, we also request Chronicle to report the issue as news to draw more attention.

I also want to urge your support on the activities either by dropping your opinions online or leaving comments on Perkin's comments book.If you have further suggestions, pls feel free to let me know.

Finally, I want to thank Zhao Wei and Luo Jun for their contribution.

Jiayu Song

elected president of DCSSA

Problem Solving

How do you solve the following problems? Outline your assertion.

1.What is the purpose of the follow up letter?

2.What kind of follow up letter is it?

Section C Format Writing

Acquaint yourself with the following. Finish the exercises that ensue.

Evaluation Meeting and Report 評估會議和評估報告

Sample 1

Objectives of the Meeting

☐ To ascertain strengths and weaknesses of the fair

☐ To improve future programs

Activities

Review the goals of the section as stated in the Units.

Discuss the following questions：

a.Were these goals met?

b.If they were not, why not?

c.What were the reactions to the sharing sessions？ （Identify the reactions as specifically as possible.）

d.Were the resources and facilities adequate?

In the light of the above discussion, discuss the following questions：

a.What areas of sharing need to be strengthened?

b.How can this be done?

Summarize the discussion

Sample 2

TO：

Directors and all Sales, Finance, and Technical Staff

FROM：Alain Nikro

Re：

Report on the Fifth Annual International Computer Exhibition, Hong Kong, 1-8 April

The exhibit was extremely successful for us again this year, as it has been in the past.Our new models received an enthusiastic response and orders were high.There were, however, two problems we should address before they begin to adversely affect out business at the exhibition.

First, the size of our stand at the exhibition was the same as last year's （700 square feet）, even though we added three new models to our line.This made our exhibit extremely crowded.

Second, our exhibit was staffed only with sales representatives. Therefore, when customers—who are becoming increasingly sophisticated—had a technical question, the sales reps were usually unable to answer it.

Therefore, I suggest the following.Next year we should increase the size of the stand to 900 square feet in order to accommodate the new models and to give customers sufficient room to examine them.

We should also make sure that there is at least one technician at the exhibit at times, to provide technical information and advice to customers.Please let me know your reactions to these suggestions.

Questions about the Samples

Complete the statements or choose the best answers to the following questions based on your understanding of the format writing.

1.Who will value the results of the survey?

A.The convention center

B.The convention center and hotels

C.The hotels

D.The convention bureau

2.What are the goals of the evaluation meeting?

A.To evaluate the bills

B.To evaluate the profits and losses and future chances

C.To evaluate the bills and performances

D.To evaluate the performances

3.At the international computer exhibition, the company put on three _____ at the stand.

4.The reporter suggested the company should have a _____ at the stand at the next exhibition.

5.The reason to increase the size of the stand is _____.6.The reason to have a technician at the stand is _____.

Notes of Format

Always bear in mind the following.

Evaluation Report

評估報告格式說明與註解

```
                           Memo
FROM：
TO：
SUBJECT：
DATE：

                          （Body）
```

Notes：

1. 成功之處。

2. 不足之處。

3. 改進意見。

調查問卷

調查問卷是一種常見的商務文書，廣泛地應用於各種商業企業市場營銷活動之中。調查問卷通常用來瞭解顧客對某家企業的某種產品或者服務的意見和建議。是企業對其現有市場的一種真切瞭解，同時也是預測其未來市場潛力的一種有效的工具。

會展業中調查問卷的使用是會展承辦單位維繫與會展主辦單位之間長期合作關係的一個很重要的方法，根據對調查問卷所收集的顧客資訊的正確解讀，會展承辦單位可以進一步完善其服務，以維持與會展主辦單位之間的長期合作關係。設計調查問卷時應該注意以下幾點：

1. 格式整齊美觀。

2. 必須註明發出調查問卷的單位名稱以及負責人姓名。

3. 必須註明發出調查問卷的具體日期和時間。

4. 需要顧客評估的項目要切合產品與服務的實際情況。

5. 應該向被調查對象說明回收問卷的方法。

6. 應該給調查對象留有一定的自由發表意見的空間。

Do It Yourself

Work out a questionnaire.

Suppose you are the executive of Sales Department of Marriot Hotel.You are to design a questionnaire soliciting convention attendees' reactions to the service and performance of your hotel.

Reference Answers

Answers to Questions about the Samples

1.D

2.B

3.new models

4.technician

5.to accommodate the new models and to give customers sufficient room to examine them

6.to provide technical information and advice to customers

Reference Answer to Do It Yourself

A detailed post-convention questionnaire asks the customer to evaluate the service and performance of a variety of different departments in the hotel :

To _____ Date _____

Re：_____ Date at C.H.H._____

Anthony M.Rey

President & Managing Director

Marriot

Detailed Evaluation	Excellent	Good	Fair	Poor
Confirmed Reservations	_____	_____	_____	_____
Attitude of Room Clerks	_____	_____	_____	_____
Attitude of Cashiers	_____	_____	_____	_____
Attitude of Bellman	_____	_____	_____	_____
Attitude of Sales Personnel	_____	_____	_____	_____
Banquet Meals	_____	_____	_____	_____
Public Dining Rooms	_____	_____	_____	_____
Cocktail Lounges	_____	_____	_____	_____
Room Service	_____	_____	_____	_____
Meeting Room arrangements	_____	_____	_____	_____
Housekeeping	_____	_____	_____	_____
Attitude of Chambermaids	_____	_____	_____	_____
Elevator Service	_____	_____	_____	_____
Exhibits	_____	_____	_____	_____

Any comments on service of Departments not listed will be appreciated and may be made.Would you recommend our Convention and Exhibition Hall?

_____

Chapter 16 Handling Problems and Complaints 會展問題與投訴處理

Section A Reading Assignment

Warming-up Activity

Go over the following terms with your teacher.

exhibitor 參展商	attendee 參加人員	convention 會議	complaint 投訴	resolution 決定	attentive 關心的	hostility 敵意
organizer 組織者	satisfactory 滿意的	category 類別	concierge 接待員	recur 反覆發生	log 記錄	defer 延期
monitor 監管	defensiveness 防衛心理	tabulate 製成表格	proactive〈心理〉前攝的（指先知資料較後知資料佔優勢的）			

Pre-reading Qestions

Answer the following questions without referring to the text.

1.What problems may exhibitors or attendees complain about?

2.What resolution guidelines should be kept in mind when convention and exhibition staff handles guest complaints?

3.What's the follow-up to guest complaints?

Text

Handling Problems and Complaints

Exhibitors and attendees will occasionally be disappointed or find fault with something or someone at the convention and exhibition center and make complaints of the recurring problems.The organizer should be especially attentive to those with complaints and should seek a timely and satisfactory resolution to the problem.

Guest complaints can be separated into four categories of problems : mechanical, attitudinal, service-related, and unusual. Guests may complain about the electrical service, the Internet and telecommunications services, utilities （air, water and drain） services, computer rentals, and parking service.They may also find difficulty in the ATM, gift shop, concierge service, and business center.

All complaints deserve attention.When exhibitors and attendees find it easy to express their opinions, both sides benefit.The organizer learns of potential or actual problems and can resolve them.And by handling those problems positively, the organizer can avoid such problems recurring.

When it comes to the art of handling guest complaints, convention and exhibition management and staff should keep some resolution guidelines in mind.The staff must not react personally : he/she is a representative of the convention and exhibition center seeking a solution to a difficult situation.When attacked, the staff must stay calm and avoid responding with hostility or defensiveness.The staff must not argue with the guest.The staff must be aware of the guest's self-esteem, show a personal interest in the problem, using the guest's name frequently and taking the complaint seriously.The management and staff's undivided attention must be given to the guest.The staff must concentrate on the problem, not on placing blame or insulting the guest.Whenever possible, complaints which are complicated or threaten to cause a crisis should be delivered to a manager with time to isolate the complaining guest.

The staff must demonstrate that he/she is proactive and sincere about solving the problem.The staff must initially allow the guest to explain the situation fully and "let off steam" without interrupting.The staff must attempt to bring the conversation around to the specific cause of the complaint, discarding unimportant elaborations.

Notes should be taken : it slows the guest down, forcing him to order his thoughts rationally and it demonstrates a sincere intention to take action.The staff must ensure that a note has been generated to the guest prior to departure, signed by a person in authority, expressing regret for the incident.The staff should avoid complicating the situation or allowing the guest to do so.The solution must be in balance with the situation, must not be "overkill".5

The staff must tell the guest what can be done and offer choices. The staff must not promise the impossible or exceed his authority. The time must be taken to check the feasibility of the solution before the staff takes action.The staff must set an approximate time for completion of corrective actions, but not underestimate the amount of time it will take to resolve the problem.

The progress of the corrective action must be monitored even if the complaint was resolved by someone else.The staff must follow up to ensure that action has, in fact, been taken at the time convenient to the guest.The staff must contact the guest to ensure that the problem was resolved satisfactorily.The staff must ensure that no elements of the original complaint will recur in the solution.

The staff must report the entire event, the actions taken, and the resolution of the incident.The incident must be documented fully and becomes a permanent record.

Log books can help convention and exhibition centers identify complaints, as can guest comment cards or questionnaires.6Specific departments of convention and exhibition centers provide comment card questions.Within each department, it lists the specific questions guests are asked, with their individual responses tabulated.

Convention and exhibition centers may also use log books to initiate corrective action, verify that guest complaints have been resolved, and identify recurring problems.This comprehensive written record may also let management contact guests who may still be dissatisfied with some aspect of their stay at tear-down.After the guest has departed, a letter from the customer affairs manager expressing regret about the incident is usually sufficient to promote goodwill and demonstrate concern for guest satisfaction.It may be a good policy for the customer affairs manager to telephone a departed guest to get a more complete description of the incident.

Only in this way can the convention and exhibition center staff solve the problem for the guest and get the satisfactory solution to the problem.

Check-in

Do you have any questions about the text? If any, ask your teacher.

Important Vocubulary

complaint	[kəm'pleɪnt]	n.	投訴
exhibitor	[ˌeksɪ'bɪtə]	n.	參展商
attendee	[əˌten'diː]	n.	參加人員
recur	[rɪ'kɜː]	v.	反覆發生
timely	['taɪmlɪ]	a.	及時的
mechanical	[mɪ'kænɪkl]	a.	技術上的
attitudinal	[ˌætɪ'tjuːdɪnəl]	a.	態度的
utilities	[juː'tɪlətɪ]	n.	水電氣等設施
rental	['rentl]	n.	租賃
concierge	[ˌkɒnsɪ'eəʒ]	n.	接待處
hostility	[hɒ'stɪlətɪ]	n.	敵對態度
defensiveness	[dɪ'fensɪvnɪs]	n.	防衛心理
self-esteem	[ˌselfɪ'stiːm]	n.	自尊
proactive	[prəu'æktɪv]	a.	主動的；積極的
discard	[dɪ'skɑːd]	v.	剔除，拋棄
elaboration	[ɪˌlæbə'reɪʃən]	n.	渲染，說明
rationally	['ræʃnəlɪ]	adv.	理性地
overcomplicate	['əuvəkɔmplɪkeɪt]	v.	過分複雜化

overkill	['əuvəkɪl]	v.	懲罰過度
feasibility	[ˌfiːzə'bɪlətɪ]	n.	可行性
underestimate	[ˌʌndə'estɪmeɪt]	v.	低估
monitor	['mɒnɪtə]	v.	監視，留心
identify	[aɪ'dentɪfaɪ]	v.	明確，找出
tabulate	['tæbjuleɪt]	v.	表格化
initiate	[ɪ'nɪʃɪeɪt]	v.	提出
tear-down	['tɛədaun]	n.	拆卸

Useful Expressions

find fault with	找毛病，挑剌
be attentive to	關注
resolution to	解決方案
keep in mind	謹記
show a personal interest in	表現出對……感興趣
undivided attention	全神貫注
let off steam	出出氣，發洩一下
bring the conversation around to	引導到……話題上
take action	採取行動
prior to	在……之前
be in balance with	與……相當
set an approximate time for	設定合適的時間
log books	工作記錄
corrective action	改正措施
customer affairs manager	客戶服務經理

Language Focus

1.When attacked, the staff must stay calm, avoiding responding with hostility or defensiveness.

受到投訴時，員工要保持冷靜，不要採取敵對或防衛的態度。

2.Whenever possible, complaints which are complicated or threatening crisis should be deferred to a manager with time to isolate the complaining guest.

比較複雜的投訴問題或者重大的問題盡可能轉交給經理，由經理與投訴者單獨溝通。

3.The staff must attempt to bring the conversation around to the specific cause of the complaint, discarding unimportant elaborations.

接待投訴者的員工應該設法在談話中找出投訴的具體原因，剔除那些無關緊要的敘述與解釋。

4.The staff should avoid overcomplicating the situation or allowing the guest to do so.

接待人員應該避免使問題複雜化，也要避免客人這樣做。

5.The solution must be in balance with the situation, must not be "overkill".

解決方案應該以能解決問題為適度，不可過度。

6.Log books can help convention and exhibition centers identify complaints, as can the guest comment cards or questionnaires.

工作記錄有助於管理者找出問題。客人的評價表和問卷也有同樣的功能。

Group Discussion

Discuss the following topic in group. Select one on the team to make a presentation before the class.

How would you receive a complaining guest?

Guidelines for Discussion

__ How would you greet the guest?

■ What attitude would you adopt toward the guest?

■ What would you say if the guest is angry?

■ How would you find what the problem is?

What would you do when the guest is complaining?

■ What would you do after you find the cause of the problem?

What would you do if you have reported the problem to the manager?What else do you think is necessary to win the guest over?

Writing Activity

Summarize the text by outlining major points.Write a few lines about handling guest complaints using the following expressions.

Vocabulary

make complaints of 抱怨	be attentive to 認真傾聽/觀察	the comprehensive written record 完整的記錄
be a representative of 代表	be aware of 留意	handle the problems positively 積極正確處理問題
the recurring problem 反覆出現的問題	argue with 爭辯	a person in authority 主管者，有職權的人
identify complaints 弄清楚投訴內容	take action 採取措施	order his thoughts rationally 理性地考慮問題
resolution guidelines		處理方針
react personally		親自回覆
stay calm		保持冷靜
take the complaint seriously		認真對待投拆
concentrate on the problem		把注意力集中在問題上
full explanation		完整的解釋
the specific cause of the complaint		投訴的具體原因
take notes		作記錄
an alternative solution		另外一種解決方案
the solution in balance with the situation		與情況相匹配的處理
monitor corrective action		監督補救行動
report the entire event		報告整起事件

Expressions

· It may be a good policy for the customer affairs manager to telephone a departed guest to get a more complete description of the incident.

· A letter from the customer affairs manager expressing regret about the incident is usually sufficient to promote goodwill and demonstrate concern for guest

satisfaction.

· Time must be taken to check the feasibility of the solution before the staff takes action.

· The staff must ensure that no element of the original complaint will recur in the solution.

· When it comes to the art of handling guest complaints, convention and exhibition management and staff should keep some resolution guidelines in mind.

Section B Case Study

Read the following passage before solving the problems that ensue.

ABC Convention Corporation Guest Satisfaction Questionnaire

Dear Guest,

We are delighted to have you with us and hope you are pleased with our facilities and services.It is our aim to create and maintain a courteous and friendly atmosphere for you to enjoy.

We are always looking for guest feedback and would appreciate it if you could take some time to fill in this questionnaire.Whether you leave the completed questionnaire at the reception desk or mail it back to us, I can assure you that it will receive my personal attention and follow-up.

Thank you for your kind assistance.

John W Howard

Customer Affairs Manager

Registration Services. Was it prompt and courteous?

Excellent	☐
Good	☐
Satisfactory	☐
Insufficient	☐
Below standard	☐

Your comments：

Venue Services. Were your exhibits well looked after?

Excellent	☐
Good	☐
Satisfactory	☐
Insufficient	☐
Below standard	☐

Your comments：

Move-in Services. Was the staff helpful?

Excellent	☐
Good	☐

Satisfactory   ☐

Insufficient   ☐

Below standard   ☐

Your comments :

Telecommunication Services （Telephone and Internet）. Were your messages handled efficiently?

Excellent   ☐

Good   ☐

Satisfactory   ☐

Insufficient   ☐

Below standard   ☐

Your comments :

Temperature, Lighting and Plumbing Services. Were you comfortable?

Excellent   ☐

Good   ☐

Satisfactory   ☐

Insufficient   ☐

Below standard   ☐

Your comments :

Move-out Services. Was the staff helpful?

Excellent	☐
Good	☐
Satisfactory	☐
Insufficient	☐
Below standard	☐

Your comments：

Concierge Services. Did we do everything to assist you?

Excellent	☐
Good	☐
Satisfactory	☐
Insufficient	☐
Below standard	☐

Your comments：

Restaurant Services. Was it to your satisfaction?

Excellent	☐
Good	☐
Satisfactory	☐
Insufficient	☐
Below standard	☐

Your comments :

Room Facilities. Was it clean, comfortable and properly supplied?

Excellent ☐

Good ☐

Satisfactory ☐

Insufficient ☐

Below standard ☐

Your comments :

In-house Services （including porter, laundry etc.）. Were your personal possessions well looked after?

Excellent ☐

Good ☐

Satisfactory ☐

Insufficient ☐

Below standard ☐

Your comments :

Individual Employee. How well did we respond to your needs?

Excellent ☐

Good ☐

Satisfactory ☐

Insufficient ☐

Below standard ☐

Your comments :

Check-out Services. Did it go smoothly?

Excellent ☐

Good ☐

Satisfactory ☐

Insufficient ☐

Below standard ☐

Your comments :

Shuttle Bus. Was it on time? Did it run frequently enough?

Excellent ☐

Good ☐

Satisfactory ☐

Insufficient ☐

Below standard ☐

Your comments :

If you return to this location, would you choose to stay with us again?

Yes ☐

No ☐

If no, please comment ： ☐

Do you have any further suggestions or comments which would help us to make your next visit more enjoyable?

Did you miss any services or facilities?

Your name （please print） _____

Home address _____

City _____ State/Province _____ Postal Code _____

Date of Arrival _____ Room No _____.

E-mail ： customeraffair @ ABCCC.com

Internet ABC Convention Corporation

Http://www.ABCCC.com

Check-in

Do you have any questions about the case study? If any, ask your teacher.

prompt	[ˈprɒmpt]	a.	及時的
courteous	[ˈkɜːtɪəs]	a.	禮貌的
insufficient	[ˌɪnsəˈfɪʃnt]	a.	不足的
plumbing	[ˈplʌmɪŋ]	n.	（布置）管線
possessions	[pəˈzeʃnz]	n.	財產
shuttle	[ˈʃʌtl]	n.	通勤車
follow-up	[ˈfɒləʊˌʌp]	n.	隨訪・回訪
feedback	[ˈfiːdbæk]	n.	反饋
in-house services			店內服務
be delighted to			高興
Customer Affairs			客戶服務部
stay with			住在
take some time to			花時間
postal code			郵政編碼

Problem Solving

How do you solve the following problems? Outline your assertion.

1.The guest thinks the registration service is insufficient.

2.The guest complains about the negligence of the venue service.

Section C Format Writing

Acquaint yourself with the following. Finish the exercises that ensue.

Reply to a Guest Complaint 回覆投訴信

Mr.Jeffery Jones

2800 Founder Drive

Florence, SC 29501

June 19, 2005

Dear Mr.Jones,

Thank you for your letter regarding your recent attendance at our convention and exhibition center.

We were dismayed to learn of the difficulties you encountered during the exhibition.You are absolutely correct in saying that an exhibition can be marred by poor service.The lack of attentive service which you described is totally contrary to ACEC standards of courtesy and etiquette.Please accept our sincere apologies for any inconvenience.Please rest assured that your letter has been forwarded to the general manager, and will be the focus of his immediate attention.

We hope that this incident does not diminish your favorable regard of ACEC.We would like to have the opportunity to better serve you, and look forward to welcoming

you again soon.

Sincerely yours,

Consumer Affairs Manager

Michael Longfellow

Cc : general manager

Questions about the Writing Sample

Complete the following statements based on the sample.

1._____ is the man who complained to the company.

2.The complaint is about the _____ at ACEC.

3.The complaint letter has been given to _____ who will deal with the complaint.

4.The complainant lives in _____.

Notes of Format

Always bear in mind the following.

投訴信格式說明與註解

```
Address


                                                            Date
Salutation
Body
    ( express thanks
    acknowledge the complaint
    explain the corrective action
    express intention to maintain business )


Signature
Cc：
```

Notes：

1. 投訴信回覆時應使用恰當的稱謂；

2. 儘量避免長篇推託之辭或進行複雜的解釋，因為客人對服務方的法規和政策並不感興趣；

3. 儘量安撫客戶；

4. 如果可能的話給客人提供適當的補償以示誠意；

5. 承諾下次不再發生類似情況；

6. 誠意邀請客人能再次光臨；

7. 投訴回覆信應由會展服務中心負責人來寫並且要簽名。

Do It Yourself

Work out an answer to the complaint letter with the Chinese prompts.

紐約會展中心客戶服務部經理 Rodger Johnson 回覆客戶 Jeffery Jones 關於會展租用設備的投訴。請根據投訴回覆信的格式，以客戶服務部經理 Rodger Johnson 的名義給客戶 Jeffery Jones 寫一封回信。

Interpretation

Read the following to your partner for him or her to put them down in Chinese or English.

1. 如果您對預訂有什麼特殊要求，請與預訂經理聯繫。

2. 為表示我們的歉意，我為您下一次惠顧本店提供 200 元的優惠。

3. 酒店對客人的隨訪信函應該在三週內發出。

4. 請相信，我們的總經理很快就會與您聯繫的。

5 您在酒店房間內的個人物品丟失了。對於您的不滿我們深表理解。

6.As a matter of policy, the hotel cannot compensate you for your loss, as the hotel cannot be held liable for the care and custody of valuables not placed within the hotel's safety deposit boxes.

7.The claim should be directed to the appropriate insurance carrier, or the guest should be notified whether the claim will be honored.

8.We hope we will have the opportunity to welcome you back to our hotel, when we can demonstrate our usual high standards of service and facilities.

9.I would like to point out that the brochure also makes it clear that we require adequate notice because we need to make special arrangements.

10.Complaining customers can become your most loyal guests if dealt with correctly and can also point out problems you may be unaware of.

Translation

Read the following passages to yourself and render them into Chinese or English.

Passage 1

Two common complaints of exhibitors are the hours of the exhibit hall scheduled to be open and the method in which guest rooms are assigned.Exhibitors feel that exhibit hours should be shorter and that delegates should have free time from meetings during the day to browse through the exhibit area.Many are annoyed at the long days of sitting all day and that there is too little time left to make their important business appointments, which is why they came to the convention.

The assigning of guest rooms is another source of exhibitor discontent.When forced to stay in a different hotel other than the delegates, the exhibitors naturally find it more difficult to transact and close, important evening sales.One solution is for the hotel to rent its smaller meeting rooms to exhibitors for evening hours.This arrangement would help delegates, exhibitors and hotels.

Passage 2

來信收悉。信中談到您來本酒店下榻期間遭受裝修噪聲干擾一事，對此我們深表關切。我們一直努力為客人提供完備的設施，也努力做到環境的安寧。但是，酒店為保證質量和形象，需要定期進行維修。我們一般是在每年的 4 月 10 日至 9 月 10 日之間進行，這期間是本地的淡季，住店客人較少。儘管事出有因，但我們還是對給您造成的不便，真誠地表示歉意。希望這件不愉快的事情不會影響您對本酒店的惠顧。希望您能再次光臨本店，享用本酒店引以為豪的各種設施。我們期待著再次為您服務。

Reference Answers

Answers to Questions about the Samples

1.Mr.Jeffery Jones

2.poor service

3.the general manager

4.Florence

Reference Answer to Do It Yourself

Mr.Jeffery Jones

2800 Founder Drive

Florence, SC 29501

June 19, 2005

Dear Mr.Jones,

Thank you for your letter regarding your recent stay at our convention and exhibition center.

It was with dismay that we learned of the difficulties you encountered.You are absolutely correct in saying that all the facilities should always be functioning in the exhibition floor.Proper maintenance and engineering should always be present in a superior convention and exhibition center.Please accept our most sincere apologies for any inconvenience.

Please rest assured that your letter and comments have been forwarded to the general manager, Mr.Smith, and will be the focus of his immediate attention.

We hope that this incident does not diminish your favorable regard of our convention and exhibition center.We would like to have the opportunity to better serve you, and look forward to welcoming you again soon.

Yours Sincerely

Roger Johnson

Consumer Affairs Manager

Cc：general manager

Reference Answers to Interpretation

1.Should you have any special requests for your next booking please contact the Reservations Manager.

2.As a sign of our concern, I would like to offer you a 200-Yuan voucher towards the cost of your next visit.

3.The guest should receive the follow-up letters from the hotel within three weeks.

4.We are confident that the general manager will be in contact with you very soon.

5.We quite understand your frustration at the loss of personal items in your room.

6. 根據規定，本酒店不能賠償您的損失。因為酒店對沒有存放在酒店保險櫃內的貴重物品沒有看管保護的責任。

7. 客人的賠付請求應該提交相關的保險機構或者告知客人其賠付請求能否得到滿足。

8. 我們希望您能再次光臨本酒店，我們將為您提供我們的優質服務和良好的設施。

9. 我想指出的一點是我們的宣傳冊上明確說明了需要一定時間的提前預訂，因為我們需要作一些特別準備。

10. 如果處理得當，投訴的客人會成為最忠誠的客人，客人的投訴也會幫我們找出自己尚未注意到的問題。

Reference Answers to Translation

Passage 1

參展商常常抱怨的有兩件事。一件是展館開放的時間。一件是旅館住房的安排。他們認為展館開放時間應該縮短，會議代表在白天開會間隙應該有時間參觀展館。許多人抱怨一天到晚坐在展臺旁，沒有時間去和會議代表們進行溝通。而這才是他們來參展的主要原因。

酒店客房安排是參展商投訴的另一個問題。參展商如果跟會議代表住在不同的酒店，他們就很難進行商務談判，進行銷售。一個解決的辦法是酒店晚間出租小型會議室給參展商，這樣對三方都有利。

Passage 2

Thank you for your letter regarding your recent stay at Imperial Hotel.

We noted with concern your comment regarding construction noise due to renovation in progress at our hotel.We do attempt to have all our facilities available year round, and attempt to preserve peace and quiet for our guests.Regrettably, renovations are necessary from time to time to maintain the high quality and appeal of the hotel.We always attempt to conduct these renovations during the low season, between April 10 and September 10, when fewer guests are on property.That fact notwithstanding, we hope you will accept our sincere apologies for any inconvenience.

We hope that this incident does not diminish your favorable regard of Imperial Hotel.We hope that you will someday return and experience the full array of facilities of which we are proud of.We look forward to serving you again soon.

國家圖書館出版品預行編目（CIP）資料

會展實用英語 . 讀寫篇 /「會展實用英語編委會 編」
. -- 第一版 . -- 臺北市：崧博出版
：崧燁文化發行 , 2019.04
　面；　公分
POD 版
ISBN 978-957-735-699-4(平裝)

1. 商業英文 2. 讀本

805.18　　　　　　　　　　　　　　　108002148

書　　名：會展實用英語 . 讀寫篇務

作　　者：「會展實用英語編委會 編」

發 行 人：黃振庭

出 版 者：崧博出版事業有限公司

發 行 者：崧燁文化事業有限公司

E - m a i l：sonbookservice@gmail.com

粉 絲 頁：　　　　　　　網 址：

地　　址：台北市中正區重慶南路一段六十一號八樓 815 室

8F.-815, No.61, Sec. 1, Chongqing S. Rd., Zhongzheng

Dist., Taipei City 100, Taiwan (R.O.C.)

電　　話：(02)2370-3310 傳　真：(02) 2370-3210

總 經 銷：紅螞蟻圖書有限公司

地　　址: 台北市內湖區舊宗路二段 121 巷 19 號

電　　話:02-2795-3656 傳真 :02-2795-4100　　網址：

印　　刷：京峯彩色印刷有限公司（京峰數位）

定　　價：550 元

發行日期：2019 年 04 月第一版

◎ 本書以 POD 印製發行